D LIGHTNING

DRAGON DREAMER BOOK II

J. S. Burke

LIND PRESS
Athens, Georgia

Library of Congress Control Number: 2016915553

ISBN-10: 0-9960425-6-3
ISBN-13: 978-0-9960425-6-7

Printed in the United States of America

First Edition

This is a work of fiction. Names, characters, places, and incidents either are products of the author's imagination or are used fictitiously. Any resemblance to real people, living or dead, or to actual events or places, is entirely coincidental.

Lind Press: www.lindpress.com

Author Site: www.jennysburke.com

Dedicated to everyone who visits the worlds of the Dragon Dreamer.

ACKNOWLEDGMENTS

For useful insights and suggestions, thanks to Diana, Jan, Janice, Jennie, Laverne, Lisa, Melissa, Roger, Stephanie, and Veronica. I'm very grateful to my editor, Carol. Thank you to Lind Press. Thanks to all of you who helped in the dragon and undersea worlds!

How many dragons?

CONTENTS

CHAPTER 1: BLACK LIGHTNING

Bright red lightning crackled above the mountain, sparkling through a dark plume of smoke. The Volcano roared with a thunder beyond any storm and sharp rocks rained down on Drakor. The young dragon gripped an icy rock ledge and shrank back into a narrow mountain crevice, choking on the thick stench of sulfur.

The mountain shook violently. Drakor's teeth rattled together like dry bones while the earthquake rumbled on and on. He felt like an ice-fish shaken to death in the jaws of a dragon.

Suddenly, the safe ledge broke loose. The white dragon stretched his long, leathery wings and pushed against the falling rock, trying desperately to fly to safety. He was hammered by a storm of rocks.

A boulder slammed into Drakor and his mind went white. He crumpled in on himself, writhing in agony. His right wing hung limp and useless.

Drakor fell from the heights and tumbled down the steep mountainside. He reached the base and kept rolling, onto a peninsula of ice. He barely missed the sea on either side.

He shook his head, trying to focus. Winter was ending, so this ice sheet would be dangerously thin. Drakor tried to stand up, but his arms and legs slipped away. He must reach the solid shore! He crawled unsteadily toward land, battered and bruised, dragging his useless wing.

Craaacckkk! A jagged line raced across the blue-white tongue of ice. Dark gray water welled up through the rift as the small ice sheet floated free. It was grabbed by a strong current and yanked away from shore.

Drakor reached the edge of the ice and struggled to his feet, ignoring the pain. Could he jump the gap to shore? He dug his sharp claws into the ice, measuring the distance with his eyes. It was too far. If only he could fly! A gulf of deep, icy water separated him from the shore, and he could not swim with a broken wing.

Drakor collapsed onto his fragile sanctuary. How long would this thin ice last? Not that it really mattered, since he'd starve long before his floating home melted away. No one would look for him at sea. A dragon, skimming above the water to hunt ice-fish, would not notice him.

Drakor blended beautifully with the ice floe. His entire body was covered with diamond-shaped, moon-white scales. Each scale had a crystalline edge that glittered like diamonds. Like ice. He gazed longingly at the disappearing shore as he spun farther out to sea.

* * *

Several leagues to the south, afternoon sunlight glinted off golden wings and dragon scales. Arak's sharp claws gripped the icy-damp wood of the skiff, as he sailed through a narrow passage between ice-mountains. Towering walls of ice crowded in from both sides, and the salty air was so cold that it burned in his lungs. He inhaled slowly, noting the distinct scent from each type of wet wood.

The long wooden skiff was dwarfed by ice, and the hold below had a honeycomb of extra supports to strengthen it against these floating mountains. Arak and Taron designed this skiff, and the dragon clan built it to search across the sea for a crucial supply of copper. Now they were questing for legends. Where were these long-lost cousins, the ice dragons?

Arak studied the crystal walls. "This is a true ice world."

Ice-mountains filled the sea like sharp-edged clouds, carved into fantastic shapes by wind and wave. Most were white, but a few glowed like clear aqua glass with an inner light. The skiff screeched and groaned, grating against the hard ice.

Taron winced and flexed his claws. "Will the ice armor hold?"

Arak flicked his long tail uneasily. "We tested the metal plates again and again. The armor has to work. Of course, we didn't have real ice-mountains for the test. And these are amazing, like ice sculptures! I wonder why some are blue?"

Taron laughed. "That's another question for the ice dragons."

Dorali, the third dragon crew-mate, nodded. "I wonder

what they'll ask us?"

Adult golden dragons were about nine feet long from head to tail. The skiff measured fifty feet from pointed bow to straight stern, and it could easily carry eight dragons. Two small octopus passengers, Scree and Orm, rested in tubs of seawater. But there were only three dragons onboard, and it felt rather empty.

The skiff had a polished wood deck, railing, and a deep keel for stability. There was a sturdy rudder with a tiller for steering. The hold was an open area below deck. This was nearly filled with supplies, but a cramped space remained. Dragons went below deck during the worst weather, and to sleep.

Traveling north was risky. A low shelter was set into the deck so that one dragon could sleep topside, ready to wake and help in an instant. A second windbreak, made from wooden ribs and fish leather, was collapsed behind the octopus tubs. This shelter could be unfolded to cover and protect the octopus passengers.

Arak looked up and frowned. A huge skiff-wing was attached to the towering wood mast, sewn from many silvery-white fish-skins. Icy-white scales of frozen fog sparkled across this wing, and it hung as stiff and heavy as wood.

Dorali followed his gaze and stretched her golden wings. "This ice grows on everything!" She flew to the top and swept her way down, clearing swath after swath of ice from the skiff-wing. The ice crystals made musical plinking sounds as they hit the deck.

Cleared of ice, the skiff-wing filled with air and they lurched forward. Arak slid on the damp boards, barely keeping his balance. He gripped the slippery deck with his copper claws. "Thanks, Dorali! That really makes a difference. This ice grows faster than barnacles on a hull." The young captain adjusted the tiller to catch the wind and the skiff spurted ahead. He breathed a sigh of relief as they moved out from between the frozen monsters.

Arak closed his eyes to better feel/see the curve in the magnetic lines. The silvery-gray magnetic shadow in his mind revealed another world. "Land is near." He had secretly visited the mythical island, using his unique gift of seeing while in trance. But his trance-sight was blurry and he had seen no dragons.

Arak peered closely at every white cloud and every sparkling ice-mountain. "Where are the legendary ice dragons?" he muttered.

Taron squinted into the light, searching the odd white clouds sprinkled across a deep blue sky. "Look! Is that one?"

Dorali studied Arak's tantalizing dragon-cloud as it slid behind a larger cloud. "It moved fast. Is that a dragon or just another cloud?"

Arak exhaled his own frosty cloud of frustration. "I wish I knew. Everything is white. Legend says they can hide on snow, in clouds, even in moonbeams. Are they watching us?" He glanced down at the shimmering, gray-green sea. A school of tiny fish roiled the water, and the sea rippled as if it was raining up from below.

Dorali sighed. "It's my first voyage, and I've seen the stuff of dreams. It's peaceful here, far from home. I can't remember feeling so content." Each of her golden, diamond-shaped scales was tipped with emerald and her eyes were blue. Just like every other dragon-lady. Each dragon-lord had golden, diamond-shaped scales edged

5

with ruby. But she alone, of all the dragons, was covered by knotty white scars.

Taron used a sturdy pole to fend off the craggy outcrop of ice. He gave Arak a friendly clout on the shoulder, tilting his sharp copper claws away. "Cheer up. We're farther north than any other dragon."

"Except the ice dragons," Arak replied, scanning the white clouds and ice. His eyes burned with the strain. "Where are they?"

Dorali gave the tiller to Taron and stretched her cramped arms. She ladled water from a barrel to fill the copper tea kettle. Then she added shaved red root, cinnamon, nutmeg, and her own blend of herbs. Dorali breathed a thin stream of fire onto the kettle, waited while it steeped, and poured five mugs of tea through a strainer. "We all need this," she said, handing Arak a steaming mug of red root tea.

Arak closed his eyes as he inhaled the earthy-spicy aroma. "Ahhh. Driana taught you the secret of perfect tea."

"Thanks to you, we now have enough copper to make a proper tea kettle." Dorali dropped ice into two smaller mugs to cool the tea. She handed these to the octopus crew-mates.

Scree held the mug of tea with one of her eight arms. Her golden eyes held a dreamy expression as she sipped the traditional dragon drink. She wore the normal red-brown octopus skin color.

Scree gazed at Arak. "Patience, my friend," she said, by gracefully weaving two of her flexible arms to sign the words.

Orm grinned at Scree from his basin of seawater.

"And what would you know of patience?" He stretched his arms wide to get the kinks out. Five octopi would be about as long as one dragon. "I've learned from dealing with you," Scree replied testily. She tilted her head back. "I think I'll take up cloud-watching. Those look like a swarm of white jellyfish, just hanging in the sky."

Orm scrunched his eyes and stared up into the bright blue sky. "I think I see the stingers on their tentacles." He pointed to a lumpy cloud. "And that's your favorite brain coral."

A shaft of lightning tore down through the sky and struck the base of the mast. BOOM! The instant thunder was deafening. Fire erupted. Hungry flames ate the wood.

Arak and Taron lowered buckets into the sea and threw water on the flames. Dorali beat the flickers to death with a fish skin. Orm and Scree shrank to safety below the water in their basins.

"Where did that come from?" Taron yelled.

Arak's eyes blazed with anger. "It was black! I've seen black flames, but never black lightning! That's dragon lightning!" He eyed the deck, checking the fire damage. "What a nasty greeting."

Taron's voice rose sharply. "Ice dragons? How could anyone make black lightning?"

Arak circled the mast, pushing gently, testing its strength. "Last spring I experimented with color. I put metals into flames, trying to make every possible fire color. I wanted a special rainbow fire for my dragonlet. When I used a pinch of titanium powder, the fire glowed black and sparkled like diamonds. Titanium's rare, and you'd need a lot to make black lightning. That's an

7

expensive warning." His tail slumped to the ground. "All my life I've wanted to find ice dragons. Made of moonbeams and starlight . . . so beautiful . . . I love the legend-stories. And they don't want to meet us."

"They weren't expecting us, and I doubt they've ever seen a skiff," Scree said. "Maybe they're afraid."

Arak flicked his tail in surprise. "Of us? An ice dragon should be nearly twice my size. We'd be more at risk if we fought."

"This skiff could be frightening. Giant squid weren't sure what to make of it, and they're huge." Scree made an image on her skin, using her color cells. She showed the skiff next to a squid that was almost as long.

Arak nodded agreement. Scree was normally a plain red-brown. But millions of tiny color cells in her skin could make almost any color, any picture, if she concentrated. And Scree was very good at concentrating. The life-like image on her body was terrifying. A giant squid had attacked Scree's underwater village and killed octopi. It was many times her size, with long snaking arms and saucer eyes.

Scree had attacked the monster with a poisoned spear, and then tried to save it. She became friends with Vorm. Arak shivered. How could you be friends with a giant squid?

Orm eyed his mate's body-picture. "I'll never feel comfortable with squid, and ice dragons may be just as deadly. Arak, you can breathe flames and talk mind-to-mind. They can't, at least not in your legends. I'd bet on you in a fight."

Arak glanced up at the white clouds. "I hope it won't come to that. They can gather lightning without a storm and throw with deadly accuracy."

Scree felt the seawater that was still running across the deck, and stared down into the icy sea. "This water has an odd feel/taste that reminds me of our volcano. It's changing, and I'm worried."

Orm shuddered. "I've noticed. Is it waking up?"

Arak poked into the charred wood to check the depth of the burn. He pulled against the mast again, testing. "The mast is damaged, but we can brace it for our return journey."

Taron nodded agreement. "And the holes must be filled. Everything we need is in the hold."

"We also need this skiff to hold still." Arak drove a metal anchor into an ice-mountain and tied off to it. Dorali used pine gum to fill the burn holes, while Arak and Taron strengthened the mast with bent metal braces.

In the early evening, Arak cautiously maneuvered the skiff through a field of sharp, craggy ice. His eyes were alert as ever but his tail drooped with defeat. "We're limping home in a battered skiff without even meeting our mythical, long-lost cousins. But our skiff still works."

Taron glanced at the burn spots. "We finally have proof that ice dragons are real."

The sun sank lower and lower as they journeyed toward home. A vivid sunset with raging reds and fiery golds was reflected across sea and ice. Ice-mountains burned above midnight blue shadows. Even the huge, silvery skiff-wing was awash with glowing colors.

Arak gazed at the sky. "I'll never tire of sunsets at sea. It's time to call home." He sighed. It would be hard to share this failure with his mate, Zarina. She had encouraged him to follow his dream quest, even though she couldn't come. This was no place for their dragonlet. He lifted his aquamarine trance-stone from his chest-pouch, sat on the deck, and focused into the blue-green ball.

Arak entered a calming trance, relaxing as his tide of frustrations drained away. This was the first stage of their mind-to-mind communication. He sank deeper into trance as he stilled his mind and focused into the translucent aquamarine globe. He felt peaceful nothingness. Then he was looking down at his limp, empty body.

His trance-mind soared across the sea to the distant dragon shore and spied the shimmer of a trance-mind, waiting. As the shimmers overlapped, Arak heard a voice deep inside his mind. This inner voice was a flat monotone.

Arak. How is the quest

Zarina. We found ice dragons. It is not what I expected

*   *   *

Drakor lay huddled on the ice, shivering, surrounded by flaming colors. If only the sunset could warm him! He ate the last bite of food from his chest pouch and, still hungry, took a small sip of water from his silver flask. How long could he make it last?

A thin crescent moon rose, bringing little light, and the diamond stars hid behind wispy clouds. No light, no heat, no food. He laughed. No shortage of ice! Drakor packed more ice around his mangled wing. There was nothing more he could do, so he ignored the throbbing pain.

Drakor took a huge diamond from his pouch. This heavy, eight-sided crystal was as clear as ice. His dragon-dam found the diamond on a distant volcanic island, shortly before she died. This gift was all he had from her, and it always seemed warm and real. In legend, diamonds brought the First Dragon to life.

Drakor automatically looked around to be sure no one was looking. A dragon shouldn't need any comfort. He cradled the white diamond, softly crooning a half-remembered lullaby that his dam had sung to him. Then he curled up miserably for the night, carried farther and farther from home by the sea.

Drakor's rumbling stomach woke him at dawn. Movement caught his eye. Glancing up he spied a huge, silvery wing on the horizon. A single wing made no sense! He rubbed his eyes and looked again. The huge wing grew larger, moving closer. It must be real.

Drakor struggled to a crouching position and steeled himself for a fight. He'd rather face a monster than starvation . . . much more interesting.

* * *

A modest breeze from the unseen land filled the skiff-wing. Arak moved the tiller gently, carefully skirting the base of another ice-mountain. Even with copper plating, sharp ice could slice through the side and sink the skiff. He sniffed the frosty air, noting the rotten egg smell mixed with salt. They were so close to the ice dragons! He had found success and failure in one black lightning bolt.

Dorali took her turn at the helm, threading the skiff between two more ice-mountains.

Arak flicked his tail with approval. "That's excellent steering."

"You taught me well." Dorali sighed contentedly. "I

love this journey."

Arak glanced at the damaged mast. "Even after the lightning strike?"

Dorali tilted her head. "The journey isn't over. Who knows what will happen? I've seen skies with green fire and floating ice-mountains. Most are white, but some look like they're carved from blue glass."

"Now you sound like Scree. The sea and sky are amazing, but you're the only dragon who wanted to join Taron and me on this adventure. I wonder why?"

Dorali shrugged her wings. "When the clan was suffering, many dragons wanted to help. Then you crossed the endless sea and found the copper we needed. Now the dragons are healthy, pain-free, and content to stay home."

Arak nodded. "Zarina said you've become a true Healer."

Dorali shivered.

Arak noticed her curled toes and hunched wings. Dorali must be remembering the experience that changed her life, when she was nearly ripped to pieces by a pack of ravenous dweer. They were each the size of a dragonlet, with rust-colored scales and sharp teeth. Normally, dweer left dragons alone. But an undersea volcano killed fish and spawned a famine.

Arak helped rescue Dorali. He and his sire carried the dragonlet by her wings as they flew to the clinic. The Healers Driana, Zarina, and Scree sewed her back together. It was a miracle that Dorali had survived. Even her torn wings had healed enough to fly. After her long stay at the dragon clinic, she became an apprentice Healer.

Dorali straightened her wings. "This is where I want to be."

"We're lucky to have you along." Arak scanned the sea and pointed. "That's a very flat piece of ice. Land ice."

"Arak, that's like the ice floe you landed on." Scree flashed an image of their first meeting, when Arak had crashed onto ice far out to sea, far from his home on the dragon-shore.

Dorali stared at the ice. "The whole clan knows this story. A chunk of storm ice knocked you from the sky, Scree healed your wounds, and you've been friends ever since."

Orm juggled five dragon-candies with three arms; the balls flew in overlapping arcs. "Now octopi trade with dragons. We get your spices and chocolate . . . for seaweed!" He expertly tossed a candy to each crew member. Scree caught her piece with a curled arm.

Arak bounced his candy from claw to claw and then caught it in his mouth. "We also get your black pearls," he said, with a grin. He took a closer look at the ice sheet and flicked his tail. "Something moved on that ice. Dorali, bring us closer."

Arak studied the small, drifting plate of ice. The broken edges were still sharp, not yet smoothed by the sea, so land was near. That was not news. He could feel/see this land in the curving magnetic lines, smell land shrubs in the air, and feel it in the black grit that dusted his skiff. Orm had tasted earthy, fresh land-water in the sea.

Arak was so close to the land of the fabled ice dragons! He ran his eyes over the pile of snow in the center of the ice floe and sighed. Nothing. As he turned away, an odd glint of light caught his attention.

Arak glanced once more at the lump of snow, sparkling like glass and fine white sand. "It's just a pile of snow and ice," he said dejectedly. Then he snapped his tail. "And two black eyes!"

CHAPTER 2: ICE DRAGON

A huge white dragon looked up and locked eyes with Arak. His eyes were stormy gray, not black, and there was not a hint of fear. Afternoon sunlight glinted off diamond-shaped scales of white opal. Iridescent rainbows rippled across the dragon's broad chest. Everything was just like the legends, but his right wing was tightly bound and covered with snow.

Arak and Taron quickly lowered a long, narrow ladder to the ice. "Climb aboard."

The jostling climb must have hurt his injured wing, but he never even winced. This dragon was made of stern stuff. Their large guest stepped easily over the railing, stood firmly on the deck, and looked about with a commanding presence. He spied the octopus tubs and darted forward, sharp claws extended.

His intent was clear.

Arak and Dorali leapt between the dragon and their friends. "No!"

The dragon knocked them aside, intent on his prey.

Orm sensibly slid into the water and camouflaged, instantly changing his skin color and texture to match the wood basin.

Scree stood her ground, gazing steadily at the onrushing dragon, and raised three tentacles. Thwack! She struck him on the neck with the tip of her middle arm. The other two arms wielded thick metal rods that struck the offending claws, knocking them away. The white dragon staggered back and collapsed.

Dorali and Arak struggled up. Taron joined them, all rushing to protect Scree. And the ice dragon was already down.

Arak laughed. "I see that you kept the toxic tips I made for your giant squid encounter." The wax balls were filled with neurotoxin from a deadly octopus relative, and tipped with a sharp, hollow needle.

Scree displayed one of her poison balls, which fitted perfectly into a sucker near the tip of an arm. "These helped with our last adventure, and I thought they might be useful again. Each poison ball has a different dose. I broke the safety on this one when the dragon looked too arrogant to listen. As long as he's sedated, let's fix his wing. I hope it's not beyond our skill."

Orm twined tentacles affectionately with his mate. "You do realize he just tried to kill you."

"So did Vorm. He needs help. He's young and simply mad with hunger. I calculated the dose in advance, so he should be asleep for at least an hour."

Orm shook his head in a dragonly gesture. "I thought I was the practical one."

Scree grinned back. "Sometimes, practical and improbable overlap." She slid another arm around her mate. "Like us."

Dorali and Scree untied the twine around the ice dragon's wing. They carefully stretched the wing, feeling the multiple breaks and the shattered bone. Dorali flicked her tail in dismay. "Wings are my specialty, but this is even worse than I thought. How does he stand it?"

Scree grabbed her Healer bag. "Arak, could you tie off to that ice-mountain? We need a still place to work."

Scree's bag was made from indestructible cloth-of-gold, woven from the thin, wiry roots of pen shells. The bright fabric was covered by tiny brown shells. The four compartments held a treasure-trove of supplies: seaweed herbs, blue-ringed octopus venom, kelp bandages, a spool of wiry gold thread, fish-bone needles, a carved coral box with oily salve, and a sharp surgeon's knife of glittering black garnet.

Dorali opened her Healer bag, made from fish leather. It was filled with dried herbs, vials of ground metal, knives made from rare green garnet, needles, thread, bandages, poison for anesthesia, rods and strips for braces, and more.

Scree ran two arms gently over his damaged wing. She tasted the wounds, felt the fever, and sighed. "We'll need everything we have." She put four live leeches around the break while Arak and Taron looked on with interest. The sturdy slugs latched on immediately. "These will suck out the swelling so we can move his wing safely."

Dorali mixed herbs in a pot of boiling water and left the potion to steep. "Boneset leaves will speed healing, the iodine in this seaweed fights infection, and flame-weed numbs pain," she explained to Arak, who was watching with interest. "You finally found your ice dragon."

Arak nodded. "He looks just like the legends, white as new snow and sparkling like ice. I didn't know that ice dragons were so . . . dramatic."

Orm pointed. "He's more spiky than I expected. Look at those sharp claws on his wings!"

Scree and Dorali designed a moveable wing brace with thin, strong ash wood. Arak cut the pieces to size and Taron inserted the small, adjustable screws. Arak and Taron held the brace in place while Scree and Dorali sewed it onto the wing. Then the Healers used cloth-of-gold thread, carefully avoiding the veins.

Orm handed them another spool of thread. "That's a strange dragon ornament. I wonder if he'll appreciate the artwork."

The skiff-wing flapped against the mast and sea spray blew across the deck. The skiff began to rock. Dorali flicked her tail nervously. "That wind is not making this any easier." She tied off the last stitch. "I hope this works."

Moments later, the ice dragon opened his eyes and looked about groggily. "Whaaat . . . happened?"

Dorali leaned closer to catch his slurred words and strange accent. She pointed to the octopus. "Scree."

The ice dragon shook his head. "How could . . . something . . . small, helplesss . . . stop me?"

Dorali laughed. "Helpless? Scree? She's tackled a

shark and a horde of giant squid. Size is irrelevant. You're as strong as your mind." She helped her patient to a sitting position.

"Giant . . . squid? Big. Daan-jur-uss." He looked at Scree again and shook his head. "Size isss always re-levant." He noticed the wing brace and alarm sparked in his eyes. He twisted his long neck around, peering at the brace from every angle. "What isss this?" he hissed, reaching over with his opposite arm.

Dorali put both hands on his arm and shook her head. "No! It's a brace for your wing. It will hold the broken bones together while they heal. And I will help the bones grow back together."

He dropped his arm and stared at her. "How?"

"I'll pulse energy into your bones at just the right frequency."

The ice dragon sat up straighter. "What isss an energy pulse?"

Dorali tilted her head. "We use the energy our body makes. What do your Healers do?"

"We heal ourselves. We learn which herbs to eat and how to wrap breaks."

Arak nodded. "Self-sufficient. But some problems require help. I'm Arak. Your dragon Healer is Dorali. Scree is your octopus Healer." He introduced Taron and Orm. "We all helped. Your wing should heal if you obey your Healers."

The ice dragon displayed his impressive teeth and flexed his long, razor-sharp claws. "Obey?" he growled.

Dorali flinched but replied soothingly, "Just listen to what we say. Drink this . . . it will help." She handed him a mug of healing herbal tea.

He took a sip from the mug, spat it out, and snapped his tail like a whip. "This isss not water."

"It's water with herbs. It will help your wing heal." Dorali took a sip to show it was safe. "Drink it . . . please."

After he finished his potion, she gave him a sack of crab claws. He cracked them open with his teeth, used his claws to extract every last shred of meat, and relaxed his snapping tail. "You live here? Floating on water, like an ice sheet. What isss this?"

Arak patted the mast proudly. "We call it a skiff."

The ice dragon shrugged his shoulders and winced with the pain.

"Scree had the original idea of making a fancy wood raft with a pole and a fish-skin wing, to fly on the water. Orm said the design must be part shark, part dragon. Now, octopi can skiff-fly across the sea. We made a bigger skiff for dragons."

Arak grabbed the railing and pushed. It didn't move. "We keep improving the skiff. This railing is much stronger, and the hold now has a weather-room."

The ice dragon shook his head. "Yellow dragons are strange."

Wind gusted across the deck, knocking icicles off the lines like leaves off a winter tree. They plinked musically on the deck. The wind grew fierce, pelting them with hard grains of ice. Arak furled his wings tight to protect them. The white dragon ignored this assault as if he did not even feel the wind.

"I'm Arak. What's your name?"

"Drakor." He looked Arak up and down. "In our legends, small yellow dragons were afraid to fly north."

"Not afraid. We had no need to leave. Our land suits us."

Drakor sighed. "That isss my problem. Our island suits us. But that will change when the new Volcano erupts. The old one isss growing a new cone that smells and acts different. I have studied this but no one cares."

Arak nodded. "Minds open slowly. What have you found?"

Scree watched closely, eyes focused, body tense. She flushed green with interest as Taron translated the conversation into their mutual language.

"The land-ice isss thinner. The ice fish are moving away. The magnetic wrinkles over the new and old Volcanoes are very different. I made jars and collected Volcano breath from the old and new cones. Then the mountain shook me off."

Taron looked toward the unseen island. "What are magnetic wrinkles?"

"They are small, wiggly, magnetic lines. Their energy pattern isss important."

Arak flicked his tail. "Why do the other ice dragons ignore these signs? Are they just too tough? Can't they imagine the danger?"

Drakor threw back his head and laughed. His deep, booming laugh rolled on and on like thunder. "Both? We learn to be . . . self-su-fi-shent. Food can be scarce. Dragonlets learn to find lichens and rock limpets soon after they hatch."

He gently stretched his good wing. "Tough isss required. But I was not encouraged to use my . . . i-ma-gi-na-shun." He mouthed each syllable as if the word tasted strange.

21

Arak grinned. "Actually . . . neither was I. At least, not by the clan, but my dam encouraged me. It's good to push beyond the borders. I was teased until I became a practical dreamer and helped the clan. Now I try to think like the beyond-dragons who live in the stars, to remember the ancient past and contemplate the distant future."

Scree turned one eye to the sea. "This seawater has a feel/taste like a volcano. As long as we're stopped, I want to collect better samples from the ice abyss and compare them with Drakor's samples from the island. Then we'll know if this whole area is a new volcano waking."

Arak translated.

"That would be great!" Drakor glanced over the side, at the cold gray sea. "But the ice abyss isss dangerous."

Scree shrugged. "Maybe." She opened her Healer bag and chose three collection jars that were carved from a thick stem of black coral. She added them to her small travel bag. "I'll collect water near the vents below. Orm, when we get home, we need a new sample from *our* volcano. It's changing, and we need to know if our volcano is part of this."

Orm twined arms with Scree. "You have to see for yourself, don't you? Giant squid hunt here."

Scree plucked a huge pink pearl from her bag. "I have *this*."

Orm sighed. "You faced a horde of giant squid once before, and this pearl was given back to you in peace. You're a friend-of-squid. But are all squid truly friends-of-Scree?"

Scree smiled brightly. "One way to find out!"

She grabbed her bag with one arm and a heavy rock

with two more. Then she slipped over the edge into the sea.

CHAPTER 3: THE ICE ABYSS

Scree turned white with shock as she hit the freezing water. She sank like the stone she held, slipping through a sunset cloud of tiny red shrimp. A long, clear fish snaked out of her way as she plummeted down.

The floating ice-mountain was even larger below the waves. Salt drifted down, squeezed from the frozen sea above, blurring the water like thick, wavy glass. Her arms curled away from the salty brine.

The thick, slushy sea was nearly frozen. Scree sank into a world that grew steadily darker and colder; it was like falling through black diamonds.

Threads of ice grew through the water like spider webs in the air, catching unwary sea life. The doomed creatures were quickly bound in a cocoon of ice. Scree stretched out one arm and shattered a prison made of sharp, crystalline needles. The starfish escaped and sank to freedom.

The water grew slightly warmer as she neared the sea

floor. Scree nodded with satisfaction. That warmth must be from volcano vents. She pulsed sideways to avoid a sharp, crumpled patch, landing instead on a dark boulder.

Scree discarded the rock weight and gazed in wonder at the exotic life of the abyss. Glowing jellyfish hung in the sea as living chandeliers. Black fish with pink lights brightened the darkness like stars in the night. Blue-and-yellow lobsters stalked past a tangle of purple starfish.

Scree pulsed toward a stream of smoky-gray bubbles. Her arms twitched as she moved closer to the horrible feel/taste rising from the volcano vent. This crack in the sea floor seemed like an entrance to a secret cave. She filled three jars with the stinky water, pushed in the stoppers, and placed them in her bag.

A cluster of glowing, flower-like animals lit the sea. Each anemone had an outer ring of thin golden petals; green strands filled the center. Their glow attracted tiny, shrimp-like prey. A golden petal whipped out and snared one.

Scree flowed just above the rocks, barely touching, searching. What else would she find here, in this alien world beneath the ice?

Suddenly she froze. Scree felt no shift in the currents, but her skin prickled with warning. Something was watching her. She changed color while her skin cratered and dimpled with sharp edges like broken eggs. In the blink of an eye she disappeared, perfectly matching the volcanic rocks. What was it? Her arms could only taste the overwhelming sea-smells of rotten egg, weathered rock, and old melted ice.

Scree focused her mind on the thousands of tiny eyes in her skin; it was like looking through a wall of glass bubbles at a puzzle image. He was lurking in the shadows behind her. The red mountain had huge saucer eyes that glowed yellow in the pale light. This towering giant squid was watching her, so hiding as a shape-shifted rock would not keep her safe.

Old memories surfaced of her first meeting with Vorm, the giant squid who attacked her undersea village and killed three of her pod-mates. She had fought back and won.

Scree smoothed her skin and changed color to a bright warning-blue, the blue of rare creatures that could be poisonous. She stretched as tall as she could and became a different, more intimidating octopus in less than a heartbeat. Then she turned to face the giant squid. She clutched her huge pink pearl, holding it out like a shield.

The squid pulsed forward.

"Tarm!" she signed with relief, making red and yellow spots on her arms to spell his name. Fear drained away, like a wave slipping back to the safety of the sea. She had met this giant before. Scree became a normal red-brown octopus.

Tarm's eyes focused on the pink pearl. "Scree. I thought it was you." He flashed a series of glowing light spots on his arms: "May you surf the tangled currents of the sea forever."

Scree answered with the same traditional squid greeting and added, "Tell Veera that I miss your abyss, but it's also beautiful below the ice-mountains."

"So you do love the dark abyss," Tarm said approvingly. "Veera will be pleased."

Scree vividly remembered his terrifying mate Veera, and the almost paralyzing fear she felt before they understood each other. "Everyone should see the abyss. It's not truly dark; life speaks with lights." Scree smiled as she quoted Vorm, remembering that scary, complicated, enriching friendship.

"Come see the vent worms," Tarm said, flashing his lights enthusiastically. He pulsed away.

Scree jetted after him, carefully noting landmarks to find her way back to the dragon-skiff. Normally she could taste her way home, but not in this intense soup of flavors. A homing snail would be quite useful, since they always found their way home. If only they weren't so slow . . . The rotten sulfur feel/taste grew even stronger as they traveled, and her sensing arms wriggled with irritation. How far would they journey?

Tarm passed another bubbling vent and kept going. Finally, he stopped. This vent was surrounded by a riot of giant worms. Most were longer and thicker than her arms, with white shell tube bodies and bright scarlet heads.

Tarm swept a swath of tube worms into his beaked mouth with one tentacle. He gave a satisfied grin. "Small tasty treats."

Scree shuddered, remembering the attack on her village and the long, powerful tentacles. She smoothed the fear out of her tense arms. Giant squid had terrifying power, but they were also immensely fascinating. They traveled the world, searching, pulsing from place to place. Home was wherever they were.

In an odd way, these squid were kindred spirits. They matched her restless need to explore, something few octopi would ever understand. She ate a smaller tube worm, one that grew farther from the vent, and made a shell picture on her skin. "This tastes like scallops."

Scree collected water from the vent, since another sample could be useful.

A huge, white king crab stalked onto the field. She studied its stately walk. Tron had mimicked this crab's unusual dance at their New Moon festival. Tron was her only friend who loved to explore and travel the seas like squid. He was dead now, killed in an earthquake when their undersea volcano woke. She flushed gray, reliving sad/fond/happy memories of her good friend. There were layers and layers of memories, like the shimmering nacre of a pearl.

Tarm scooped up the crab and it disappeared into his mouth. "There is always good hunting near the vents."

Scree shivered . . . his dinner crab was exactly her size. She gave an octopus sigh. Now she would never see the real dance of the king crab.

Tarm pointed to a rocky field.

Scree took a closer look at the sausage-shaped rocks, which were barely visible in the dim light. "Sea cucumbers!" She picked up one of the small, crusty animals. Its brown skin was covered with an elaborate design of pink and white lines. There were tiny tube feet along one side and tube threads around its feeding end.

"The sea cucumbers near our reef are solid brown, and rare." Scree pulled an empty sack from her bag and stuffed many of these brainless snacks into it.

"These are too small for me," Tarm said. His long tentacles rippled nervously. Then he bent low and looked her in the eye. "Scree, the seas are changing. Many fish have moved away. We have other food, but some of the younger squid want to hunt octopi."

Scree went rigid. "They would ignore our

agreement?"

Tarm looked away, but the lights on his arms continued to speak. "These squid did not meet you, so they say the treaty does not include them. It's a game to them, to prove they are superior to the older, cowardly squid. They don't see the danger because you are so small."

Scree sighed. The volcano was changing, the squid were threatening, and even her octopus pod had rumblings of dissent. Was everything going to blow up? Could her pod stop a determined attack by a horde of giant squid? Tarm was watching her closely, as if measuring an opponent for battle. This was a warrior race. Friendship with squid would never be simple, and it was time to challenge back.

Scree coiled her arms as if to strike, to remind Tarm of their last encounter; she had temporarily disabled two of his tentacles with her hidden poison. "We'll deal with any squid foolish enough to attack us. Our treaty protects both sides. Because of your warning, and because I value our friendship, I'll try to keep my pod from retaliating and hunting you all down."

Tarm flushed a paler shade of red. "We'll discuss this at our next gathering."

Scree relaxed her arms. "Good." She glanced north. "Have there been changes up here since last year?"

Tarm tapped the sea floor. "It's warmer than last season, and the water tastes different. Ice fish are leaving. Did you find your ice dragons?"

"They found us."

* * *

Scree climbed up the side of the skiff, hooking her

29

arms over the rungs of a special ladder worked into the side. She squished thin and slipped under the railing. Then she pulled jars made of polished black coral from her bag.

Drakor snapped his tail. "You have samples!"

"And I met an old friend, Tarm." Scree used her color cells to paint a giant squid across her skin.

Arak laughed, Orm sighed, and Dorali looked on with relief.

Drakor's eyes bulged. "And you returned?" He reached eagerly for a jar. "This isss great!" He pulled a glassy black container from his sack, carved from obsidian. He sniffed both jars. "The Volcano breath I caught in my jar smells almost the same as your sample."

"Orm feels chemicals. He can tell if they are the same," Scree offered.

Drakor watched closely as Arak translated. "That could help. I must learn your language."

The unreliable, gusting wind was replaced by a cold, steady wind. Arak reached for the furled skiff-wing. "Prepare to cast off. We can fly if we're careful." Dorali and Taron pulled the anchor from the ice while he adjusted the skiff-wing to catch the rising wind.

Arak pointed to the sky. "How do you make lightning?"

"We gather sky energy. What can yellow dragons do?"

"We control our inner energy." Arak tossed a chunk of ice into a ceramic bowl. He breathed a small stream of brilliant fire, melting the ice. The air held a pleasant burnt smell.

Drakor felt the water. "It isss warm. Water isss why

yellow dragons make fire?"

"It *is* a quick way to get water from ice, and hot water for tea. We also make smoky fires to preserve fish for the winter."

Drakor shrugged, still looking at the water. "There isss always water at our hot springs. But this could be useful. How do you make fire?"

"Dragons have two stomachs. We eat nuts and fish that have lots of oil. During our first two years, all of our food goes to the first stomach and we use it to grow. After that, the extra oil is stored in the second stomach, with carbon. To breathe fire, you spit the oil mix and light it with sparks from a copper claw."

"I will learn to do this," Drakor said confidently. He wrinkled his nose and glanced at the fire-damaged mast. Then he scanned the deck. The charred spots were filled in, but still as obvious as black rocks on snow. "Lightning?"

Arak nodded. "Black lightning."

Drakor looked up. "Black? That was a warning to leave."

Arak narrowed his eyes. "The message was crystal clear. Why?"

"This huge wing isss like a monster invading our territory." Drakor looked out to sea and noted their heading. He snapped his tail angrily. "Wrong way. My home isss sooner. I must return now."

"Your clan would not welcome us. And, thanks to black lightning, we must return to *our* home to fix the skiff," Arak replied firmly.

Drakor's eyes blazed with anger. He struggled to his feet, wobbling a little. He flexed his claws, gripping wood that was slippery with frozen saltwater. "No."

Arak looked up at the hulking dragon and stood his ground. "We'll help you heal so you can fly again. Then you can return."

Drakor bared his long, sharp teeth. He cleared the deck around him with one sweep of his powerful tail to make a clean fighting circle. "No. I challenge you."

Arak locked eyes with Drakor. "Move back," he ordered his crew-mates. He balanced gracefully on the balls of his feet. "I'm smaller than you, but I'm not injured. If we fight, I will win. I don't want to hurt you."

Drakor took a menacing step forward and growled, "No. I will win." He whipped his tail to strike. Arak leapt above it.

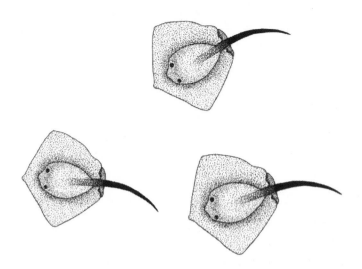

CHAPTER 4: LIGHTNING SWORDS

Dorali jumped between them and put both hands on Drakor's chest. "Stop!"

He looked down at her, eyes wide with surprise.

"Even if you win, what can you do with a broken wing? What happens to an ice dragon who can never fly? I will help the bones grow together and take off the brace when your wing is healed. Then you can return home."

Drakor flinched as if struck. He stared at Dorali. "To fly isss to be free." Then he asked Arak, "How long isss it to your home?"

"Almost two five-days."

Drakor flexed his claws in frustration. Then he said, "I will come." He sat down on the cold deck and gazed silently across the sea, staring at his unseen home as it slipped away.

Arak's battle focus drained away. He squinted as ice crystals were driven into his face by the rising wind. If a strong wind filled the entire skiff-wing, the stress could break their damaged mast. He grabbed a rope and yelled, "Taron! We need a smaller wing fast!"

Arak, Taron, and Dorali struggled to shorten the skiff-wing.

Drakor turned away from his homeland and sat in silence, watching them work. They carefully maneuvered the skiff past another ice-mountain, keeping an eye on the fragile mast. The sky darkened into a night filled with sparkling stars and shimmering lights. Finally Drakor said, "I will help."

"I'll show you how. And I'll teach you how to make dragon-fire," Arak said.

Scree tilted her head back to gaze at sheets of emerald fire that hung in the night sky, dancing in the distant star-breeze. "Orm, this alone is worth the journey north. Auroras are as beautiful as glowfish in the dark abyss."

Orm studied the sky. "It's an artistic display of darkness and light with no giant squid. That *is* a bonus!"

Drakor glanced up. "Storm, stars, black funnel clouds . . . the sky isss always beautiful. The aurora isss even more beautiful when we fly very high in the wind-stream. That isss a fast ride, like an air slide." He stood up. "The wind isss steady. Now isss a good time to learn. I am ready to make fire."

Arak rubbed his forehead. "Drakor, if you can understand the wind, fire will be easy."

"Is this wise?" Scree asked with her silent sign language.

He shrugged and signed back, "I think he'd learn anyway, by watching our clan. This way he learns as a friend." Arak placed a ceramic bowl in a safe spot, away from the mast and rails. "First, you must learn to zap.

Then you can make fire." He held out his claws, and a bright spark flew into the exact center of the bowl. "Concentrate on your inner energy to zap."

Drakor furrowed his brow. His face was a storm cloud of concentration and his claws sparkled like the edge of lightning. But there were no sparks.

Arak pointed to the stars. "You learned to gather lightning energy from the sky. I'm sure you can learn to gather body energy to make a spark."

"Gathering from inside isss not the same as gathering from clouds," Drakor growled. He tried again and again while stars moved across the night sky. Finally, a small, starry spark flew from his claws. It barely hit the rim of the bowl. "Yesss!"

By the end of the day, Drakor could zap like a pro. Spark after spark landed in the center of the bowl. Then Arak added oil to the bowl. Drakor zapped a spark into the oil and stared hungrily into the flaming bowl as if it held the last fish in the sea.

Orm turned golden-orange with a pattern of red sparks. "Fire that burns."

Scree laughed. "Add some scales and you'll look like a dragon."

The next day, Drakor learned to spit oil and spark it. He made streams of fire. Then he blew rings of fire. The smoke clouds smelled like grilled air. "This isss interesting. It isss good to learn new ways." He stretched his good wing and glowered at the wing brace. "But it isss hard to get used to this."

"But worth the effort," Dorali said sternly. "Not flying is much worse." She set down a tray with mugs of spiced red root tea.

"Thanks! Perfect timing," Arak said as he sipped the ruby warmth. "Drakor, where do you get your lightning metals?"

Drakor swallowed a steaming mug of tea in one gulp and picked up another. "There are rare metals near our hot springs. When we toss titanium into a lightning shaft, it glows black and sparkles like diamonds. Beautiful. Black lightning isss special."

Arak snapped his tail. "Should I feel honored that an ice dragon attacked us with black lightning?"

Drakor shrugged his wings. "Probably. They wanted to drive the point home."

Arak stared at the charred wood on his skiff, feeling an inner storm of anger. Then he laughed. "Definitely driven home."

Drakor clouted Arak on the back, nearly knocking him over. "Now I will teach you to gather lightning with no storm. First, stand tall. It helps to be higher in the sky."

Arak stretched taller.

"Tilt your claws toward a sparkle in the clouds. Feel the tingle." Drakor gestured with his claws. "Gather charges of energy. A small energy ball in your claws pulls in more energy. It isss like a snowball rolling down a hill. The snowball gathers more and more snow. Soon you have enough energy to make a lightning bolt."

Arak tilted his copper claws and concentrated. Nothing happened. "Drakor, you're right. Gathering sky energy to make lightning is very different from focusing body energy to make sparks." He tried again. And again. Late in the evening, Arak finally held a tiny pearl of fire. He had a happy/proud/exhausted expression on his face.

Scree's eyes twinkled. "You look just like a dragon-lady gazing at her first egg."

Arak gathered more energy and the fire pearl grew. "It's like holding a star."

Scree watched closely. "I can't see magnetic lines, but I can feel energy. I want to hold a star."

Drakor nodded to Arak. "That isss good. Let the lightning ball grow bigger. Then we will learn to find wrinkles so you can hit a target. This turns the bolt into a lightning sword."

Arak looked up from his star. "What?"

"Wrinkles are wiggly magnetic lines. They attract lightning. I use my inner sight to find a magnetic wrinkle near the target. Wrinkles are small and do not hold still. When the wrinkle isss on top of the target I toss the bolt. The wrinkle will attract the lightning bolt and I will hit my target."

"That would be more accurate than the way we toss lightning bolts onto the beach," Taron said, frowning at the shadowed corridor between floating ice-mountains.

Arak followed his gaze. "Dorali, grab that pole. We may need it."

Drakor eyed the channel and stood taller. "Why do you hit sand?"

Taron adjusted the tiller, carefully guiding the skiff down the middle. "The sand melts and makes glass rods. Octopi love them and trade us beautiful pearls, seaweed, even oyster spat."

Drakor grimaced. "Spat?"

Arak laughed, but his eyes were glued to the ice-mountains. "Spat is oyster seed, to grow oysters. They're tasty, and oysters make a strong reef. The tsunami tore up our shore under the sea. We put oyster spat on rope nets and placed them on the dead sand, weighted with rocks. This has grown into an oyster reef."

Taron added, "Octopi planted new eelgrass below the waves. This and the oysters helped bring back the fish, and our undersea shore is alive again."

Thick, blue-gray shadows filled the channel like dense smoke. Pale afternoon light slid along the knife-sharp edges of ice.

Arak laid his ears back instinctively as he faced this menace. "How do you find magnetic wrinkles?" he asked, almost as an after-thought. The ice danger sucked him in as surely as a bog of quicksand.

"The same way I gather sky energy: I concentrate." Drakor flicked his claws out and a bright pearl appeared. It quickly grew into a glowing, twisting ball. "Magnetic wrinkles are small, and they wriggle."

Arak glanced at the energy pearl for just a moment. "I watch sparkles in the magnetic field to judge the strength of storms. I follow curved magnetic lines to find land. But I can't see wrinkles . . . yet." He stared at the towering walls of ice as they entered the narrow channel.

Taron carefully adjusted the tiller, steering the dragon-skiff down the center.

An ice-mountain tilted, creating a powerful whirlpool that sucked them into the ice. Taron lifted the wood pole and stared hopelessly at the falling giant.

Time slowed. The sky disappeared. Dragons stretched their wings to fly. Orm and Scree flowed to the edge of the skiff, ready to drop into the sea. All too late. The air grew heavier as the mountain rolled over, crushing down.

A ball of blinding white light flew to the ice, stretching, growing into a lightning sword. The tip gouged deep into a crack, boiling the ice from within. The iceberg shattered. Ice chunks rained down and skittered across the deck as the skiff slipped past to safety.

Everyone stared at Drakor.

He flicked ice off the deck with his long tail. "This isss good practice for the ice game Slam." Chunks flew overboard, skimming just above the rail, one after another. It was a precision drill.

"You knew that ice-mountain would fall?" Arak asked.

Drakor shrugged his wings. "Not sure. The ice-mountain was old, worn on top, so I was watching. Old, white mountains are more likely to flip over. After it flips, the ice isss blue like the sea."

Arak clapped him on the shoulder. "So that's why some are blue. That was a useful lightning bolt."

Drakor grinned. "I make lots of lightning swords to practice for the games."

Taron hit ice chunks with his tail, but they merely slid beneath the rail. "How do you play games with lightning swords?"

"Many ice targets are put on an ice field. Then the drum beats slowly. Each player has one turn. There are ten drumbeats to hit targets with lightning swords. The winner is the dragon who hits the most targets in the least drumbeats." Drakor's eyes glowed.

Dorali wiped cold sea spray off her face. "Have you won?"

Drakor studied his sharp claws in silence. He flicked them out and started growing a new lightning sword. "Yes."

Arak stared at the open sky. "I think I'll find some

wrinkles now."

Scree scrunched her eyes, concentrating as she adjusted the tiny mirrors in her cells. The shining image of a lightning bolt flew across her body. "Orm, imagine throwing a lightning spear!"

Orm shook his head. "Underwater? We don't even have copper claws."

"The dragons are learning new ways to control energy. Maybe we can, too. We're not always under the sea and we do have copper blood. I want to hold a star."

Orm smiled. "You've always loved stars. That's why I made you a star ceiling. Scree, are you ever tired of trying the impossible?"

"Never. You started the first farm, grew the first pearls, and saved Arak's dragon-dam. I'm no more tired of trying than you are. We just choose different impossibles." Scree curled and stretched each arm. "I won't know what I can do until I try."

Scree entered a light trance and focused on the sky. After hours and hours of staring into the sky, she slumped down into her basin, as limp as a jellyfish. "I can't see *any* sky energy. I may never hold a star." Then she popped up, arms straight and strong. "Maybe octopi can't find sky energy. But I can talk mind-to-mind and feel the lightning inside my blood. I'll try to find my inner electric energy."

Scree looked at Orm. "If an eel can give an electric shock, then an octopus can zap. I *will* learn to do this."

Orm made his skin sparkle. "I have no doubt. You'll learn to control your natural electricity and then teach this to others. I'm trying to imagine a whole pod of octopi zapping like eels."

The next day, Arak squinted into a bright blue sky,

working to keep his eyes open while he also looked with inner sight. He quickly pointed to one magnetic wrinkle after another.

Drakor eyed Arak's invisible wrinkles and nodded. "Good."

"There's nothing like a near disaster to motivate me to learn," Arak said.

"Now, gather energy and grow a lightning ball. Find a magnetic wrinkle near your target. Wait for the wrinkle to move over the target. Then throw the lightning."

There was a flash of light and a small, nearly melted ice-hill exploded. Drakor clouted Arak on the back. "Well done."

The sea turned lumpy white, with the color and texture of summer clouds. Thousands of cloudy, pulsing umbrellas bounced off the skiff.

Dorali stared. "It's a huge swarm of jellyfish."

Drakor gazed into the sea. "I have not seen this before." Then he looked due north, absently tossing a tiny spark between his claws. His eyes were focused on the horizon.

Arak followed his gaze. "We'll bring you safely home."

"But will I get back in time to warn the clan?"

"You said they wouldn't listen to you. It's hard for anyone to believe in a danger so rare. But, if you're right about that volcano, we may all have a problem."

* * *

Early dawn shimmered with rainbow brush strokes across the watery gray sky. Scree grabbed Orm's arm. "Look!"

Orm glanced up and stared. "It looks like an abalone

shell!"

Arak studied the iridescent display. "It's an abalone sky. I've never seen one before. These must be cloud colors of the north."

Drakor grinned, showing his long, sharp teeth. "They are rare even here."

Arak nodded. "What's in your bag?" He pointed to Drakor's silver-blue sack. The supple, fish-skin leather had shimmering scales with colors that rippled like ice-water.

Drakor opened his bag. "A water flask, a diamond crystal, and metals. Titanium to make black lightning and cobalt for blue." The silver flask reflected the colors of the sky. He lifted a large silver-gray crystal, carefully, as if it was a precious dragon egg. "Titanium isss a rare, magic metal."

Dorali's wings rustled with excitement. "Could I see your metals? I'll be careful." She took a pouch of dried, gray-green herb from her Healer bag. "Nettle herb has a metallic taste, and stings when it's fresh. Nettle tea helps heal dragon bones and scales. Orm, could you check this against Drakor's metals?"

Orm held the herb with one arm and touched Drakor's metals with another. "I feel titanium. Nettle concentrates this metal."

Drakor leaned down and sniffed. "I only smell plant."

Arak took a close look. "Titanium is rare. If nettle could make a black fire, it would be much easier to use the plant than to find metal crystals."

Orm plucked a bristly plant from Dorali's bag. "What's this?"

"Horsetail. I use this in a tea to help with swollen

joints, and to scrub out the tea kettle."

Orm ran an arm across the stalks, feeling with his sensitive suckers. "There's titanium and gold in this plant. Horsetail is a very fancy scrubber."

Drakor looked up at the sky. "Now would be a good time to practice gathering lightning and finding wrinkles."

All three golden dragons took turns working with him, trading off for skiff duty.

As the day drew to a close, Scree watched the horizon. "We should get back in time for our New Moon Festival."

"Maybe." Orm dropped a piece of wood overboard and counted how long it took to travel from bow to stern. "Five knots. We're not moving very fast, but we could get home in time."

"Orm, stop analyzing. Watch with me. I love to see the sun melt into the sea. It never seems to set; it just dissolves like dragon candy." The red ball shrank ever smaller on the horizon, as cherry-red light spread across the evening waves. "This is a treasure of the mind. I don't need to stuff it into my sea cave. Vorm was right. Memories are all we truly own."

Orm changed his body color to mirror the sunset. Colors drained down his arms and disappeared as he turned a star-sparkled midnight blue. "About that dragon candy . . ." He tossed something to Scree and she grabbed it out of the sky. "I saved two pieces of chocolate. This is a treasure of the mouth."

Scree turned happy-green.

The skiff flew south, passing smaller and smaller hills of floating ice. Then there were none. Winter was still in the air, but frost no longer fouled the skiff-wing. The sky was deep blue, and the wind was so steady that Arak lashed the tiller, letting the skiff fly on its own. They all took a break, together, and it felt like a holiday.

The sea sizzled as every dragon on the skiff hit the same floating piece of driftwood with a bolt of lightning. Thunder boomed.

Taron grinned. "Wrinkles make a difference."

Dorali made a glowing pearl. "It's interesting energy."

Arak laughed. "You're a good teacher, Drakor. We can spear a target with lightning on a day with no storm."

Drakor flared his nostrils as salty smoke blew across the skiff. "That isss a new smell. Now learn to find *all* the wrinkles, fast, so you can hit many targets."

Arak tilted his head, considering. "That would take this game to a whole new level. I'd love to see that."

Drakor had a gleam in his eyes. "Toss ten pieces of wood on the sea and I will demonstrate."

Soon, ten wood targets were scattered across the sea.

Drakor stood tall. His eyes held fierce determination. Then sword after sword flew from his claws. Within minutes, every target burned on the sea.

Arak snapped his tail. "You must win many games!"

Scree and Orm applauded with brightly colored arms.

Then Scree pointed to the sea, where three stingrays flew across the waves. "The sea has fiery swords, too. Orm, I can't see magnetic wrinkles or gather outer energy. I can't hold a glowing star or make a lightning sword. But I *can* gather inner energy." She placed the tip of one arm into a bowl and the water shimmered.

Orm eyed the bowl. "Sparkling water. I'll bet you have more inner energy than a thunderstorm."

Dorali took a close look. "Touch my arm." Scree did as she asked. "That's a micro-zap! Keep practicing and

I'll teach you how to use this for healing."

The wind shifted slightly. Taron checked their heading and adjusted the tiller, as automatically as breathing. "I think you could fly this skiff in your sleep," Arak said.

Taron nodded. "So could you. The wind and waves are inside us now."

Drakor studied the sparkling water bowl. "Interesting. Healing isss good but I am more interested in fighting."

Dorali tilted her head. "Why?"

Drakor looked to the north. "Mardor isss our leader because he won every fight."

"You choose a leader by fighting?" Arak asked.

"A big, strong dragon isss always the leader. How do you choose?"

Arak stretched his wings, considering. "When the clan leader wants to stop leading, she suggests a new leader. If most of the clan wants this dragon to lead, she is chosen. It's a hard job and she's not an absolute ruler."

"The leader does not tell you what to do?"

Arak shook his head. "I think she would like to. The leader tells the clan what we should do, and we discuss this. We meet and make decisions with consensus. Each dragon has a cone dipped in salt. If I agree, I toss my cone into the basket. All these cones are tossed into the fire together. If there are enough cones, they make a blue-green fire that means yes."

"Kon-sen-sus?" Drakor clicked his claws as he puzzled over the word.

"We talk things over until most of us agree that it's a good idea."

Drakor frowned. "That sounds very sloppy. Our

leader just tells us what we must do."

"It sounds like you have no choice, even if your leader has bad ideas," Dorali said.

Drakor threw back his head and laughed. "That isss true." He warmed the tea kettle with dragon-fire, and scented steam filled the air. Then he poured tea for everyone. "Arak, you were right. Flames are useful. What else can you do?"

Arak sipped his tea and flicked his tail as he studied the big white dragon. Finally he said, "We can speak mind-to-mind, without words."

Drakor stood straighter and his eyes glowed with interest. "That could be *very* useful."

*   *   *

The long swells of the open sea were gone, replaced by smaller waves that tugged at the skiff. Arak filled his lungs with the reassuring smells of home: old seaweed washed ashore, early spring buds, smoked fish. His home had everything: the sounds and smells and colors of the sea, a limestone cave that could hold the entire clan comfortably in bad weather, a forest with wood for skiffs and fires. A smile lit his eyes. Best of all, soon he would see Zarina and their dragonlet. He felt a pang of sorrowful understanding for the ice dragons. Of course they didn't listen to Drakor's warning. It would be hard for anyone to leave their home forever.

The dragon-shore appeared on the horizon. Drakor pointed north, toward the long white edge that sparkled. "You still have big ice?"

"Some. In winter this land is completely covered with snow and ice. Our Winter Festival has games, cloud sculptures, ice sculptures and feasts."

Drakor nodded. "Our Winter Festival has ice games on a frozen lake. We use our tail to knock a stone into the goal. Dragon pairs carve huge ice sculptures with lightning. And, we compete with lightning swords."

"That would be an amazing sight," Orm said.

Arak translated and added, "I'd like to see your festival."

"We're home!" Arak guided the skiff to a soft landing at the dock. He helped Taron tie the skiff to solid pilings, feeling the change in the rhythm beneath his feet. Ice crystals sparkled in the sand beyond the waves.

Dorali set the wood plank between skiff and dock and walked carefully down.

Drakor followed her off the skiff, with his eyes scanning everything. He stepped onto the dock and lurched. His legs moved in a strange way. "Why isss it so hard to walk?"

Her eyes twinkled. "Your feet expect the land to rise up and meet them. Arak says that when you're on a skiff, you walk with the sea. You move as the sea moves and soon you have sea legs. Now you need to find your land legs."

Drakor walked slowly down the dock, heading for shore, still lifting his feet higher than necessary. "It feels like the land isss moving." He glanced at the rowdy crowd of golden dragons that lined the shore, jostling each other, staring at him. "What do they want?"

"They're eager to see a real, legendary ice dragon," Dorali said.

Drakor snorted. "We were always real."

CHAPTER 5: SHARK RIDE

Scree tied their octopus skiff to a raft that was anchored above her village. A fiery sunset gleamed across the damp logs. The raft was a gift to the pod to honor Orm and Scree. They had solved a mysterious illness, identified a poison in the copper mine, and saved the dragons.

A wax-filled ceramic bowl was fastened to the top of a tall pole, to hold signal fires, to call the dragons in time of need. This signal had been useful when the pod was attacked by a giant squid.

But now, octopi could talk mind-to-mind with dragons, in trance. That was far more efficient than a signal fire. Still, this raft was an excellent place to dock their skiffs.

Scree wrapped one arm through her Healer bag handle while Orm checked the knots. They both grabbed sacks of food and slipped over the side. Scree and Orm twirled down through the sea together, arms sensing, feeling the feast through the water.

"This will be our last pod celebration before the Trading Festival. Orm, feel the foods. I taste abalone and spices," Scree said.

"Abalone meat is a rare treat. Abalone skies are splendid and Arak found his ice dragons, but I've missed our village." Orm turned happy-green. "There's chocolate! Just wait 'til the pod sees these cherry clams. Kragor likes growing them in his sea farm."

Scree rippled with laughter. "I think Kragor just wants another excuse to stick his head underwater. He loves to make glowing gardens beneath the waves."

Orm nodded. "Sometimes I wonder if he's part octopus. You can tell he's Arak's sire, with his love for the sea."

Scree tapped her bag with one arm. "The pod won't expect these sea cucumbers from the ice abyss! Tarm showed me where they gather . . . food too small to interest him."

Orm twined an arm with Scree as they landed softly on the sand near the dance floor. "I'm glad Tarm decided *you* weren't food."

The beat of pounded giant clam shells pulsed through Scree's body. Sound traveled through the sea much faster than through air, and she marveled at the difference. There was a shell drum in the center of her village to call the pod. This beat would reach everyone faster than she could shape-shift.

Scree gazed into the sea. Far beyond, there was a warning circle of tall kelp trees with dangling shells. If a giant squid pushed through this kelp forest, the shells would clang together and the unique sound would warn the pod. Would they be ready?

Pairs of young octopi twirled through the water above newly raked sand. The dancers had changed their arm skin to bright colors: orange, teal, yellow, red-violet, and more. Their swirling arms matched the drumming pulse of pounded shells.

Scree was caught by the light current and pulled from side to side as she pulsed, moving in a pattern with the dancing water. "I'll put my Healer bag away," she told Orm, and squirted to her cave. An elegant garden of red, green, and brown seaweed surrounded her home. It rippled with the sea and seemed to wave a greeting. She flowed into her cave.

Orm's glowing tunicates made stars in a night sky on her ceiling. He had even added a group of anemones with long arms that glowed in reds and greens, waving through the water like northern lights. Scree ran an arm over the rolls of gray-green kelp bandages, tasting to determine freshness, and nodded with satisfaction. Krees must have replaced these recently.

Scree added food to a bowl filled with live limpets and checked the shelves along both sides of her cave. A sparkling, green garnet jar held poison from the deadly blue-ringed octopus; this made an excellent sedative. A small box that was carved from dark red coral had sharp, hollow needles. These were spines from the fin of a dead lion-fish. In life, this beautiful fish could inject poison through its fin.

There were rows of hinged containers made from scallop shells: yellow, orange, red, and purple. These colorful boxes held iodine-rich seaweed, sponges, oily salves, herbs, and supplements. Silvery shell boxes had the dragon spices: cinnamon, pepper, garlic, and more. These had a great feel/taste and Healer uses, too. She checked the knives, testing for sharpness. Everything was in its proper place.

Scree flowed out of her cave and joined Orm, heading for the feast. Purple sea fans, dark blue starfish, scarlet barrel sponges, seaweeds, and schools of fish covered the reef with a riot of color. A crab ambled across the coral, covered by dozens of orange-and-pink anemones. "That crab likes to decorate with sunset colors."

Orm pointed to a burgundy starfish draped over living lilac coral; its crusty skin had a jewel-like pattern of tiny scarlet bumps. He mimicked the color and texture on his octopus body. "That starfish looks like a garnet carving covered with red seed pearls. Maybe Taron could make one."

"He'd carve one for his dragonlet." Scree slipped sideways to avoid a stinging jellyfish; layers of cloudy flounces hung below the pulsing bronze umbrella. Sounds of the sea passed through her, and the vibrations of fish grinding their teeth. A parrot fish took another bite of coral before swimming away. "I've missed the reef. I wish those fish would stop chewing it!"

Scree slid slowly toward a dull coral boulder, the color of dead seagrass. It was dotted with tiny, bright flowers of pink, orange, or blue. Scree pulsed closer. The frilly flower-worms disappeared into their tubes, reacting instantly to the ripple in the water. "Our flowers move fast."

"They're like bursts of colored dragon-lightning. No land flowers could match this," Orm said proudly.

The watery light from the sun faded away with the day and glowing fish appeared, giving their living light to the reef. Tall poles were set in the sand, making circles within circles like a full moon. Baskets filled with food were fastened to the top. The New Moon Festival was lit by glowfish that swarmed around the poles, feeding on treats.

The pulsing beats continued. An elderly octopus removed a large white pearl from his sucker. It flashed through the water, shining like the moon, tossed from arm to arm as he whirled. This ancient dance celebrated their Mother, the Moon.

A change in drum beat announced the important, traditional circle dance.

Scree grabbed Orm's arm. "Hurry! We're just in time!" They slipped through clusters of purple sea fans that edged the dance floor. This level field of sand had been cleared for dancing long ago. She twined one side arm with Orm and the opposite side arm with another octopus, becoming part of a huge circle. Three arms were behind each octopus, serving as anchors, and three arms were ahead to twirl the dancers.

Eight dancers took their places inside the circle, facing the outer ring. Each dancer gripped three arms of an octopus in the ring. On the beat, they were flung to the next pod-mate in the circle. The dancers quickly released their former hold and grabbed three new arms. Boom. They were flung again, releasing and grabbing arms. Boom! They were flung again. Boom-Boom-Boom. The beat grew faster. Dancers were flung again and again, twirling about the inside of the circle, spinning like tops.

The drumming stopped and the dancers melted back

into the ring. Scree was one of the eight new octopi who took their places inside the circle. Scree loved the flying sensation as she was whirled about, twirling in circles within the big ring. She released three arms and grabbed three more.

All too soon, the rhythmic beating stopped and the dance ended. Scree leaned contentedly against Orm. "I love the circle dance. It's like flying on a dragon."

"And so much safer," Orm said, twining arms affectionately.

An octopus musician took her place on a coral head. She played three instruments at once, beating two giant clamshell drums with red coral sticks. Riss made a sharp crack of thunder on the larger shell and muffled rumblings of distant thunder on the smaller shell. She scraped across grooves on a third instrument, adding the sound of surf-waves pulling back into the sea. The performance was a rhythmic blending of sea, sky, and shore. Scree felt the vibrations as they rippled through her body; the last pulse fled into the darkness beyond.

Then three strong beats announced the feast. Orm turned gold. "Feel those dragon spices! It's enough to make anyone hungry!" They squirted to the feasting table, which was made from hundreds of coral rocks. This kept the food above the sand stirred up by the octopi.

Gigantic clam-shell bowls were filled with temptations. Ground peppercorn was worked into abalone meat, releasing a tide of flavors. Carved coral shakers were filled with dragon herbs and spices. There were crab claws, scallops, lobsters, shrimp, and seaweed salads. A huge shell, big enough to hide an octopus, held succulent oysters decorated with colorful sprigs of seaweed. Orm and Scree added their cherry clams and sea cucumbers to the table. Then they joined the octopi gathered in lines at the sumptuous buffet.

Orm sighed. "I was right. Chocolate!" Bright orange scallop shell pairs were clustered together on the table, holding balls of chocolate within their hinged wings. The candies were coated with nut oils to protect them from the sea, so they wouldn't dissolve until eaten.

A jar of red-root tea had curls of cinnamon bark and a spigot. Scree filled her glass, pushed on the rubbery top, and put her stem straw through a hole in the lid. "Ahhh. Perfect."

Scree and Orm filled shell plates with tasty treasures. Then they settled onto the sand, joining a circle of friends. Orm leaned forward eagerly, talking with his apprentices, signing while he ate. "How are the abalone crops? And the pearls?"

Stur, the pod leader, joined their group. He greeted Scree and Orm with the double clasp of friendship. "It's good to have you back. What did you learn in the northern sea?"

"It's so cold that the sea is nearly frozen. It has a slushy sound and I could see ice crystals growing in the water. I met Tarm in the depths, and he still fears my magic arms." Scree twisted an arm upside down, showing the hidden wax balls that held a potent poison. "Our treaty holds, but some of the younger squid don't respect it. Are we ready for an attack?"

Stur turned a paler shade of brown. "Ever since you warned me in trance-mind, we've had daily spear-throwing practice. I'd like to discuss this attack with you, and other problems. Later."

Scree pulled a sample from the small pouch tied to the upper part of one arm. "As a former Healer, I thought you might be interested in this new seaweed I found."

Stur felt the thin, golden-green leaf, delicately tasting and sensing with his suckers. "What does it do?"

"When I squished a piece, it made my arms numb. This could be a useful sedative."

Orm laughed. "So if you squish this seaweed, you can't talk?"

Scree gave him a wicked smile. "I can always use pictures." She flashed an image on her skin for barely an instant. The head of the monstrous viper-fish had long, sharp, curved fangs. This body-picture appeared and disappeared so quickly that only an octopus eye could see it.

Orm blanched white. "Naturally. But arms are so civilized. Less graphic."

Stur flowed upright and gave a general nod to the group. "Later?" he said, facing Scree and Orm.

"Yes."

Krees waited respectfully until their leader left. Then she proudly displayed her Healer bag, which was made from cloth-of-gold and covered with hundreds of tiny shells. "It's finally done. I thought I'd never finish sewing all these shells on! I mixed tan, brown, and dark brown shells to make a better camouflage pattern."

Scree inspected the shell covering and each inner compartment. "Perfect. The design is lovely and everything is well organized."

Scrim and Tor silently held up their Healer bags for inspection.

"Tor, how clever of you to put slip knots on the

compartments."

Tor turned happy-green.

"Scrim, where did you find *blue* sea fans for dividers?" Scree asked.

Scrim pointed southeast. "They grow on the slope that leads down to the abyss."

She twined two arms with each of her three fosterling apprentices. "I chose well." Scree was like a sun in the center, with arm-rays linked to her friends and loving warmth in each embrace. She untied an upper-arm pouch with her remaining two arms. "These are the surgeon's knives I promised, one for each of you. Jade is sturdy and holds an edge."

Krees stared. "Purple jade. It's almost too beautiful." She turned the knife from side to side, running the tip of an arm along the blade before adding it to her bag.

Tor bowed and put the gift carefully into his surgeon's compartment.

Scrim held his knife by the point and tossed it high. The sharp blade spun up through the water, turning over and over as it fell. He caught the rounded handle and smiled. "It's perfectly balanced."

"Why does that matter?" Scree asked as he slipped it into his bag.

"A weapon can be useful."

Scree looked meaningfully at his bag. "You're a Healer."

"You used a poisoned spear on the giant squid when it attacked the pod," Scrim said.

"I used poison as a sedative to stop him."

Scrim nodded. "So would I."

Scree studied her apprentice. He held himself tall and

proud, but she felt no meanness inside. "And then you'd help."

Scrim blinked both eyes. "Of course. I'm a Healer."

Scree clapped two arms on his octopus shoulders. "You should lead a pod defense squad. I'll talk to Stur."

Orm jetted over just as a large fish with bright golden scales appeared, seeking scraps. Scree drew in the wet sand with three arms that moved so fast they were a blur. She decorated the sea floor with an accurate sketch of the fish. "It's good to see bigger fish again; our reef felt empty after the last eruption. Now the volcano taste is growing stronger and changing." She curled her arms nervously.

Orm grabbed Scree's arm. "We can discuss this later. It's story-telling time. Let's go!" They pulsed to a boulder surrounded by raked sand.

Tall poles, each topped with a basket of smashed crabs, made a circle around the boulder. This food attracted reef glowfish to light the story-teller. Farther out, at the edge of darkness, a circle of glowing jellyfish lit the water. Light pulsed down their long tentacles, rippling like an aurora, as they devoured tiny shrimp from more poles. Scree pointed to the shimmering jellyfish lights. "This is new, and I like it."

Scree and Orm were almost buried as current and former fosterlings flowed over and twined arms with their mentors. The enthusiastic greetings overlapped, as tangled as the branching arms of a basket starfish.

Stur, the pod leader and Scree's former fosterling, flowed up onto the stage. Three arms hung down in front, close together, to extend his body-screen. Three arms were behind for balance. He raised two side arms high, and stillness settled over the pod. "This is the legend of Sorm, the First Octopus."

Scree grabbed Orm's arm. "What? That's your special story!"

He grinned. "I have a new one to tell."

Stur made pictures across his body-screen while one arm on either side wove words through the water. "Our mother, the Moon, ruled the seas and created the tides. But she was lonely. She wanted a child. So she gathered rich mud from the bottom of the sea and formed a round head like the moon. Then she made two arms for each of her four moon phases."

Stur closed his eyes. His head turned white like a full moon. He twisted each pair of arms together until they seemed like four. Then he lifted his arms high and unraveled the pairs into eight octopus arms. "She showered her child with moonlight, and his arms danced with life! But he could not see. So she gave him eyes."

Stur opened his eyes.

"When he saw his beautiful mother, he bowed before her. The Moon was pleased and gave him more ways to know her world. He could taste subtle flavors and feel the most delicate touch. He could feel-hear the beating sounds in the sea. His mind could remember and imagine. She named him Sorm. 'What must I do?' he asked."

"'You must prove yourself by performing four tasks, one for each of my phases. Then you will be worthy to be called my child and I will give you a home in the sea,' the Moon replied."

Stur held a bag made from the flexible purple skeletons of sea fans.

Scree stared. That was Orm's precious legend-sack!

Her mate had searched for years to collect all the shells and rare stones from his favorite legend.

Stur described the first task of finding a shell that swims. The Moon was pleased and scallops became their first food. The second task was to find a ball of sky living in the sea. Sorm finally found sky living inside seaweed floats, and seaweed became their second food.

"The third task was more difficult, to create the Moon's image on his skin and of his skin, to show he was her child. Sorm painted dyes on his skin, but they faded away and were not truly of his body. He could change his skin colors to match almost anything, but it happened without thought. Then he made a dark circle on white sand and concentrated when his body naturally made a circle. He tried and tried, until he could make the full moon circle at any time. The Moon approved, and Sorm learned a new way to communicate."

Stur imaged a simple moon circle on his body.

"The fourth and last task was the most difficult, to find the most beautiful stone. It seemed easy, for there were many lovely stones in the sea. Red coral was a living jewel the color of a sunset sky. Black garnet was a rare, glittering gem like a star-studded sky. Coral agate looked like a storm cloud, with lightning colors running through its lumpy white surface. Sorm trembled with excitement when he found a white marble ball in a sea-flooded cave. It looked just like the full Moon. But it was dull."

Stur reached into Orm's legend-sack and raised four arms. He held a branch of polished red coral, sparkling black garnet, colorful coral agate, and a white cave pearl.

"Almost two years had passed. Sorm yearned to complete his task, to earn his place in his mother's heart

and in the sea. He was tired of traveling. He wanted a
home. But he was afraid to bring the wrong stone. No
stone seemed quite perfect enough for the Moon. As Sorm
pulsed through the water, searching, a flash of silver
caught his eye. A fish thrashed, struggling desperately. Its
fin was caught in the seam of a large oyster shell. 'Help
me!'

"Sorm pried the shell apart, just a little, and the fish
swam free. But it did not leave, even though it feared him.
'You saved me. I am in your debt. How can I help you?'

"'I must find the most beautiful stone for the Moon,'
Sorm replied.

"'Open this shell, and you will find what you seek,'
said the grateful fish.

"Sorm opened the oyster and found a big, round,
gleaming white pearl. This was the perfect stone! It
looked just like the Moon. Sorm gave her the pearl.

"'You are indeed the child of my heart,' the Moon
said, and gave him a beautiful cave in the sea. Because
the fish helped, octopi do not eat fish. And even today, all
newly hatched octopi must prove themselves. They leave
home and live a dangerous life on the waves for almost
two years before they return. Survivors are welcomed
home, just as Sorm was. Octopi celebrate our Mother with
the New Moon Festival. We feast, to remind her to grow
full and bright again. We dance with pearls to celebrate
her beauty."

Stur lifted a huge white pearl, shining like white fire
against his red-brown skin. Then he danced with the
pearl. It slid down one flexible arm and was flipped to the
next, caught and flung in a pattern. He tossed the ball
high, whirling like a top beneath it. He caught the pearl,

paused, and bowed.

The watching octopi lifted their arms high above their heads. The arms changed to rainbow colors and wove words of praise through the sea.

"He did well," Scree said with pride in her former fosterling. "But I'm used to your story-telling. That was nice, lending Stur your legend-sack."

Orm shrugged his octopus shoulders in a dragonly gesture. "He needed it." Then he pulsed forward, settled on the stage, and gazed at his audience. The octopi lowered their speaking arms respectfully and sat in stillness. All eyes were fixed on Orm. "This is the story of the giant squid." He spoke like a dancer, with eloquent gestures.

Scree glanced at the audience. Every octopus eye was focused on Orm. Even their skin seemed to shimmer with concentration, seeing through the thousands of tiny eye-cells.

"This is also the legend of Scree. Not so many moons ago, a giant squid attacked our First Village. Long arms crushed caves and grabbed pod-mates to eat." A horrific movie played across Orm's body-screen. "Scree made a poison spear and attacked this monster. It caught her, studied her, and then collapsed from the poison."

Scree blushed purple as many pod-mates turned one appraising eye on her, while continuing to watch Orm with their dominant eye. Everyone knew the basic story, but Orm was a master storyteller. He made this experience vivid, terrifying, and real.

"Almost everyone wanted to kill the giant. But Scree did not want to kill. She wanted to learn more of this being . . . and she is a Healer. So the squid was bound with strong cords." Orm showed an image of a tiny octopus facing the giant squid. "Scree learned the squid light-language. When you understand someone, you see with new eyes. His name was Vorm." Orm made a series of yellow and red light spots on his arms.

"Vorm shared squid customs and legends with Scree, and she missed him when he died. The pod carried his body and released it to the dark abyss, following squid custom."

Orm showed the pod carrying Vorm's long body. Then the squid tumbled over the ledge into darkness.

"Scree explored and learned that more squid were leaving their abyss. She feared an attack and wanted to challenge the giant squid in their home. Arak made a plan for Scree. Dragons and octopi worked together to help. Scree fought one giant in the abyss and then made a peace pact with the squid. It is important to know your enemy, both the dangers and the possibilities."

Orm grabbed a food container with one of his arms and tossed the contents up into the sea. A cloud of glittering, glowing reef fish gathered around him in the night sea. "Life speaks with light in the dark abyss." He covered his body with images of strange, glowing deep-sea fish. "Now we will share the dance of the giant squid." Orm turned dark red and transformed his body. He stretched his head twice as long, making it flatter and pointed, and reached a long red arm to Scree.

Scree turned surprise-orange. She hesitated. Then she transformed into a squid. Bright yellow light-spots appeared on her arms as she joined Orm on the stage. She adjusted her tiny cell-mirrors to reflect maximum light through the color spots. Scree and Orm flashed a rhythm of lights that matched the drum beats. They twirled side-by-side in tight, glowing circles, moving ever closer until they almost touched. Their arms meshed perfectly as they spun. Yellow light-spots flared at the tips and flowed upward in unison. Red spots flashed another pattern.

Orm and Scree twirled faster and faster until their light-spots blended together. Shimmering rings were spun from the sparkling spots, and they moved inside this. They stopped spinning, and their arms wrapped around each other in graceful curves.

Scree spoke with the light-spots of squid language while Orm translated with his dancing arms: "May you surf the tangled currents of the sea forever." Scree shifted back into octopus form and spoke again. "Giant squid are dangerous, but they are also intelligent and interesting. They glow brightly through life. When I stopped Vorm, I only did what needed to be done. Any one of you could do this. It is a choice. We are each capable of choosing to do what is needed."

The audience turned brilliant dragon-gold to signal appreciation, waving arms with dragon-scale patterns. Some octopi changed their arms to traditional, jewel-toned patterns. They waved arms with rose-and-gold diamonds, copper-and-turquoise spirals, and more. A few pod-mates shape-shifted into squid and twirled away through the sea.

Scree jetted off the stage and Orm followed. Her arms were stiff and her eyes sparked with anger. "You gave me no warning."

Orm looked into her angry eyes. "You would not have stayed if you knew. You can face a giant squid but not the legend this becomes. The juveniles must know what has come before. This is our history. You should want them to learn the value of seeing with new eyes."

Scree slumped to the sands as her anger drained away. Her arms lay in loose, random coils like seaweed washed ashore. "Everyone needs to see with new eyes. They also must know that we can make choices. They should seek their inner strength."

Orm spiraled one of his arms affectionately around Scree's closest arm. "You found your courage early. Now you're a legend."

She turned an irritated/challenge blue. "I'm just an octopus."

Orm turned a matching blue. "I'm just a normal blue octopus, looking for sharks to ride."

Scree rolled her eyes.

Young octopi squirted past them, gathering to play a game of Mimic. The lead octopus transformed to become the most unusual creature he had seen. The other players copied him perfectly, and the stingrays they became were quite realistic.

"I've always loved this game," Scree said.

Orm grinned. "So a squid dance was not enough? You've seen beings no one else has. You could join the game. Would you become a deep-sea glowfish, glass sponge, or maybe a purple sea pen?"

Scree shape-shifted and became a cloudy white ball with stripes of iridescent rainbow hairs.

Orm matched her in a drumbeat. Only an octopus could follow the rapid transformation of a shape-shifting octopus.

"Why did you choose to be a comb-jelly?" Orm asked, after they changed back into their normal octopus shape.

"I love their rainbows. Remember the comb-jellies when we skiff-flew on the southern seas? We need to travel again. You have felt the new flavors in the sea. The feel/taste of our volcano is changing faster, and it seems to match the ice abyss near Drakor's volcano island. I need new samples."

A river of fish swam by and turned back upon itself, churning into a silver ball that shifted across the sea.

"An underwater cloud," Scree signed.

Orm copied the fish on his skin. "Arak says every gray cloud has a silver lining. Does every silver cloud have a gray lining? Let's go see Stur."

They squirted back to the meeting circle.

Stur twined arms with Scree, his former mentor, and Orm. "Thank you for coming. Spar's visiting our village and may join us."

Scree settled onto the sand. "What's the problem?"

"This new generation is acting more and more like dragons. More like you."

"This is bad?" Scree asked.

Stur sighed. "I don't know what to do. Every octopus has a wax poison ball, a few have coral knives, and they can throw spears, so they feel safe. Some have learned to speak mind-to-mind. They can call home from far away, so they aren't afraid to travel. They're not careful. Some aren't even worried about giant squid."

Orm looked from Scree to Stur. "Meeting the dragons has been good for the pod. We have dragon spices for our food, skiffs for traveling, poison balls for protection, and chocolate."

Stur wrung his arms, with one arm snaking around

another. "But the pod is changing so fast. This new generation won't listen, and they fear nothing. How can I manage them?"

Scree hid a smile. This change was inevitable. She had sparked a quiet revolution and this was the future: dragon-octopi, a new type of life. Just wait 'til she taught them to zap. That should be interesting!

"Talk with Arafine; she manages dragons. Put them in charge of a new farm. Make them leaders of pod defense squads and hold drills until we can defend our village in our sleep. Ask them to work together and solve a real problem. And I'm afraid there is one. Our volcano is acting up again, and this eruption might be much more powerful. It could destroy our village and the reef. We need a plan to move."

Spar, the leader of their first octopus village, flowed slowly into their circle. He greeted everyone formally. When he twined arms with Scree his skin pulsed gray.

"What is it?" Scree asked.

Spar wove his arms carefully to reply. "It's just some arm stiffness."

"When you have eight arms, stiffness is a real problem. We use arms for everything, even to talk, so I've been working on a solution." Scree reached into her Healer bag, found a stoppered coral jar, and gave it to Spar. "Take two quithra eggs each day, no more. It's like a bitter oil pill that stops stiffness and pain. Taking the tiny eggs every day is more effective than using the salve I make from them. Quithra are rare, so Orm's trying to increase their numbers."

Spar accepted the orange jar with an octopus bow. "That's a wonderful achievement. What were you saying about the volcano?"

* * *

Darkness faded away and dawn colors bled through the sea. Scree pulsed to the surface, twirling as she rose, noting the many farms scattered through the coral reef . . . clams, abalone, oysters, and more. These farms had grown. Now they even had quithra sanctuaries, where they fed the young of these brightly colored sea slugs. When quithra grew into adults they wriggled up to the surface to spawn, during the first new moon of winter. Scree harvested a careful portion of their toxic eggs for her medicines.

Change one thing and you change the world. Scree had said this before. Maybe Stur was right to be concerned. Had they changed too fast, grown too much for this place? Lost in thought, she failed to notice a swift dark shadow.

Bump.

Her heart jolted and Scree nearly jumped out of her skin.

The huge sea turtle bumped her again, smiling playfully.

"Tara!" Her heart resumed its normal pumping. "How are you?" Scree spoke the turtle's language, using body tilts and fin gestures. Tara had been badly damaged in a shark attack, Scree had healed her, and they had been friends ever since.

Tara looked meaningfully over her left shoulder.

Scree added skin pictures to their conversation. "There are gaps between your plates. It's time to add new shells. Orm, could you wait at the surface with Tara? I need to treat her now."

Scree jetted to her cave to collect additional supplies. She rummaged through a box of abalone shells and chose the largest, thickest ones. Then she grabbed kelp leaves, with baby barnacles growing on them, and stuffed this into her bag. These barnacles would be easy to move to the turtle, which was a crucial step in fixing the shell.

Scree chose a curved bone needle, another spool of cloth-of-gold thread, and sped back. She turned one eye downward and pointed her other eye up as she rose to the surface, watching what was behind and what was ahead. Past and future. Change happened but this volcano could bring the final change, the end of her pod.

Scree straightened her arms. Not if she could help it.

She shaped her head into a point and turned a smooth, shiny black. Then she jetted to the surface, moving so fast that she flew up into the air. She fell back down with a splash, landing right beside Orm and Tara.

"You're in a good mood, leaping like a ray," Orm said.

Scree gazed into a morning sky of deep periwinkle blue. "What will be, will be. And we will be ready."

The sea tasted odd, mixed with water from a recent rain that had flattened the waves. She could see forever across the flat, glittering expanse, all the way to that tantalizing horizon. It drew her like a magnet.

Scree ran an arm over Tara's back, checking the abalone shell plates that she had used to replace the original, damaged turtle plates. Tara had grown considerably and these were now too small. She sawed five abalone shells into hexagon plates, used a file to improve the fit, and smoothed the shell edges. "Perfect." She drilled tiny holes at the edges.

Scree sewed the plates together while Orm held them in place, leaving slack for Tara's body to grow. She fitted this onto the turtle. Then she peeled baby barnacles off their seaweed home and attached them to the plate edges. "These barnacles will grow their own glue to hold the pieces together, and sea moss will cover her new plates. Soon she'll look all natural."

Scree and Orm rode on the turtle's back for one last, friendly trip together. Tara dropped them off at the log raft that was anchored above the pod. Eight small skiffs were tied securely to the raft. They pulled up into a skiff, arm over arm, and untied the ropes. Orm raised the skiff-wing. White clouds scudded across the sky as the wind picked up, and their skiff leapt across the sea.

"Scree, do you remember when Tara was our only skiff? Times have changed."

"They certainly have," Scree said, and paused. "And I usually think change is good."

"What's on your mind?" Orm asked.

"I like the farms, but we seem to be taking over the coral reef. I think the village has grown too large. We all need to move, anyway, but have we come too far from what is natural? I do think the giant squid may attack, in spite of all I tried to accomplish. And, I don't think either pod leader believes the volcano threat is real. They don't want to believe."

Orm twined one of his arms with hers. "That's a lot on your mind. Let's take one thing at a time."

Scree trailed an arm in the sea, sensing, while Orm flew their skiff. They passed right above the Old Village and traveled on, gliding south-west.

"Sometimes I miss the old pod," Orm said.

"We should visit again." Scree wiggled her arm against the strong current. "We're making good time. Is there anything better than skiff-flying?"

"What about flowing over a reef with living rainbows, or watching rivers of silver fish swim by?"

"I'm glad the reef fish are back." Her eyes grew wide and her wiggly arm became as stiff as a trunk of black coral. "The volcano scent feels strong here. We must be right above it."

Orm turned the skiff in tight circles, shortening the skiff-wing to free the wind, until they stopped. "It's too deep to anchor, so the skiff will drift."

"I'll keep one eye on the skiff shadow while I collect a jar of volcano's breath from the vents." Scree slipped over the side and disappeared beneath the waves.

Scree pulsed through watery green light toward the dark mountain. Everything near it must have died in the last eruption, but the slopes were already covered with new life. There were long strands of seaweed, splashes of purple algae-paint, scarlet scallops with tiny blue eyes, and mustard-yellow corals with colorful tube worms. Orm would love this! Some rainbow colors disappeared as she pulsed deeper and deeper; the sea ate the light. Soon there were no reds or yellows. Feathery, fern-like corals appeared in shades of blue, like a snow-covered meadow beneath a midnight sky.

A curtain of bubbles rose from the vent. Scree caught the stinky air in her red coral jar and used a tight stopper.

A swift current brushed her skin, stronger than the flowing sea. She froze, instantly matching the pitted rocks and corals. Loose bits of skin stretched thin to become seaweed. The sleek gray shape turned and slid closer. Its long, pointed tail slashed through the water.

The shark circled back.

Scree did not move. She was invisible. But sharks could sense the electricity in life. It swam slowly toward Scree, moving its tail from side to side.

Suddenly the shark charged.

Scree waited until the last moment, when the shark would close its eyes. She jetted up, landed on its head, and fastened her powerful suckers onto its sandpaper skin. She dangled one arm in front of the shark.

The shark shook its head repeatedly, trying to shake her off. Then it focused on the wriggling, tempting treat just beyond its teeth. It surged forward.

Scree hung on with all suckers and tilted her dangling arm higher, directing the shark. They flew through the sea together, faster than dragon-flight! The shark followed her uncatchable arm, faster and faster, up to the light. And there was the shadow of the skiff. She flung her body off the shark, catapulted through the sky, and landed neatly inside the skiff.

"Another shark ride. That was quite the entrance." Orm stared over the side as the shark circled, thrashing its tail angrily. "Why didn't you use your poison and put it to sleep?"

Scree shook her head. "Sleep would kill a shark. They need to keep moving."

Orm rolled his eyes. "So you had to protect it?"

"Of course. It's a fish! And that was one terrific ride. You could call it a very efficient way to travel."

"Efficient, yes, but I still prefer slower and safer. What did you learn?"

Scree pulled out two jars. "The volcanoes match."

CHAPTER 6: MANTIS LIGHTNING

The water was every possible shade of orange, reflecting the flaming sky. A bright yellow ribbon started right below the setting sun and split the sea in half, running from horizon to shore. The strong sea breeze felt wonderfully cool.

Drakor walked carefully down the dock, still feeling as if the ground moved beneath him, and into a boisterous crowd of dragons. He stopped and stared. How did they function? No ice dragon would act that way. There was no order, and they were as noisy as a spring gathering of smidgers!

Drakor's tongue flicked out and back. Those plump lizards were so tasty, but hard to catch. They scurried as fast as a waterfall and lived in long Volcano tubes that were much too narrow for dragons.

Smidgers were brown-and-white, like the patchy ground-and-snow of his home. But they could turn all brown or all white in a heartbeat to match any change on the ground. When a smidger held still it was almost invisible. In the depths of winter they turned as white as ice dragons. Their color change was effective camouflage but simple, nothing like Orm and Scree's amazing ability to match anything and make pictures.

Drakor stepped off the dock onto a patch of crunchy grass. Long blades with coats of spikey ice crystals lay tangled on the ground, like wooly caterpillars swarming on a berry bush. He eyed the sparkling frost patterns and dug his claws into the frozen ground. At least this felt like home.

Arak landed on the shore beside his mate and broke into Drakor's thoughts. "This is my family, Zarina and Arwina."

Drakor bowed to the dragon-lady and smiled at the small dragonlet, who stared silently up.

"She's never this quiet," Zarina said, as she handed Drakor a huge ceramic mug. The white and blue clay were marbled together like an icy sea. There was a ring of gemstones on the side, surrounding a clear diamond: ruby, orange topaz, yellow citrine, emerald, blue topaz, and amethyst. "I mind-talked with Arak during the journey. He told me that diamonds are important in your legends, but we didn't know your trance-stone. So I made a rainbow circle of gemstones around a diamond."

Drakor snapped his tail in amazement. "This isss the most beautiful thing I have ever seen."

Zarina smiled. "It's yours to keep. A gift."

Drakor bowed low. "I will treasure it."

*　*　*

Dorali was glued to Drakor's side, guarding his

injured wing as a dragon-dam guards her egg. "You must see our artwork in the cave. We practice micro-zaps by changing water patterns, but we grow fantasy snowflakes to learn how to manipulate energy. Then we turn them into gemstone ornaments to decorate our Winter Solstice tree. We'll share shadow-stories later."

Spicy aromas and the scent of char-grilled fish permeated the air. Dorali inhaled deeply and smiled, but Drakor wrinkled his nose. "What isss that smell?"

Every dragon turned toward the loud, brassy sound that shimmered through the air.

"Fish. That's the dinner gong! It's time to eat."

Dorali, Arak, and Zarina made a protective circle around Drakor as they walked to the stone tables. Arwina hopped happily between her sire and dam, beaming at the world.

Dorali gave a warning look to anyone who crowded too close. "The clan gathers every evening. Each dragon brings something to share. The dragon who brings a big fish or a well-spiced dish is respected. This is a true feast to honor you."

Drakor stared down at her. "To honor me?"

"You are the guest," Dorali said firmly, leading Drakor to a long, stone table. It was covered with dishes of hot food, and the stone was warmed by dragon-fire. A thick, spicy fish stew, steamed oysters with seaweed, grilled white-fish, charred sturgeon fillets, rock crab claws, baked yams, crispy tubers, sliced carrot crisps, and more covered the table. Steaming hot cocoa and spiced red root tea added an earthy scent to the air.

Drakor's eyes were huge. "There isss so much food!"

Dorali nodded. "There's always enough, but a

welcome feast is special." She ladled spicy fish stew into a bowl and handed it to Drakor. "This is our traditional main course. These are steamed crab claws and stuffed clams." She added servings to his plate.

Drakor gagged on the stew. "It tastes strange."

Dorali hid a smile. "It's cooked with pepper, sea salt, and herbs. You eat plain food, but I think these spices will grow on you." She added roasted tubers, sweet mashed yams, and toasted almonds to his plate. "These are clan favorites."

The second stone table was filled with cold dishes: fish rolls, mushrooms, pickles, raw oysters, fish eggs, and fresh red-and-green seaweed salads. Platters of brown seaweed had dragon designs made from thin-sliced almonds and finely ground turquoise.

Dorali filled another plate with creamy oysters and seaweed salad. "Here. This raw food will give you a taste of home."

Drakor sniffed the oysters and a huge smile spread across his face. "Thank you. What isss that?"

The third, smaller table held chocolate candies, honey-roasted almonds, a honey-sweetened compote made with dried berries, and the traditional snow pudding.

"That's for later."

Drakor balanced his stack of plates and followed Dorali to the seats, which were woven from branches. Arak and Taron joined with their families, forming a protective cocoon around Drakor.

A rock tossed into still water makes a series of rings that ripple out from the center. The white dragon was the rock that brought this change. The clan surrounded Drakor in rings that rippled out, chattering to each other but always with one eye on the dragon legend in the center.

"They stare. At home, no one watches me."

"They're curious," Dorali said. She repeated this softly, looking at her scars. She hated it when dragons stared at her, but how many of those stares were just curiosity? "Tonight you can answer their questions. Soon they'll be used to you."

After they fed, Dorali scrubbed her plates and stacked them on the shelf under the table. Drakor copied her.

"Now it's time for deserts." She hurried to the small table and picked up two scallop shell plates, one yellow and one purple, each larger than her hand. "Meals are more colorful since we began trading for these plates."

Drakor gave her a puzzled look. "What are dee-zerts?"

"We'll try them all," Dorali said with a grin, putting a chocolate snowball on his plate. She added a crystal bowl with blue-green snow, laid on red seaweed, covered with oily-black Sturgeon eggs. "This is our traditional desert: snow pudding. It's made for the Winter Festival, but we wanted you to have some. You'll like the raw fish eggs."

Drakor ate the chocolate snowball, chocolate-covered almonds, and a slice of dried green melon dipped in dark chocolate. His dark eyes sparkled like a night sky. "This isss a-ma-zing!"

"Zarina makes them. Orm calls her a chocolate artist. Everyone looks hopeful when she brings her dish for dinner." Dorali took both plates and cleaned them.

Drakor cradled his rainbow mug like a priceless treasure before stowing it carefully in his pack. "I want to see more of your art."

"You must see our amber snowflakes!"

"You have orange snowflakes?" he asked, following her.

Drakor halted at the narrow cave opening. He peered into the dank shadows, sniffing the pine-scented smoke and earthy-damp limestone. He closed his eyes and his forehead wrinkled with concentration. "I sense many rooms beyond. I hope I will fit." Drakor crouched down, protecting his injured wing as he entered the dragon cave.

The cave opened into a huge chamber that could hold the entire clan. Rust, tan and white stone flowed across the damp floor. Glow-worms hung from the ceiling, lighting the cave with a soft, yellow-green glow that gleamed off the water-slick rock.

"It isss cool in here. I like that."

Dorali nodded. "All year long, winter or summer, it's just like this."

A few dragon-lengths in, Drakor stopped to admire a round pool with a frosty rim of white limestone. The still water was as clear as a sheet of new ice. Six large fungus flowers were spread evenly around the circle, and each flower glowed in a different color: red, orange, yellow, green, blue, purple. This living rainbow was reflected in the water mirror. Plink! The reflection changed as ripples spread from a drip; the colors wriggled and blended together.

"That isss art," Drakor said in a hushed voice.

"Orm would agree. Arak found those fungus flowers in the New World. Orm added bacteria that glow in different colors. He never gets tired of playing with natural light. You should see the glowing walls of Orm's sea cave." Her voice echoed softly off the stone walls.

Dorali pointed to a small chamber on the other side. "That room is for dragon-ladies with dragonlets. Older siblings sometimes stay here and help look after them."

They walked through a stone forest. Creamy-red limestone columns reached from floor to ceiling. Drakor ran a hand over the long, flowing stone drips. "This looks like hot lava on our Volcano, but it feels like melting icicles."

They walked farther into the cave. A tall limestone column had sprays of rock like a waterfall, frozen in time and growing across the ages. It glistened in the light from glowing fungus flowers that were artfully placed. The next chamber had a low ceiling covered by hollow rock straws. Each straw had a twinkling drop of lime-water dangling from the tip. The walls had a pale greenish glow that lit the sparkling drops.

Dorali pointed to the walls. "I helped paint this room with a glowing fungus."

A bright streak of light splashed across the floor from an open chamber. "This is the game room," Dorali said, answering the question in his eyes. "It's very popular when we're cave-bound during long snowstorms. Our snow can be wet and very deep."

Drakor nodded. "We live near the sea, where the snow isss usually dry, and most of it blows away. Ice dragons build shelters between short trees that are always green and smell nice. We each make a tall circle of stones and put fish skins across the top. We scrape off the fish scales and rub in oils until the skin isss like cloudy ice, so we can see the sky. At night we fall asleep watching auroras."

Dorali flicked her tail gently. "That would be a lovely way to sleep."

He grinned. "Sky art isss always beautiful."

They entered the game room. A fire was lit beneath the natural chimney hole, lending an orange glow to the walls. The enchanting aroma of popped red-corn filled the room. An elderly dragon-lord with bronzed scales sat near the flames, leaning into the warmth, munching on salted popcorn. Dorali nodded politely. He looked the ice dragon up and down, silently, and returned to watching the fire.

Dorali whispered, "He's our oldest dragon. His mate and most of his friends have become dragon-stars in the sky. He lives in his memories, and our gatherings no longer interest him."

A huge maze stood in the corner, taller than a dragon, made of bright silver wires. "This is fun." Dorali dropped three gemstone balls into a hole at the top of the maze. Amethyst, ruby, and blue topaz marbles rolled along silver runners, weaving and spiraling and dropping through random holes. They spun through the maze. The blue gem rolled out first.

Drakor thumped his tail. "Blue isss first. Good. Sky should win."

There were five limestone tables covered with dragon-games. Each table was surrounded by carved benches that were worn smooth by generations of dragon scales. Bags with polished white, red, or black stones rested on wooden game boards. Flat, painted puzzles showed the world from a dragons-eye view. One game had five levels of ice-clear quartz boards, held together by black coral. Pearls filled some of the hollows carved into each level.

"This game's new," Dorali said. "It's one of Orm's inventions. He calls it Arms and Claws. Each of the five dragon-claw levels has an eight by eight octopus grid, with cups to hold black or white pearls. I think Orm and Kragor are the only ones who understand the rules. Kragor is Arak's sire, and a great artist."

Drakor clicked his claws on the crystal boards. "This game isss well made." He lifted a clawfull of lumpy, shiny black stones from a pile on the table. "What isss this?"

"Puzzle pieces. Each puzzle bag holds many tens of carved onyx pieces. When all the pieces are put together the right way, they make one sculpture." She connected several puzzle pieces and studied the outline. "I think these pieces will make a dragon."

"Not all puzzle sculptures are dragons?" he asked, trying to fit a piece into the beginning sculpture. "All of our ice sculptures are dragons."

Dorali shook her head. "There are puzzles to make a crab, sturgeon fish, octopus . . . that's the real challenge. All the pieces are black. You don't know what the puzzle sculpture will become until you've put enough pieces together. It's a bit like real dragonlets. What will they grow up to do?"

"This isss an interesting idea. You have games for the mind. Our games are all to make us strong, to fight and survive." Drakor frowned. "I must try puzzles, later. Where isss the art?"

"It's in the next room."

They walked on through a dark maze of rippling limestone draperies. Drakor sparked his claws and the glistening rock reflected this like stars. Dorali added spark-stars of her own to the hanging sky. Soon they were sparking star after star, laughing, filling the stone sky with stars.

"I did not know zaps could be so much fun!" Drakor said.

Dorali reached her arm into a dark space. "This must be the place." She took a torch from the metal wall sconce and lit it with a spark from her claw. Wavering torch light showed a space that was barely large enough to hold three dragons. "Here's the storage room. Watch your head."

Drakor pointed to a stack of large ceramic bowls. "That isss like the beautiful cup Zarina made. What are they?"

Dorali smiled wistfully. "Nest bowls." She picked up two stunning bowls. One was made from red clay, with gold wire wrapped around each cut ruby. The second bowl looked like the sea. It was made from blue clay spun with thin silver wires, and the frothy rim was studded with small white pearls.

"Each dragon-dam makes a ceramic bowl for her egg, following clan tradition. A dragon egg must hatch in a nest that combines land, water, fire and air. The First Dragon was born of these four elements; now all dragons are born within them. The nest bowl is made of clay, softened by water, and hardened by fire and air. This ancient magic nurtures the dragonlet. The nest is heated with dragon-fire to keep the egg warm." Longing pierced her heart, but her voice barely shook as she put the bowls away. This was not for her. No dragon-lord would choose a scarred dragon-lady.

Drakor nodded. "Nest bowl art. How do you make cloud art?"

Dorali turned away from the nest bowls. "Dragon-ladies grow snowflakes in the clouds for the Winter Festival. We each choose a tiny snowflake growing inside its water sac. I put a copper claw into this crystal sac, into the heart of the crystal snowflake. Then I pulse energy into the flake."

She demonstrated by putting one claw into an open circle made from her thumb and first finger. "The energy attracts more freezing water to the six snowflake arms, and the flake grows. I use my energy and chemicals to control the pattern as it grows. Each snowflake gets as big as a dinner plate."

Drakor shook his head. "That isss too much to understand."

Dorali opened one of the boxes in the corner. "These are the amber snowflakes. When we put a snowflake onto liquid pine sap, the golden sap takes the flake pattern. We turn this sap into solid amber with a zap of electricity."

Drakor picked up an ornament made of many tiny dragons. He peered through the warm, translucent stone and traced the six-pointed pattern with his claw. Another snowflake had leaping swordfish, and two swords made each of the six points. One had octopi.

"Stone snowflakes. This isss an excellent use of the zap. Which one did you make?"

Dorali picked up another flake with a strong geometric pattern. "I call it Mantis Lightning. I used an insect for the pattern, a preying mantis that was jade green and moved as fast as lightning. One moment it was standing still and then it held a moth to eat. I didn't even see the mantis move."

Drakor held her flake near the torch light, where it glowed in rich amber colors. "Lightning speed would be useful in a fight."

"Is everything about fighting?"

"Fights are very important to us. We choose our leader by fighting. Our games are a special kind of fight for status." He turned the flake from side to side in the light. "This isss a complicated design. It must have been a challenge to grow your snowflake." He handed it back. "Why are you the only dragon-lady with a pretty frost pattern on your scales?"

Dorali flinched. The white pattern was her scars. She looked up, meeting Drakor eye-to-eye. "Pretty?"

"You are the first yellow dragon-lady I met. I thought they would all look like you. But the others are plain."

"Thank you," she said, not answering his question.

* * *

Arak felt happy down to his last scale. He had spent the entire day with Zarina and their dragonlet, catching up on everything. His mate was so clever, always finding new Healer remedies, and Arwina was growing so fast! As soon as she was old enough, both of his special dragon-ladies could join him on a voyage.

He stopped by the shore to watch evening colors paint the sky. Sunsets were always more beautiful here, reflected in the sea. Rose and violet flowed across the waves, gradually replaced by darker amethyst and indigo. Then stars emerged to light the darkness. Arak flicked his tail, surprised by how much he missed the shimmering green and purple auroras of the north. He turned away from the sea to find Drakor.

Sometime during that long day, dragons had built a bigger-than-normal domed shelter for their large guest. Branches were woven together with vines, and fish skins lined the inside to seal it from the wind. All dragon shelters were built within thick clumps of bushes, making them warmer and almost invisible. It was not yet spring, so the nip in the air became frost at night.

Arak found Drakor by the new shelter, testing the ropes, peering inside. He handed the ice dragon a stack of blankets. "These are from Zarina. See you tomorrow." Arak yawned and stumbled away, dragging his tail through the dead leaves. He nearly fell into his own shelter.

Arak woke early the next morning, before the sun, but the ice dragon was already up. Drakor pointed to the leafless forest, which had been coated by a freezing rain. Sunrise colors bloomed like fantasy flowers through the icy twigs. "This isss beautiful."

A dragon landed beside Drakor with a summons for both of them. The frosty ground crunched beneath their feet as they walked to the meeting circle. Arak flared his nostrils, inhaling the welcome aroma of toasted almonds. Exhaustion and cold made him ravenous, so he scooped up a generous handful and crunched blissfully.

A bright fire crackled cheerfully in the center of the circle. Arak leaned into the welcome warmth. He took a second look and his eyes grew wide. These flames were pure blue, not the standard greenish-blue.

Drakor stared into the fire. "It isss the true color of our sky."

"I think they used cobalt metal to make a special fire just for you," Arak replied quietly.

Arafine, the leader, was waiting with Healers Zarina, Driana, and Dorali. Kragor, Arak's sire, was seated on a bench with Taron. Three more dragons landed with a flurry of wings and dust; greetings and questions filled the air.

Arafine raised her wings high for silence. "Drakor, we welcome you here. Arak said that your volcano may erupt soon in a new way. Could you tell us more?"

"Our old Volcano rumbles and smokes, then bleeds down the sides. The burning red blood hardens to black rock. It isss always the same. There isss a magnetic spider web around the Volcano. This energy has a simple pattern. It isss as predictable as the tides."

Drakor looked to the north.

"A new cone isss forming in the side of our old Volcano. Magnetic wrinkles dance above the new cone with a twisted pattern. There are sharp energy spikes and new smells. The rumbling heart of this Volcano beats faster."

Drakor shuddered. "We have legends from long, long ago, from a time before we lived in your land. I have seen all the warning signs of that deadly Volcano eruption. The rhythm and smells have changed, the ground isss swelling, and the big fish are leaving. The next eruption will be different. It will destroy my world."

Arafine asked, "Why aren't the other ice dragons worried?"

"They follow our leader, and he does not listen to the old legends. He does not want to believe." Drakor flicked his tail nervously. "I have seen our Volcano explode, in my mind. Then our home isss gone. I have future-sight. This will happen."

Only the crackling fire interrupted the silence of dragons.

Finally, Arafine asked, "When will your volcano erupt?"

"I do not know."

She studied the ice dragon. "Thank you for coming."

Arak motioned to Drakor and they left.

Drakor glanced back at the dragons who remained by the fire and he snapped his tail. "It isss real. This will happen."

Arak gave him a level gaze. "I believe you, and I think Arafine does, too. But you're an unexpected visitor, a legend with a dream warning. This will be hard to believe." He turned and looked north. "Where will you go?"

Drakor's tail drooped to the ground. "I do not know."

Arak gazed out to sea. "Dreams are important, but you also need a plan."

CHAPTER 7: SQUID STORM

Scree and Orm flew their skiff back to the village, beneath a bright sliver of moon. They tied off to the raft and slid overboard, splashing through starlit waves. After they disappeared, the wave pattern reformed as curved gray scales with silver rims.

"Only two eight-days until we leave for the spring festival," Orm said cheerfully, as they sank to the sand below. "I can hardly wait for Kragor to see my new glowing tunicates: violet and gold. His undersea garden will be the wonder of the dragon world."

Scree twined arms affectionately. "It already is." Kragor and Orm had painted a picture of dreams below low tide, with rings and swirls of small tunicates that glowed in red, blue, and green. This living tapestry lit up the sea at night.

"Orm, our sea sample matches Drakor's volcano. Our volcano is waking. I feel this danger in every pulse of my body. We must move."

Orm sighed. "Our reef is beautiful, the farms are doing well, and we've completely settled in. This is home. Even my snails go back to their homes when I move them."

Scree ran an arm gently along his. "So we're like homing snails? I do love this place but anywhere that you are, is home. We moved here when we needed a new home. The New World reefs could make another new home."

Orm turned one eye to the west. "That would be a faraway move." He slipped into his cave and Scree pulsed to hers.

Just before dawn, Scree ate a hearty breakfast of clams and knobby red seaweed. She watched as sunlight filtered down through the sea, bringing color to the gray reef. Orm was right, their reef was beautiful. The tentacle petals of anemones flowed back and forth with the waves like dragon flowers in a summer breeze. These animal flowers decorated a nearby rock with mint, green, and lilac. A carpet of bright pink-and-red anemones filled the valley between coral heads, waving short pink tentacles around fiery centers. It was a lovely undersea meadow.

Scree was checking her medicinal supplies when a manta ray swooped in to see her. She ran an arm along his fin, feeling for lumps and tasting for infection. The torn fin was healing perfectly, but he brought a disturbing message about giant squid. She informed the pod leader.

Stur immediately appointed Scree as defense leader for the entire pod. "You were the first octopus ever to use a spear, the first to fight back. Now you can organize everyone to fight back."

Scree wanted to scream in every shade of red. This was a dangerous distraction from an even bigger problem. When their volcano exploded it would destroy everything. You couldn't escape unless you left before it was real.

She straightened her arms. "So now I get to be the first to lead an army?"

Stur chuckled. "That's a good name for octopus defenders, with so many arms." He turned a sober brown. "We'll need all those fighting arms. The pod has practiced throwing spears, but we don't even know for sure how many giants will attack. We need a strong defense plan. We need you."

Scree sighed. "Then I accept. Squid are deadly, but this volcano is more dangerous and there is no defense. We can only survive if we leave before it erupts."

Stur looked into her eyes. "Before it seems real."

Had he read her mind? Scree gave a wry smile. "That is the challenge. And if I'm in charge of defense, I will also be in charge of prisoners. I will not kill."

Stur gave her a hard look. "This is not one starving, sympathetic squid. These monsters will attack together, as a game, to prove that they can kill us."

"Stur, I'm a Healer and I will not let them change me. I will change them and that is the ultimate victory. I fight for peace."

The leader blinked. "How?"

Scree stared into the distance, and her eyes were a thousand years old. "It seems that peace must be won more than once. Communication is the key, and killing these giants would waste an opportunity. They will learn to respect us. Then we'll release them, alive, to spread our warning. Each battle we fight this way will create ripples of change into the future, to protect octopi not yet hatched."

Stur nodded slowly. "I accept your terms." Then he curled his arms with frustration. "But these monsters make my blood boil."

"Hotter than a volcano?" Scree smiled. "I'll go prepare for our squid visitors."

And so, the day after her shark ride, she was checking their early warning system. Both villages had one. Scree pulsed around the circle of golden-brown kelp trees that grew well beyond the village borders. This sturdy seaweed normally grew in cold water, but Orm had bred a variety that could live in the warmer waters of their coral reef. The ring of kelp now reached from the sea floor to the surface, and it made a unique warning barrier.

Scree shook a kelp tree violently, as if a squid was passing through. Shells that were tied to the long, leathery leaves clanked together, making enough noise to wake any sleeping octopus. Only a squid or the most violent storm could make the shells clank. These unique sound vibrations would pass through her entire body, waking her arm-minds first and then her main brain. There were spears leaning against the inner wall of each octopus cave, and waking arms would grab them. In the blink of an eye her troops would be up, armed, and ready.

Scree poked her head into the cave that Orm had built for his newest creations. Jellyfish pulsed around the darkness within the deep cave, glowing brightly in unusual pinks and turquoise, like true flowers of the sea. These were bred from the normal white variety. Colored light gleamed along cloudy flounces and tentacles; they glowed like ice sculptures beneath an aurora borealis.

Orm was busy feeding them.

Scree squished her body thin and slipped between the rods across the entrance. "I see you're having some fun here. Kragor will love them! The squid will probably attack at night, so these jellyfish could also be useful."

Orm tossed the rest of the jellyfish food up into the water. "I suppose that squid would be so entranced by their artistic beauty that they'd stop an attack just to watch?"

Scree laughed. "Probably not, but they could light up the squid. Then we could see well enough to fight back properly."

"Speaking of Kragor, we met at the raft above while you were in conference. I brought him sacks of dragon-weed, and he gave me this. Then he flew back for an important meeting."

Scree opened the box and flashed bright, happy colors. "It's full of wax-covered sodium balls. How did he know we'd need them?"

Orm twined arms. "I called him in trance-mind on our way home from the sea of ice, after that giant squid warned you. Kragor offered to make as many blinding lights as I wanted."

Scree ran her arms lovingly through the dull wax balls. "These are more precious than pearls. I was just going to ask. Were you mind-reading into the future?" She covered the box. "Arak made our spears, and now his sire made these. We're fortunate in our friends. What do you think of octopi as fighters?"

Orm curled one arm beneath his head, considering.

"Sometimes octopi are feisty rulers of the sea, and sometimes they shape-shift into invisibility. Both traits are useful."

"Squid have a serious size advantage. We need to combine our opposite talents and fight while camouflaged," Scree decided.

"A good plan multiplies the effectiveness of the resources," Orm said.

Scree laughed. "Or, in plain octopus, you can do a lot with little if you plan carefully."

She called a meeting of the eight squad leaders. "We each carry a wax ball for protection, with poison from our deadly cousins. This box has wax-covered sodium balls. I call them lightning balls, and each member of your squad needs one. Squid live in the abyss, in depths that have never known the light of the sun, so they will probably attack at night. Bright light is a powerful weapon that will stun a giant squid. Now turn away to protect your eyes."

Scree scratched some wax off the ball and tossed it up into the sea, where the sodium burned bright and fierce. Octopi spun back to face her, eyes wide, pupils shrunk to a black point. The water tasted of fright and excitement as she handed out boxes of lights. Scrim, her apprentice, accepted his lightning balls with great enthusiasm.

Scree raised two arms for attention and the squad leaders grew still. "This will be a challenge, but it could make all the difference in a fight: be invisible. Squid can't shape-shift or camouflage so they won't expect us to hide like this. Don't make yourself an easy target. Learn how to keep in camouflage even when you're afraid or angry. Don't lose your concentration, don't let your emotions take over, and don't turn blue. Hold drills day and night.

Learn to gather immediately when the alarm sounds, respond to the fight signals, and stay camouflaged while fighting."

The next day, Scree checked random caves. The spearheads were incredibly sharp, made from colorful jasper that was dragon-heated to change the rock texture. This made it possible to shape the rock into a finer point, to puncture as easily as sea urchin needles. The spear shafts were made from sturdy oak, carved and painted with a seaweed pattern for camouflage, and rubbed with wax to protect them from the sea.

The spear tips were coated with poison from the blue-ringed octopi, and they had protective caps. This poison worked as a powerful sedative, but too much would kill. The poison dose on a spear was low, so that octopi would not kill each other with a missed throw.

They each carried a poison ball in an arm sucker. They also carried sodium balls, to stun the enemy with blinding light.

Every cave had four spears leaning against an inner wall, near the door. The squid should drop like a stone, but would the poison work fast enough? Even the best plans could fail, if the enemy didn't follow along. How many squid would attack? Who would be hurt . . . or killed?

Orm found Scree in her cave, wearing an unnatural shade of gray. "What's wrong?"

"It's easy to be brave for myself, fighting on my own. It's much worse being in charge, responsible for the lives of friends."

Orm twined arms. "Scree, you are rare: a natural Healer *and* a natural fighter. You didn't ask to be in charge. Stur is pod leader and he chose you to lead defense. Some may die, but many more octopi will live because of you."

Scree leaned against Orm, feeling his unshakable belief and confidence in her. No wonder he was so irresistible, even as the years pulsed by. "Thank you." She straightened her arms. "Could you come with me to check on the decoy village?"

This village was under construction in the dance field, safely away from their real homes, and it was nearly complete. The pretend caves were solid piles of rocks. Crabs and clams were eaten here daily to create the proper lived-in tastes. Extra weapons were stored here. Scree would lead the defense from an open circle in the center of this decoy. Their true village was now well camouflaged as a lush field of seaweed, with long brown and green strands planted between homes.

Orm brushed against a cave pile and a few rocks rolled off. "These aren't very sturdy."

Scree sighed. "They don't need to last. The battle may be terrible, but it won't last long."

Orm nodded. "I dread the coming squid storm. Is this decoy village worth so much effort? It takes time away from other battle preparations."

"The bigger threat is still the volcano, which has far more power to destroy us than mere squid. When the battle is over we must prepare to move. If our village is destroyed by squid, we'll lose supplies. It will be more difficult to organize a move."

Orm grinned. "So you're thinking ahead to the next problem. That's good. But . . . 'mere squid'? That's not how I see these giants."

"It's all a matter of perspective. See you later." She flowed away.

Scree checked the practice field and observed while camouflaged. Scrim, her Healer apprentice, wore the arm band of a pod defense leader. He juggled four red coral knives, making bright, overlapping arcs in the water. After his unique warm-up, he stowed the knife blades in sheaths fastened to his upper arms. Then he threw spear after spear at a tall target.

"You're good," Scree said. "You hit the most vulnerable points every time and you stayed in camouflage."

He flushed bright red. "But will I be able to hit a moving target? The squid won't hold still like this seaweed dummy."

"You're angry."

"If they attack, then they lied about the agreement."

Scree sighed. "Squid are complicated. Most want to leave us alone, but some believe this treaty does not include them."

"Then they will learn otherwise. We will win."

"I believe we *will* win, with fighters like you," Scree said. "And then we must release the squid, alive."

"Why?"

"We must do this to show compassion for ignorance, so the squid can carry our warning to others, and because we are Healers."

Scrim curled his arms with frustration. "Do you ever find this hard to do?"

Scree gazed beyond their village, lost in memories. When she finally spoke, her arms were gray with sadness. "Yes. I was furious when Vorm killed my friends, but he was desperately hungry. The fish kills drove him to attack us. When I came to know Vorm, I could not hate him. I learned enough of his language and customs to make a peace treaty with his kind."

"And now that treaty will be broken," Scrim said. His arms were rigid with anger.

Scree nodded. "Probably. But this new group of squid will learn that we are dangerous, and that lesson will spread like ripples in a tide pool. It's better than constant attacks."

"So we must be forever on guard, even with a treaty?" His skin pulsed with emotions of many colors, changing from moment to moment: anger, fear, frustration, even a desperate need to understand.

Scree could read these colors as if she was inside his mind. She twined arms with her young apprentice. "I wish it were different. You are a fighter, a Healer, and a thinker. Maybe *you* will find the way."

She left and wandered through the village, talking with fighters, while evening came and stole colors from the sea. Scree remembered every apprentice, past and present. These were the juveniles she fostered, raised, and trained. All were precious to her, but Scrim had an intensity that she fully understood. It must be easier to experience life more lightly.

In the dead of night, vibrations from the warning shells pierced Scree from all directions at once. Giant squid spurted toward the village, stirring sand up into the dark water. Octopi poured out of their homes, wielding spears, but it was difficult to see what was happening in the cloudy darkness. Orm released his glowing jellyfish, bringing light to the night.

Six yellow moons glowed in the distance, moving closer. These were the fierce eyes of giant squid. Scree took a good look as she jetted to the center of the decoy village. Three squid were attacking at the same time, making a perfect triangle of terror. The pod was surrounded.

Scree shuddered. She struck her shell drum one time and octopi instantly followed the order. Lights that burned brighter than dragon-fire sizzled through the sea. The three giant squid jerked to a halt, flailing their long tentacles. The huge eyes were well adapted to see in near-darkness, so this blinding light was unbearable. They shook their massive, pointed heads in visible pain. They could not advance.

This delay was a crucial part of her plan. Octopi could move by slowly sliding along the sea floor, running on stiff arms, pulsing through the sea, or using their siphons as jets. Now was the time for speed. Every octopus jetted through the sea with the speed of a shark.

Long minutes later the squid recovered and surged forward, searching for prey. Row after row of invisible octopi stood before each advancing monster. All had shape-shifted to match coral heads or rocks covered with seaweed. Squad leaders had flattened their chosen speaking arms into yellow-brown leaves of kelp. Octopi squirted their ink into the sea to dull the squid's senses. They hurled rotten dagur eggs through the water, a gift from Arak to mask their octopus scent. There was nothing to see, feel, or sense.

Scree was in the center, well lit by glowing jellyfish, and her speaking arms were brilliant gold. She was the leader, the most visible and the most vulnerable, directing the defense. She could feel Orm watching her through his eye-skin, with silent worry and tangible love.

Rings of extra spears surrounded her, thrust into the sand. The spears called to her. Scree wanted to grab a weapon and charge into battle! One of her arms drifted toward a spear, acting with a mind of its own, reaching. She forced her arm back down. She *must* remain in the center. Other octopi would carry these spears to squad leaders.

Octopi took aim and spears flew, but many missed the targets. Scree noted that Stur, Scrim, and even Orm had become experts, striking these giants just below the head where the poison should work faster. But each dose was low, to protect octopi from fatal poisoning if struck by accident. The attacking squid were merely irritated by these pinpricks and ripped the spears out.

Squid probed the sand with strong tentacles, seeking their prey-toys. The invisible octopi shifted away and injected poison with a direct arm strikes.

Angry tentacles whipped through the water, making a violent undersea storm. Octopi were pulled back and forth by the surging sea and nearly ripped loose. Scree tasted fear in the water, but most octopi were able to maintain their camouflage colors and stay hidden. Then the squid began smashing the sea floor with powerful blows.

Scree watched from the center. She turned from one monstrous attacker to the next, observing a battle that shifted constantly, like a cloud of ink in the sea. She signaled defense moves and called up reserves to replace the wounded. She was like a spider in the middle of its web, feeling through every strand, directing the defense.

When octopi were struck and stunned by random

blows, they automatically changed back to a normal shape and color. Pod-mates flowed over to protect their helpless friends by covering them with their own camouflaged bodies.

Scree shuddered as one youngster color-changed to a bright terrified-blue. A squid grabbed this unfortunate octopus and he disappeared into its beaked mouth. The squid's body pulsed with pleasure as he searched for another bright, tasty snack.

His eyes locked onto Scree, the only visible octopus. Lights flashed along his tentacles as he signaled his friends. The other squid messaged back and they all charged to the center.

Scree read their lights. She stood firm and struck another drum signal. A new volley of lightning balls stunned the squid while squad leaders quickly reformed their lines. Spears flew, striking with more force as octopi gained practice. Squid tore the spears out and, blinded by the sodium light, they simply bashed everything they could reach. Fighters jetted to Scree to collect more spears.

As soon as the squid regained their sight they focused on Scree. They recognized the leader, connecting her signals with the attacks. She was now the target of angry giants.

The squid regained their sight and surged to the center, moving slower and slower as they reacted to the many small doses of poison. Scree studied the sluggish giants and smiled grimly. This would be their last defense and it would be close, dangerous work.

Scree gave two drum beats and the sea exploded with brilliant light from sodium balls. Octopi jetted forward, stabbing the stunned squid with long, needle-like knives. The enraged giants fought back despite their temporary blindness. They pushed through to the decoy village, swatting invisible octopi and smashing the caves. Scree took a moment to be glad these weren't their real homes.

Then, one by one, the giants began to tremble. They moved slower and slower, as if their tentacles were pushing through thick molasses. The poison was taking effect. At last they fell, flailing as they crashed down.

Scree knew their arms were numb, but their eyes blazed with fury. This was no longer a squid game to catch easy food and prove their elders wrong. They were determined to kill the octopus with the drum who had signaled each counter-attack, the golden octopus in the center.

The last giant squid surged forward as he fell. He broke through to the center and smashed an angry tentacle down onto Scree. She could barely see Orm cry "NO!" Then the world turned black. She felt and saw no more.

CHAPTER 8: ONE MOVE AHEAD

Orm, Stur, and her apprentices turned an angry blue and charged to Scree's defense. It was too late. She was already buried beneath the thick, snaking tentacle and flattened to a bloody spot. They grabbed the tentacle anyway, pulling and heaving together. It slithered off her.

Scree's battered body lay still and her skin was deathly gray. Orm felt a grief such as he had never known. He cradled her limp body, desperately feeling for a pulse. He ran his arms gently along hers, willing them to speak again. What would he give for one feisty reply? There would never be another Scree. Could a heart truly break?

The logical part of his mind that could never keep still quietly asked him, "Why isn't she more squished?"

Her arm twitched. Was it a sea current or her final death spasm? Suddenly, the light returned to her eyes. She moved her arms feebly, asking, "What happened? Where are the squid?"

Orm turned ecstatic shades of bright green. "The battle is over. We won. *You* won." He held Scree in his arms and looked deep into her eyes. "As you once said to me, don't you ever do this to me again!"

"What? Don't stand all golden in the center of a squid attack, or don't have the sense to plan an escape?" Scree laughed. "I wasn't really sure it would work."

"What did you do?"

"Orm, you told me to keep myself alive for you. That was an interesting challenge. I would be stuck in one place during the battle, bright gold, an obvious target. Everyone else would be moving around to fight, so camouflage was their best defense. I had to be visible, I couldn't camouflage, so I needed something new."

Scree slowly curled and uncurled each arm, testing. "Yesterday evening a new idea came to me. I dug a shallow hole in the center, where I would stand. I covered the hole with long kelp leaves and staked them into the sand around the edges. If I was struck, the leaves would give way. That squid knocked me senseless and pushed me into the hole but, as far as I can tell, I'm all right. I'm battered but not squished to a dead pulp. It worked!"

Orm winced. "You should have told me."

"There wasn't time." She struggled upright, wobbling a bit. "Stur, can you take over now? It's time for me to become a Healer again. Please send the wounded to our Healer caves."

Stur gave a deep bow and then, to her amazement, circle after circle of octopi bowed. The entire pod bowed to her. Scree had a fleeting mental image of seaweed all bending toward the center, an impossible feat with natural waves. Then Krees and Tor swarmed over, anxiously checking her for injuries.

"I'm fine," she said, gently shoving them aside. "Where is Scrim?"

Krees and Tor left for their Healer caves.

"Orm, remember my plans for after the battle? I need you to meet with the squad leaders."

Scree flowed slowly to her cave, feeling more exhausted than she would ever admit. She crushed fragrant seaweed and filled the cave with a pleasant, relaxing taste. Then she worked on one wounded octopus after another, bandaging as she went, prioritizing when a worse case arrived. Time crawled by.

Orm brought a meal and an update. "You're turning gray. You should eat something."

Scree picked at the food with no enthusiasm. The peppered oysters and seaweed salad looked excellent, but worry robbed her food of flavor. "Have they found Scrim?"

"The pod is still searching. Some octopi were flung far into the reef. Three pod-mates are dead."

Scree nodded sadly. "It was a vain hope to have no loss."

"Three giant squid attacked us at night and all are now bound, helpless, waiting for you. I expected much worse," Orm said. "I need to check back with the squad leaders." Then he was gone.

Stur arrived bearing the limp, battered remnants of an octopus. Three arms were ripped off. Who could it be?

Scree took a closer look and recognized an old scar. Her arms twisted in anguish. "Scrim!" She flushed gray with grief and moved her arms desperately over his heart, feeling for a pulse. There was a faint, erratic flutter like a dying butterfly. He was mostly dead. She flashed blue with anger at such a loss and then turned solid topaz-brown with resolve. Scrim wasn't dead yet, and she would not let him die.

"Stur, hold this seaweed compress on firmly and tie off the torn arms."

"I remember how," he replied with calm arms. "You taught me well."

"I've never treated anyone in such critical condition." His pulse was so faint, like an echo of life passing on. A strong herb could kill him. Scree poured a few drops of dark brown syrup into his mouth. It was her safest, mildest stimulant. "Scrim loves chocolate and he can't even enjoy this," she said with trembling arms.

Scrim's pulse grew slightly stronger. Now she could feel the terrifying, irregular flubbing sound of his heart. If the heartbeat was wrong for too long, he would die. Scree plucked a round, blue coral jar from her shelves and scooped out some oily salve. She rubbed this gently all over his skin, letting her arms work independently while her mind raced through every herb she knew.

"This salve will reduce swelling and help his heart pump in a better rhythm," she said to Stur, automatically slipping into her teacher role. "Can you feel it shifting?" Then Scrim's limp body turned a whiter shade of gray. Scree shuddered. "He's dying." Her eyes darted along the shelves, identifying each herb by its container, and stopped at a glassy jar. She jabbed an arm at the top shelf. "I need that amethyst triangle jar."

Stur grabbed the odd jar, feeling its triangle base and three triangle sides. He used an extra arm to yank out the gemstone stopper and recoiled. "What *is* this?"

Scree counted three drops into Scrim's mouth and massaged to help the herb slide down his throat. Three of her arms encircled his body, checking for changes in his pulse and tasting the chemicals in his skin. He was slipping away. How much longer before his death color was forever?

Scree was barely aware of the world beyond Scrim. Her arms answered, speaking almost on their own. "It's a gift from Zarina, an extract from a New World flower that can strengthen a heartbeat. She made the jar from amethyst to match the purple foxglove flowers. She carved it into this fancy shape to match our Healer triangle sign . . ."

". . . with a broad base of Healer knowledge and the tipping point where healing occurs," Stur finished. "I remember. I've never seen a jar like this. The herb has such a sharp feel/taste."

Scree nodded. "Foxglove is powerful. Too much can kill, so the jar is unique."

Why wasn't the herb working? She glanced at the amethyst jar and her skin sparkled with a new idea. Purple had the greatest energy of all the rainbow colors. She focused a micro-zap through the crystal jar right over his heart. Scree was monitoring her arm sensors so closely that she nearly missed the change in his skin color. His body jerked violently.

"He's back!"

Scrim's eyes found Scree and his arms whispered, barely moving, "I saw you fall."

"I had an extra defense: a hole hidden beneath kelp leaves."

Scrim gave a weak smile. "You always were one move ahead. I should have known."

Scree smiled sadly. "It wasn't enough. There were losses, and we nearly lost you."

Krees and Tor appeared at the entrance to check on

Scrim. He was still in critical condition. One arm had been torn off into the mantle and would never grow back. Scree read their subtle, almost-controlled color changes. They were thrilled that Scrim was alive but horrified by his injuries. What would it be like to have such a gap, to move with an odd number of arms?

Krees bowed to Scree and gave a hidden sign: "We will take care of him now." Openly she said, "The pod needs both of you. We'll stay here and entertain Scrim."

Scree twined arms with all three of her apprentices, sending and receiving unqualified love. Then she and Stur left.

Scree stopped just outside the dance field and watched through the gritty water. Three prisoners lay tightly bound on the sand, struggling mightily against their ropes, surrounded by an angry pod. The water was charged with emotional flavors. Octopi were changing colors from intensity-red to scared-angry-neon-blue. Many had cuts on their skin, where the color changes were not quite normal. Orm's glowing jellyfish hung in the sea, lighting this unreal scene. So much had happened, and it was not yet dawn.

The cuts would heal but the dead would not. Anger for the dead and wounded burned in Scree, and she struggled to control it.

"As we agreed, this is your show," Stur said.

Orm nodded. "Everything is ready."

Scree pulsed to the front, stretched tall on her arms, and turned bright gold. Squid eyes blazed with angry recognition. She read their lights: This was the puny leader who had defeated them in battle. She held up the huge pink pearl. "This shell-stone was given to me by

Veera, in the deep abyss, as a sign of peace. You know this. I left as a friend with the squid blessing: May you surf the tangled currents of the sea forever." Scree spoke their language fluently, making rapid patterns of red and yellow spots on her arms. "You broke a treaty that protects both sides; it would also protect squid from octopi. If you had visited us in peace, we would have welcomed you. But you came to kill for sport. Now you will pay the price."

Scree struck her shell drum and the giants flinched. The remaining squad leaders pulsed to her side. She noted that there were only six of her original eight leaders; one was dead and Scrim was in critical condition. She would not give in to hatred. "Killing you would be too easy," she said to the captives, with angry arms.

Scree nodded to her squad leaders. They whacked the giants on the end of each long tentacle, using their octopus arms to inject venom from the wax balls. The hidden poison made octopi appear to have a magical power. This was an impressive display, and she knew that both sides would remember it forever. The poison was perfectly placed, far from the head, and soon the giants stopped struggling. Three squid bodies lay as still as death . . . but their minds were awake.

The giant squid watched in fear, unable to move. Octopi stalked forward on long, stiff arms, carrying bright crystal jars of starlight . . . Orm's glowing bacteria. The octopi used hollow fish fin needles to inject spots under the skin of each squid head.

"You will live, but you have been marked," Scree warned. "Your star spots will always glow, and we would recognize you on the darkest night. If you ever attack octopi or our floating wood homes, we *will* kill you."

Another group of octopi attached floats to the limp squid. "Now we will return you to the deep abyss. We carry you so that you will never again touch the sands of our village," Scree said. She raised her golden arms and the rest of the pod surged forward. Each octopus grabbed hold of a squid, using the strong suction cups of their arms.

Stur noted the communal effort and he nodded with grim satisfaction. "The arms of the entire pod are working together. You made a real army. The squid will not forget this."

"I'm at least as angry as you are. I will not kill, but they will never forget."

Scree joined the pod and helped push these limp, floating bodies through the sea. They pulsed past the slope and reached the abyss. Cold, clean currents from the dark depths flowed across her skin. "If we kill, you would learn nothing. Never return." She used her sharpest knife and easily sliced through the thick ropes that bound the prisoners. Then squad leaders cut off the floats. Three dazed, giant squid fell heavily into the darkness beyond.

The octopi were exhausted, drained of their emotional colors, and became a normal dull brown. They pulsed slowly home to bury their fallen comrades.

The pod held its traditional ceremony for the dead. Scree and Orm joined a line behind the bodies. Each friend imaged a special memory. Then they covered the bodies with branches of dead coral. The entire pod planted seaweed around the coral, until colorful strands covered the new reef. Soon the sea would reclaim them. As battle leader, Scree added a cluster of anemone flowers above the fallen.

A long stretch of dead, white coral held a regular pattern of gray rocks. A name was etched into each rock. The pod leader added three new rocks to this memory wall.

The sea rumbled ominously, and Scree shuddered. Then the sea shook. She swayed with the water, pulled back and forth, as if blown by a strong winter wind. Their volcano was waking.

CHAPTER 9: LEGENDS

Drakor climbed the northern hill, digging his feet into the patchy grass, eyes on the prize. His brace was off and today he would fly again. Thick morning fog covered the valley below like a blanket, drenched in the soft blues and purples of late dawn. Scents of the sea hung in the damp air.

Drakor reached the top of the hill, faced the sea, and stretched his wings as wide as he could. The newly-healed membrane was tight and scrunched. He ignored the stabbing pains and stretched wider, until his wings matched. Then he launched himself into thin air, far above the rocks below.

Drakor missed his stroke and tumbled down. Sharp rocks rushed up to meet him. He stretched his wings wider, reaching for a better stroke, and finally caught the wind. He skimmed just above the rocks and surged up into the sky.

Freedom! His heart beat to the tune of his wings and his eyes glowed like cut diamonds. Sea breezes blew across his scales as he danced with the wind, tilting his wings to catch every shift. He spun through the air, ignoring the pain in his rusty muscles.

Drakor swooped low; the very tip of one wing rippled along the water. He caught the warm thermal, rising with the sea mist, and soared higher. He was smoke and fire, Volcano lightning thundering across the sky.

Dorali appeared out of nowhere, gracefully matching Drakor in the air. She pointed to the ground, signaling for him to land.

Drakor flew another circle, cupped his wings like a parachute, and landed as gently as a yellow-flower seed. He promptly fell over, cradling his wing protectively.

"What were you thinking?" Dorali cried, eyes flashing. "You must let your muscles build up slowly. Do you want new injuries?"

He smiled a toothy grin. "What did you expect? You took off the brace. I needed to feel the sky again."

"If you're not careful you'll feel the ground instead. Then you'll need that brace again and be in no shape for the quest."

Drakor stretched his wings gently. "I must find a new home."

"Then do those wing exercises so you can explore the New World properly, from the sky."

Drakor bowed his head, partly to hide a smile at her concern. He *was* an ice dragon, after all. But he stretched and flapped his wings every moment that he could, to strengthen the muscles. He pulled his wings through the water and made short gliding flights through the sky.

Three days later he approached Arak. "I do not know if I will ever be here again. I want to visit the octopus village before we leave. We can fly there."

Arak shuddered. "Your broken wing is barely healed. That's much too far for you to fly; the Healers would never forgive me. I'll contact Scree and Orm, and we'll take the skiff tomorrow morning. Tonight we share shadow-stories."

When evening purples colored the sky, the clan gathered in their cave. Solid limestone benches formed a half circle around the welcoming fire. Arak, Zarina, and Arwina had seats beside Drakor. Dorali sat near them, staring into the fire, ignoring the crowd. Arak touched Zarina's arm. "She came."

Driana walked around to the far side of the fire, to the open floor between the fire and the cave wall. This flat, white wall was made of teensy, glittering crystals. It was perfect for shadows.

Driana raised her wings for attention and the conversations stopped. "This is the legend of the Flame-flower and the First Healer." She made shadow-scenes using her claws, feet, wings, and even a coiled tail. Dark and light wove together in life-like patterns.

"A dragonlet lay limp on the sand, burning with fever. He was dying."

Driana made a small, winged shadow-dragon appear on the wall.

"Ravena, the dragon's dam, begged the First Dragon for help. 'How can I save him?' A deep voice answered in her mind, 'Take five golden scales from above your heart. Plant them in a ring and breathe fire in the center.' She gasped as she pulled off each scale. The pain burned.

112

Then Ravena did as instructed and fell into a deep, exhausted sleep."

A ring of shadow scales appeared on the wall, and the First Dragon's shadow loomed above this.

"When Ravena awoke, the ring of scales was gone. A new plant with bright flowers grew in its place. Each bloom had five pointed petals that were the color of flames. Again the voice spoke in her mind. 'Boil five flowers in water. This tea will heal your dragonlet.'"

The shadow-movie on the wall followed her story.

"The dragonlet opened his eyes and stretched his wings, looking around as if nothing had happened. His dam spiraled up into the sky with joy. The Flame-flower was born, and Ravena became the First Healer." Driana finished with a bow.

Dragons thumped and snapped their tails in applause.

Arak smiled at Zarina. "I remember when you first gathered that herb. You found a new place where it grows, and then a new use for it."

She leaned against him. "And you made a musical, flame-flower ice sculpture to impress me."

Drakor stared at the fire. "We have nothing like shadow-stories."

Arak nodded. "It's another way to use fire. Driana will join us for our journey to the New World. She's an excellent Healer and a clever cook. She uses herbs for more than healing! We take turns fixing meals, but she's the best."

Arak stood up, stretched, and walked to the stage behind the fire. He looked into the eyes of each dragon, gathering their attention, and took a deep breath. "This is the story of the monster wave."

Arak shivered, remembering the day when he woke before dawn, feeling an unseen threat. He had sent his trance-mind across the sea, to a circle of boiling water. This was a hidden volcano, and the sea would send a giant wave. His mind fled back into his body to warn the clan. Many dragons were angry at being roused from sleep, and they called him a worthless Dreamer. But the leader believed.

Why had he woken so early? Why was he the only dragon who felt that threat? Arak had a secret talent, the ability to quest while in trance. Only he could see more than the shimmer of another trance-mind; he saw what was there. Sometimes, young dragons walked in their sleep. Had he dream-walked to the boiling sea, and returned to warn his sleeping self?

Arak swept one wing up slowly, creating the shadow of the terrifying wall of water. His other wing bent to form their hill sanctuary. Taron played the drum, beating faster as the water piled higher and higher.

The shadow-wave towered and crashed onto the hillside. His claw shadows were the powerful edge of the sea raking down the hill. Finally, he showed the devastation, with floating trees and an empty shore.

The audience applauded his skill, but some flicked their tails nervously.

Arak returned to his seat.

Drakor said, "That wave isss impressive."

"It was more terrifying than a giant squid."

Taron stood up and walked to the stage. "This is our journey to the New World." He waved one hand to create rippling shadow-waves against the wall. The shadow of a skiff, made from his clawed fist, slid across this sea.

Swordfish leapt and smaller fish flew.

The audience leaned forward, always intrigued by travel stories.

Taron dropped metal into the fire to make blue flames as he described the glowing blue seas. His shadow-skiff landed on the distant shore. He curved his arms and tail, creating the shadow of a short tree with plump fruit pods.

His mate, Erinite, played the flute, blending familiar dragon melodies with enticing, exotic notes. All ears were swiveled to the sound. Drakor held completely still; he looked like an ice sculpture.

Using sleight-of-hand, Taron magically produced a clawfull of fragrant cocoa beans from his shadow-tree. "This is one of the treasures of the New World." Everyone leaned toward the tantalizing aroma. A tray of Zarina's chocolate was passed around to eager dragons with dreamy expressions.

Drakor took his piece of chocolate, but he was still staring at Erinite. "I have never heard such beautiful sounds!"

Arak nodded agreement. "Taron carved the flute and she learned to make new music."

Drakor tore his eyes away from Erinite and studied the crowd. "Story-telling with music and chocolate isss a powerful combination. The giant wave isss scary, and the journey story makes me want to travel." He turned to Arak. "Why?"

"We need to find more dragons for the next journey."

Drakor had a gleam in his eyes. "But why did you share the scary wave? Does this mean you want to move?"

Arak gave the hint of a smile. "Perhaps."

Drakor snapped his tail cheerfully.

* * *

Drakor and Arak left just before dawn, and reached the octopus village in early afternoon. Sunlight slanted across the sea, making the waves sparkle like diamonds. They tied the skiff to the signal raft.

They dropped the summoning stone into the water, and it crashed onto the rock below. Scree and Orm soon popped up beside the raft.

Drakor and Arak each grabbed two rocks and plunged into the sea, using the weight to speed their descent. Then they dropped one rock and hovered above the sand, weightless in the water. Arak swam after the octopi using a special dragon-stroke, pulling his wings against the water and collapsing them to begin a new stroke.

Drakor quickly mastered this underwater skill and followed Arak to Orm's cave. He could barely take his eyes off the coral reef to look where he was headed. Octopi flashed gold to greet Arak, but they stared at the big ice dragon and kept their distance. Some octopi lived in natural caves beneath coral heads. Others had homes made from rocks that were strengthened by sturdy barnacles. Long strands of seaweed grew around them, making colorful gardens that partly hid these caves.

They soon reached Orm's cave, and Drakor poked his head inside. He stared. A glowing tapestry of red, green, blue, violet, and gold tunicates covered the curved walls. "Beautiful!" he signed.

Then Arak took his turn. "Orm, I think this is your best pattern yet. I'm glad I saw it." He began to shake as he ran out of air. Arak wrapped arm to claw in a quick farewell and swam back toward the raft. Drakor watched his friend grow smaller in the distance. Arak reached the raft, rocketed back to the surface, and disappeared.

Drakor followed his octopus escort to Scree's cave. He peered inside, gazed up at the glowing tunicates, and his eyes grew wide with surprise. "You have northern stars."

"Orm changed the pattern in honor of your visit," Scree replied.

Drakor eyed her shelves and snapped his tail in amazement, which made a tiny wave. "There are so many Healer items. And weapons!" He pointed to a stack of spears leaning against the wall.

Scree gave him one to examine. "Don't touch the tip," she warned. "We used these when the giant squid attacked."

"I heard about that. What happened to the squid?"

"They were defeated, marked, and released."

Drakor shook his head. "I am not sure that an ice dragon could ever understand why you let them go." He eyed her display of sharp gemstone knives. "Beautiful and deadly."

Scree smiled. "Healers can be dangerous."

Drakor remembered their first meeting, when she knocked him out. "And merciful. You helped fix my wing after I tried to kill you."

She nodded. "Now I have a friend. A live friend is worth more than a dead enemy."

Drakor shook his head. "That isss a strange idea, but I will consider it. I owe you a debt. Mind-call and I will help if I can." He said farewell and swam away.

Arak was waiting on the wood raft. "You can hold your breath so long."

"That isss because I am so big," he said, matter-of-factly. "Scree has many shelves in her cave. How does she remember where everything isss? Orm lives in the sea but he put stars in Scree's cave. His cave isss covered with living, glowing colors. The pattern has swirls like an aurora that becomes the sea."

Arak chuckled. "That may be what Orm imagines in his amazing mind. He and Kragor are practically legends, the best artists we may ever know."

They cast off and skiff-flew home, beneath an amethyst sunset that became a diamond-filled night. Faint scents of home were carried on the wind from the distant shore.

Drakor leaned into the wind with nostrils flared and a smile on his face. "Life isss strange. I thought I would die when the Volcano knocked me off and broke my wing. Now I have seen new worlds and new ideas. Maybe there isss hope for ice dragons when we lose our world."

The wind shifted and Arak adjusted the skiff-wing. "Dreams are powerful. A good plan can make them real."

* * *

Arak glowed gold beneath the last half moon before spring. He stared out to sea. "We're holding this festival early because of the earth-shakes. The octopi will be here any moment. I can see the tips of the masts of their skiffs."

Waves slapped the sandy shore and slipped back into the sea. A ribbon of foam was left behind, marking the reach of each new wave. Arak stood in the waves, eyes closed, ears turned forward. The music of the sea swelled, crashed, and sighed into silence, over and over. "This is my favorite lullaby."

Drakor nodded. "Always the sea. I am learning to like your spices, but sea salt isss still the best spice. I spoke with Scree about our Volcanoes."

Arak opened his eyes and stared. "You spoke to her in trance? Scree must be worried. I'm still impressed that she defeated three giant squid."

Drakor snapped his tail. "That isss impressive. Scree did not mention her part in the attack."

"Orm told Kragor all the details. Scree led the defense. Now she's focused on the volcano, so I'm trying to find enough wood to build another fleet for the octopi."

Arak stretched his wings wide and folded them back. "I remember when octopi had one turtle to carry things. Then Scree had her skiff idea, and now we all fly on the sea."

Drakor ran his eyes along the rows of half-finished skiffs. "Why so many?"

"There are two pods. Scree wants enough skiffs for all the octopi to move."

"Ah. Where will your guests stay?"

Arak pointed out to sea. "We built guest homes there. Each one has a circle of stone walls and a narrow entrance. Long pieces of coral wash up after storms, and they make a sturdy roof."

Drakor waded into deeper water and plunged his long neck into the sea. Waves ran in and fled back many times. Finally he lifted his head. "It isss a good design." Cold water sleeted off his white scales like moonwater.

Arak laughed. "You look like a melting icicle. Yes, it's a good design. Everything needs a good design. What's your plan for the ice dragons?"

"I am not sure. Look!"

Arak sucked in a lungful of air and shouted, "They're here!" He added oil and a clawfull of metals to the fire. Blue-green welcome flames shot up into the sky; the fire was the color of the sea.

A fleet of skiffs slipped up onto the shore; their wood hulls grated softly against the sand. The sea rose and fell daily, with tides that pulled like powerful arms. The pod landed at high tide so their skiffs would be safely beyond the sea.

Dragons flew to greet them, gleaming gold in the starlight. They eagerly dragged the small skiffs even farther inland and tied them to poles sunk deep in the sand.

Kragor, Arak's sire, greeted Orm with the double clasp of friendship. "I changed the design of our undersea garden. Now the tunicates glow in a star-within-star pattern of red, blue, and green. I can't wait to show you."

"Let's go now."

A gray starfish washed up onto the sand between them. The crusty creature rose up onto its five arms. It walked calmly back into the sea, octopus-style, ignoring everyone.

Orm laughed. "That's a serene starfish. Kragor, I brought you tunicates in two new colors: violet and gold."

The dragon closed his eyes tight. "I can see it. This new pattern will be amazing!"

Arak grinned. His sire and Orm were both obsessed with art, and as close as dragon nest-mates.

Arafine, their leader, formally welcomed Stur and Spar, the leaders of the two pods. Octopi carefully arranged their baskets on the beach, above the tide. Then they walked back into the water on stiffened arms and rested in the sea, near their wares. Dragons crowded around baskets of exotic seaweed, live oysters, fresh scallops, shiny abalone arm bands, vials of blue-ringed octopus venom, red coral knives, and many more items. Fires dotted the beach, lighting the night. Fragrant smoke drifted across the traders.

Six dragons greeted Scree and clustered around her baskets. One held a treasure trove of shimmering pearls. The second was filled to the brim with rare, deep-sea scallop shells. These bright purple, yellow, orange, and red shells often became fancy dessert plates, and some were used to decorate dragon nest bowls. The third basket held poison, and the attention of all three Healers.

Zarina crouched down, counting the vials. "This is exactly what we need!"

Dorali nodded agreement. "Herbs help, but nothing beats the right dose of venom."

Driana signed, "We'll take them all."

Arak put a bulging sack onto the beach and opened it. "We have lightning casts!"

Several octopi rose up on their arms, running to Arak through the gentle surf. They felt the clear rods, which were made by melting beach sand into glass with lightning. Krees, Scree's apprentice, traded pearls for five casts. "These are perfect for the entrance to my cave. The rods will make a protective screen I can see through, and squeeze through."

Scree pointed to a row of skiffs, which were not yet finished.

"We're building the octopus skiffs as fast as we can, but we need more hardwood," Taron said.

Scree curled her arms nervously. "The sea is shaking

and our volcano is waking up." She lifted one arm up into the damp air, sensing. "Your forest has lots of pines but few oaks. Most pine trees have weak wood for such a strong flavor, but I taste some yellow pines. These have a stronger wood than your other needle trees."

Taron snapped his tail. "Octopi are so efficient. That's the fastest forest survey I've ever seen! If it's acceptable, using yellow pine would speed things up."

Scree's last basket caught the eye of Arak's dragonlet, Arwina. She peeked at the collection of pearls and sighed. "They're so pretty."

Drakor gazed into the basket. "Pink, orange, violet . . . these are sunrise colors."

"Great sky colors," Scree agreed. "I collected new samples near our volcano. They match what I found in the ice abyss near your volcano. The volcanoes are connected so, if your home is truly in danger, then our reef home is too."

Drakor snapped his wings, making a gale of wind that nearly flattened Scree. "This isss bigger than I thought."

Arak clicked his claws together. "Volcano explosions would affect us, too. I told Arafine that we should move our supplies now, beyond the reach of the giant waves that would follow."

Karoon rolled his eyes. "You're afraid of a dream? Moving our supplies would just waste our time. We should be smoking fish and preparing for the winter we *know* will come."

Arak shrugged his wings. "Dreams are powerful. What we don't know for sure can still kill us. Two volcanos give signs that they will explode. Each would cause a giant wave, one after the other. If Drakor's vision is correct, there will be a monstrous wave beyond any that our ancestors ever saw. We need time to move the dragonlets and supplies beyond its grasp."

"How far do you think we should move?" asked Erinite, Taron's mate. Their dragonlet was splashing happily in the sea.

Arak looked inland. "Beyond the third mountain. We need to bring our Healer supplies, plenty of food, and blankets for everyone."

"Moving all that would take forever!" cried a young dragon-lord.

"We have more important things to do," said another, sharpening his claws in the sand.

Zarina gave the protesters a stern look. "Don't you remember the last big wave?" She turned to Arak. "We won't be able to take everything. Can we seal the cave against a wave that powerful?"

Karoon snapped his tail irritably. "You act as if you're in charge of the clan."

Arak shook his head. "Just my family."

Taron pointed at the sea. "We can debate this at the meetings. Look!"

Both pod leaders had raised bright golden arms for attention. "We have a surprise. We brought a coral reef." At their signal, all of the octopi pulsed together. Most of the octopi settled onto the shallow sea floor. Eight transformed into creamy coral heads with strands of green seaweed.

One octopus flattened her body into a lacy purple sea fan, while two more shape-shifted into blue lobsters. An orange-and-white calico crab, mustard yellow barrel sponges, and a carpet of pink-and-orange anemones appeared on the sandy sea floor.

Eight octopi remained at the surface. In the blink of an eye they were replaced by pink-and-blue jellyfish. They hung in the water, arms swaying with the waves. Then Scree and Orm became black stingrays and flew gracefully through this colorful shape-shifter reef.

The dragons stared, eyes wide, snapping their tails in amazement.

"They can become anything?" Drakor asked.

Arak shrugged his wings. "Apparently. This is the first reef I've seen that was made from octopi."

* * *

Arak woke as dawn light filtered into his shelter, which was tucked away in thick bushes. He stretched, filled his lungs with the new day, and tossed off his old, comfortable blanket. This was woven from flax, and years of rubbing against his scales had made it even softer. He slipped off the springy matt, which was made of woven branches, and poked his head out. Sea mist softened the sharp edges of boulders that were strewn among the trees. A perfect spider web hung between branches, decorated with shimmering pearls of dew.

Drakor greeted him, looking like he'd been awake for dragon-hours.

"When do you sleep?" Arak asked. When had it become normal to talk with a legend? Drakor was now just another clan dragon . . . except that he ate like three dragons and fished like six, hauling in the huge sturgeon fish.

Drakor flicked his long tail. "There isss much to see before I leave."

Arak nodded. "We'll miss you. See how small that

spider is?" He blew on the web, and the tiny spider scampered into hiding. "It weaves a sticky trap for insects but makes safe strands for itself. It has a plan to survive. You need a plan to help ice dragons survive."

"My clan only listens to the leader, and he listens to himself," Drakor growled.

"Can you convince him of the danger?"

"I will try. I think I will need to challenge Mardor, but he isss older, bigger, and stronger."

Arak clouted him on the back, hard, in an ice dragonly way. "Then you must learn a different way to fight. And when you win, where will you go?"

Drakor flicked his tail nervously. "You really think I can win?"

Arak nodded. "Anything is possible. Scree made a plan to defeat three giant squid, and it worked. What's your plan?"

Trading continued throughout the day, with new items. Orm made abalone arm bands that were popular with the dragon-ladies. Zarina made salty chocolate pecans that Orm simply could not resist. Precious dragon herbs were exchanged for rare seaweed from the ice abyss.

As the sun set, clan and pod gathered at the steeper shore. Dragons built a crackling fire, and the colored flames cast cheerful shadows. The entire clan of noisy dragons sat around the land side of the fire, while octopi filled the sea-side seats.

Dragons had pushed logs into the bank at different depths. Scree, Orm, and the other pod visitors rested on these sea seats, flowing up or down to new seats with the changing tides.

The central fire had festive blue-green flames leaping among the traditional orange and yellow from burning logs. Pine needles glowed orange and twisted like claws, climbing into the scented air.

Arak sat down next to Drakor, who was staring trance-like into the flames. "What do you see?"

"It isss a tiny Volcano." Drakor stretched his injured wing carefully and smiled. "Dorali's energy-pulse helped my bones grow back together. How can something so small be so strong?"

Arak laughed. "The energy-pulse or Dorali?

"Both. Soon I will fly home."

"That would be a long flight for a newly healed wing. It may need more time to be strong enough." Arak cocked his head. "We're leaving on another journey to the New World to harvest copper, cocoa beans, and honey. There's a cold land to the north with ice and old volcanoes. You could come along to see if this would make a good home for ice dragons. After the northern stop, we would skiff-fly directly to your home." Arak didn't mention that he had only seen this northern place while questing in trance, in his mind.

"How long will you be gone?"

"A dragon-month. Dorali could help your wing heal stronger. You must be ready to win a fight."

Drakor took a deep breath, inhaling the pleasant smoke from pine, juniper, and sweet-scented ash-wood. "I will miss these mar-ve-lus fires . . . we have little wood to burn. I will come. Ice dragons need a new home, so it isss an important part of any plan." He placed both hands against Arak's, claws tilted away, in a ritual gesture. "You are a good friend. I will not forget this."

Arafine, the leader, raised her golden wings high. Silence settled on the clan. "It's time for story-telling."

"Tell us the story of the ice dragons!" begged a dragonlet.

All eyes turned to Drakor, the living legend.

Arafine said, "Arak will share our ice dragon legend. Then Drakor will share his clan's story of the ice dragon."

Arak stepped forward. He swept his wings upward and all talking stopped.

"This is the legend of the ice dragons," he said, in a deep, dramatic voice. He wove sign language between his words, using gestures from both dragons and octopi. Everyone had learned this mutual language and took pride in new expressions. Dragons spoke of changing their colors when considering a new idea. Octopi bent two arms like folded wings to concede that the other being was right.

"Long ago, our world was white. The sun was dim and often hidden by snowstorms. Ice covered the land. The ice dragons had large, snowy wings. Their scales were white moonstones edged with glittering diamonds. They were made from snowy moonbeams and icy starlight. Ice dragons were huge, with twice my wingspan."

Arak stretched his wings wide.

"They lived on the ice, dove into the sea for fish, and played catch with lightning as we do. Ice dragons flew far above the storms. Then their world changed. The sun became hotter, the ice began to melt, and glaciers retreated from the sea."

Arak paused dramatically while his eyes swept across the sand.

"Golden beaches were seen for the first time. Their white world had color. Some dragons moved off the ice to see the new sand. The sun caught these ice dragons and turned them to gold." He gathered a clawfull of sand and held it high, letting it sift through his claws. The sand and his scales gleamed golden in the firelight.

"Other dragons stayed on the ice. They worked together, rolling huge rocks to the edge of the ice. They pushed the boulders off, building an immense wall to protect the ice from the sun. But the sun was too strong. Most of the ice melted away and the ice dragons left. Stories passed down beyond memory claim that they flew very high and found a new land of ice, where they still live. And now we know this to be true."

Arak bowed.

Dragons thumped their tails and octopi turned exotic colors to applaud. There were violet arms with orange swirls, pink arms with blue diamonds, and more. Octopi also used their arms to sign words of praise.

Arak remained standing, ready to interpret Drakor's story for the octopus guests.

Drakor stood and bowed politely. "That was . . . interesting." He stepped into the firelight. "This isss our story."

"The black Volcano rose high above the silent, endless ice. Lightning crackled through his hot, dark clouds and he roared." Drakor roared louder than thunder, startling the dragons.

"White lightning struck the glacier again and again. The bolts gouged sharp flakes from ancient ice and carved a white body. The ice dragon was covered with crackling scales, like the shattered surface of a frozen stream. A jagged ridge ran down the back. The Volcano melted long, smooth wings that flowed out from the ice body. He threw two bolts of black lightning and cut dark holes into the head for eyes. His sculpture was complete, and lifeless."

The huge white dragon crouched low, spreading his wings wide across the ground, holding as still as an ice sculpture.

"Then the Volcano gathered white diamonds, made from blood-red fire deep inside his heart. These diamonds held his fiery spirit. He ground the crystals into dust and sprinkled this over his sculpture. Diamond dust settled into the rim of each white scale."

Drakor held up a massive, eight-sided diamond crystal that gleamed with an inner light. Then he snapped his huge wings open, springing to life with a gale of wing-wind.

Arak dug his claws in, refusing to budge a scale-length. He leaned into the wind.

"The ice dragon's black eyes glowed with life and her scales sparkled. She drew in her first frozen breath, sprang into the sky and flew high above the hot clouds. She dove back through black clouds, faster than the wind. The First Dragon was born of Volcano and Ice, as fierce as fiery lava and as wild as a winter gale."

Arak nodded. This story was nothing like the gentle legend he knew, where ice dragons were made of moonbeams and starlight. But it fit Drakor much better. He had described his home with its stunted trees, biting winds, and black grit from the volcano. This grit blew far out to sea, adding dark shadows to the floating white ice-mountains.

Arak wrinkled his nose, remembering the odors of burnt sky and rotten egg that blew across the dragon-skiff. It was a dangerous, forbidding place. Ice dragons must grow up quickly in that harsh land.

* * *

The next day, Dorali shivered as storm energy sparkled through her. She stood alone at the very edge of the meadow, watching the sky with a longing so deep it sliced to the bone.

Years ago, a pack of hungry dweer nearly tore her apart. Now, the scars kept her apart. Young dragons stared at her. Others let their eyes slide away from her ugly scars, which they pretended not to see. She would never be beautiful, not with her scars. She would never be invited into the clouds by her very own dragon-lord. But she would be the best Healer the world had ever seen.

Clouds towered higher and darker, but with little wind. Lightning sparked in the clouds. It was a perfect day for storm dances. By tradition, mated pairs flew into the clouds first. Arak and Zarina leapt up, wingtips barely touching as they spiraled higher. Mated dragons became bright whirlwinds, twirling up until they disappeared. Then other couples formed and joined them. Would she ever be invited to dance?

The clouds blazed bright, lit by colored lightning. Dorali felt the vials of metal powders in her pouch. These were used to color the lightning red, orange, yellow, blue or purple. But not green.

Each dragon-lord had a precious vial of chromium powder. This red-orange metal looked like the edge of dragon-lord scales, but it would change a lightning bolt to vivid green, like the edge of dragon-lady scales. The special bolt was only made for a dragon-lady. She could accept or toss it aside. If she accepted, they were mated for life.

Dorali imagined herself in the clouds, spinning through the sky, eyes locked on her partner. She felt the rumbling thunder and tasted the burnt air as dragons tossed lightning. Rainbow colors flashed in an electric display more beautiful than an aurora borealis.

Crunching steps jerked Dorali from her dreams as Karoon walked up to her. What could he want?

"Would you like to dance in the clouds?" he asked, wearing his annoying, confident smile.

Her eyes widened in surprise. Karoon generally ignored her, but she'd caught him staring at her scars. "With you?" She studied him. He had courted another Healer for years. "Why? Because Zarina has chosen a mate?"

Karoon flicked his tail. "Maybe . . . partly . . . but you're a well-grown dragon-lady."

"And scarred."

"I can ignore your scars," he said.

Dorali's head buzzed as if lightning had passed too close. Her eyes burned bright with tears she would not release. She was a substitute, an after-thought, a damaged product. It took all her willpower to respond calmly. "That's not good enough for me."

"What? You're rejecting me?" Karoon sputtered. "Who else could you find?"

Her hands were clenched so tightly that the claws bit into her. She must leave. If only she could become invisible, like Scree!

"That doesn't matter. I'd rather be comfortably alone

than with someone who doesn't appreciate me." She turned away from the rainbow clouds.

* * *

Dorali stepped into the moonlit sea, sinking her claws into the cold wet sand. The sea rose and fell around her; silvery waves slipped ashore and slid back with a sigh. Her rapid breathing gradually slowed to match the hypnotic rhythm of the sea. She would join another quest. The dragon-lords and octopi onboard the skiff accepted Dorali so completely that she was sure they did not even notice her scars. They just saw her.

Scree relaxed nearby. Her arms drifted back and forth with the waves, like seaweed.

Dorali stared longingly at the horizon. "I must go back to sea."

Scree gave her a penetrating look. "What is it?"

"Scree, you can change to be anything you want. Any color, texture, shape. I am *always* the dragon with the ugly scars."

Scree wrapped two arms around Dorali and gave her a gentle hug. "Much depends on your perspective. I look at you and see a good friend." A bright blue stick with amber eyes landed on a bush at the edge of the sea. Moonlight glinted off its clear glass wings.

Scree pointed. "See that dragonfly? Look at the eyes."

Dorali leaned closer to the dragonfly, moving slowly, trying to not scare it away. "Each eye is like a tiny honey-comb."

Scree nodded. "A dragonfly views the world through eyes that see many different pictures of one thing. It's a bit like seeing through my skin. I concentrate on all the picture-parts, put them together, and make them into one picture." She looked into Dorali's eyes. "Each of us is made of many pictures, memories, dreams. You are so much more than any one dragon could ever see, and you're beautiful to everyone who cares about you."

Dorali sighed wistfully.

"Arafine says the seal of approval that matters is our own. That's true, but we all need acceptance from others. You are appreciated more than you realize." Scree smiled. "We'll leave for the New World in three days. I can hardly wait! I love to travel beyond the horizon. What will we find?"

CHAPTER 10: MYSTERIOUS DEPTHS

Arak rose before dawn and strolled through a glass forest that glowed in the moonlight. Every twig was coated with ice, twinkling like earth-bound stars. This freezing rain was the last blast of winter. He crunched across the frozen beach, savoring the scent of the sea . . . and adventure. Arak stretched his wings and flew to the skiff.

Taron greeted him as he coiled another rope. "We're as loaded as a rain cloud."

Arak nodded, flicking his tail. "We'll need these provisions."

"What did you see?" Taron asked quietly.

Arak studied his friend. He had finally trusted Taron with his great secret. Dragons used their trance-stone to mind-talk to someone who was far away, but Arak could mind-travel. He saw what was there. He had extended his trance-range even more, to quest across the sea.

"I've seen strong sea-storms between here and the New World. We'll travel to our southern stop first, using the currents, and gather New World food. Then we'll skirt the coast and travel north to the copper mine. Farther north, the land has thick ice and old volcanoes with no smoke. This might make a good home for ice dragons. I wish I could search with more senses than sight."

Taron just shook his head, with a gleam of humor in his eyes. "And have no excuse to journey? Be glad you can't see everything." He tossed a heavy sack to Arak. "Your sire and dam brought more smoked fish and another cask of fresh water. We can barely squeeze everything into the hold and still have our weather-space."

"Ooof!" Arak grunted as he caught the sack. "Kragor's been to sea and Arafine's a worried dragon-dam. There should be more than enough food for this journey. We could almost build another skiff with all the extra boards, rope, fish leather, and tools stashed for repairs."

Taron stretched his wings. "Octopi cleaned the barnacles off our hull and ate them as snacks. Our skiff is smooth again, almost new, so we'll fly even faster. I can't wait!"

A light morning breeze ruffled the skiff-wing as a crowd of dragons arrived to bid farewell. Shouts of "More copper!" and "Don't forget chocolate!" filled the air.

Arak's dam and sire arrived to wave a cheerful farewell.

His younger sibling, Korana, landed neatly beside them. Her scales gleamed as she arched her neck in a perfect curve. "Be sure you bring back the copper we need," she said, as if giving an order.

Arak sighed and ignored her. How could she be so smart, beautiful, and obnoxious?

Taron twined necks fondly with his mate, Erinite. "I'll bring back wood for your flutes." He wrapped his wings around their dragonlet and gave him a toy skiff. It even had a mast and skiff-wing. "I carved this for you. Be the wind. Practice blowing this skiff all over the pond and you'll learn how to skiff-fly."

Arak gazed into the eyes of his mate, the Healer Zarina. "I wish you could come."

She twined necks with Arak. "Soon."

"I'll look for healing herbs, but Dorali will probably find them first."

"She'll be happy to share. Dorali's like my first dragonlet, ever since she lived at the clinic with me while she healed." Zarina frowned. "That dweer attack hurt her in deeper ways. Your last journey seemed to draw her out of that shell she hides in, but something new happened and she's pulled back in."

Arak looked out to the horizon. "Who knows? Adventure may draw her out again." He reached down to their dragonlet. "Arwina, you're growing like seaweed! Don't grow so fast that you fly before I get back." Arak ordered.

She giggled and glanced up sideways. "Can you bring me another pretty stone?"

"For your collection? Absolutely." Arak pulled a carved crystal board and a small, lumpy bag from his sack. "Here's a special gift . . . octopus checkers with a complete set of play pearls. Orm grew them just for you.

Learn how to win as any color while I'm gone."

"I will!" Arwina poked her claws into the shallow holes and grooves on the board. "It's so clear, like ice." She opened the bag and bounced up and down, fluttering her young wings. "Oooh! White, pink, purple, orange, and black pearls. And even blue! They're all exactly the same size. These are perfect!"

"Have a safe journey. I'll be waiting for you each night in trance," Zarina whispered to Arak.

"I'll be there," he said quietly. "Soon we'll journey together."

Zarina took Arwina's hand and they moved back into the crowd.

Orm and Scree climbed a ladder built onto the side of the skiff, pulling up with one arm after another. They each slid under the rail and flowed into their water-filled tubs.

"Spring has arrived," Scree signed, pointing. Icicles lined the railing, dripping as the sky warmed to gold.

Drakor walked up and the plank, which bent ominously beneath his weight. Then Dorali and Driana came aboard.

Drakor raised one eyebrow. "Two dragon Healers?"

Arak shrugged his wings. "We'll face new challenges on this quest. Driana and Dorali are excellent Healers and experienced journey-mates."

Last of all, Karoon strode proudly up the plank and hopped onto the skiff. He tossed his sack neatly beside the hold door.

Dorali sucked in her breath. "Why are you here?"

"I volunteered. They asked for a strong dragon-lord, and I'm ready for some adventure," Karoon replied, with a wink.

Dorali spun on her heel and walked as far away as the skiff allowed.

Golden dragons lined the shore, shining bright in the early sunlight. The sky was barely blue when Taron cast off. The skiff-wing filled with wind, tugging them away from shore. The skiff bounced across short, choppy waves.

Taron sighed contentedly. "Our new quest."

Scree turned green with excitement and leaned forward in her basin. "Who knows what we'll see?"

Orm reached across and twined arms with Scree. He turned white and made an incredible design of gray sharks and red giant squid within a ring of black lightning. "Yes indeed. Who knows? How could it possibly get any better than this?"

Earthy scents of land were soon replaced by the tang of salt spray. A long strand of seaweed floated past, torn loose by a storm. The shore disappeared and a blue circle of sea was once again their entire world.

Arak felt the rhythm of the waves and walked with the sea, matching his steps to the long swells beneath him.

Drakor snapped his tail and pointed.

Manta ray fish leapt out of the water, one after another, flapping their triangle fins like wings. They flew high like huge black butterflies and splashed down into the sea.

Karoon, who was still learning how to walk on sea legs, staggered to the railing and held on tight.

Scree smiled. "It's good to see big fish. These must have been far from our volcano before it erupted, so they weren't killed by the heat and chemicals."

Drakor continued to stare. "I have never seen such

fish. I think they are flying for fun, like a dragon."

Clouds blew in and the air smelled of rain. When the wind shifted, Dorali adjusted the tiller to maintain their heading. Arak closed his eyes to better feel/see the magnetic storm lines. "This storm is north of our course," he said, with a sigh of relief.

Sunset clouds turned bright pink with a rim of gold. A dark night followed as these clouds hid the stars. Driana lit three oil lamps.

Arak searched the sky. "We have no guiding stars. This is when it really helps to have an octopus on board."

Orm took the hint. He slid down the side of the skiff and wrapped two arms securely around a narrow platform. He trailed another arm in the sea, tasting their path. "We're still headed the right way," he signed with two more arms.

The sky rumbled ominously. Random clouds glowed bright with inner lightning and then disappeared into darkness.

Dorali gazed into the distance. "It's so beautiful. We paint clouds with colored lightning and play games."

"What does the winner get?" Drakor asked.

Dorali shrugged her wings. "There's no winner. It's just for fun."

Drakor raised one eyebrow. "Just for fun? That isss an interesting idea."

Arak yawned as he checked the magnetic lines once more. "Taron, I think this storm will miss us, but I'll sleep topside just in case. Call if you need help and wake me for my shift to steer."

Waves slapped the skiff with a hypnotic rhythm. He curled up beneath a low shelter on deck and dropped into sleep, wrapped in the eternal song of the sea.

* * *

Arak woke at dawn and immediately surveyed the skiff, muttering as he wiped salt crystals from the ropes. Dried sea spray was the new frost. He turned in a circle, checking the sea, and his head jerked up. The not-so-distant sea appeared solid, like a beach of dark rocks with occasional white sprays of waves breaking against them. What could it be?

Suddenly they were in the midst of a living island made from tens of thousands of manta rays. Each fish was flat, about six feet across, with a long thin tail and triangle fin-wings. The rays overlapped like rocks on the shore, one above the next. They took turns leaping out of the water, flapping their wing-like fins. Each fish made a huge splash as it crashed back into the sea.

Dorali gazed at the lively display. "This is definitely worth the journey."

Taron snapped his tail with a loud crack. "I've crossed the sea many times, and I've never seen so many rays!"

"Maybe we could walk across the sea on their backs," Arak said.

Orm grinned. "That would be an interesting journey."

Drakor stared. "I wish ice dragons could walk to the New World."

"Everyone's talking about your volcano. Why do you think there'll be a disaster?" Karoon asked.

"I have seen all the warning signs from legends, but this isss more than a dream. I have future-sight. I saw my dam bitten by a poison lizard, in my mind, before it happened. I was not long from the shell. This happened for real the next day, and she left forever." Drakor flinched at the memory. "Then I saw my sire caught in an avalanche, before it happened, and he was destroyed."

Drakor took a deep breath and looked out to sea in the exact direction of his home. "I have seen our Volcano explode. My mind sees more than the legend. I see the glowing red eyes of the Volcano. There isss gold and purple lightning. A burning cloud reaches up into the wind-stream. Then our home isss gone."

Drakor's voice fell to a whisper. "I was warned and I did not save my dam or my sire. I failed. Now I see everyone at risk, everyone I know. Will I fail again?"

Arak followed Drakor's gaze across the sea. "You didn't fail, Drakor. When you had your first visions, you didn't know it was future-sight. Now you know, and you're making plans." He flicked his tail uneasily. "I hope Arafine can convince the clan to move our supplies inland."

Drakor stared. "She isss the leader. I still can not understand how they would not listen."

Arak shrugged his wings. "Ice dragon rules would be great, if all leaders were good. Arafine will let everyone talk and think about 'what if'. Then she'll try to guide them to the best decision."

"Ice dragons have only one voice," he said, sadly. "And it isss not my voice."

Arak looked him in the eye. "It could be. Keep working on your plans."

Scree turned to Orm. "Dragons can fly to the hills for safety. When our volcano explodes we won't have time to pulse away to safety. The pods should move now, while they can!"

"You're not a pod leader," Orm reminded her.

"I spoke with Spar and Stur and I think they listened. I hope." She twirled her arms nervously. "I understand the fear that sits in Drakor's eyes."

Orm caught one of her arms and twined his own around it. "We bartered for skiffs, and they should all be ready before we get back. Your squad leaders will make sure these skiffs are flown to the raft above each pod. They can each hold at least three adults and a juvenile. Two fast voyages would move the pods to safety. Then we can move back home."

Her arms relaxed, spilling over the side. "This must work." She gathered her arms together and popped tall like a sprouting mushroom. "Why move back? We can start another pod! We'll bring tiny abalone, clams, and oyster spat for new farms."

Orm rolled his eyes. "I assume *you* would want to join this new pod."

Scree grinned. "Naturally. New is interesting."

* * *

The night sky was crystal-clear, washed clean by an afternoon shower. Arak breathed deeply, inhaling the smell of the sea with its unique blend of life, death, and salt. He gazed up into the starry sky. Dragons passed on to this after-home. "The fires of our ancestors shine bright tonight."

Taron asked pointedly, "What about the living? Our mates and dragonlets?"

Arak looked to the east. "Yes, it's almost time to call home. Trance-mind is a great way to talk across the sea." A whiff of ozone, the storm's gift, heightened his senses. He turned to Dorali. "This is also a good night to see deeper."

142

Dorali nodded agreement. "Who knows what the depths will bring?" she said in a deep, mysterious voice. She fastened a fat, burning candle into a rock bowl and carefully lowered this onto the sea.

Karoon stared. "You're wasting a good candle!" Then he snapped his tail. "It floats! How?"

Dorali threw a rock to him, perhaps a bit harder than necessary.

Karoon caught it with one hand and his eyes grew wide. He picked two more out of the sack and began juggling, keeping a perfect rhythm. "These are so light!"

Dorali flicked her tail irritably. "This rock floats because it's full of holes, like a sponge. The light attracts strange creatures that rise from the deep at night."

Drakor kept his eyes on the floating candle. "That rock isss a gift from the Volcano. The holes are from Volcano's breath."

A patch of sea began to glow faintly as a school of small fish rose to the surface. These were creatures from another world, with huge eyes and tiny blue belly lights. They swam slowly toward the floating light.

Arak peered into the starlit water. "Those fish look like carved black onyx, and their lights are glowing gemstones."

Taron leaned over the railing for a closer look. "Hmm. They *would* make interesting puzzle sculptures."

Dorali's eyes sparkled with amusement. "If you're tired of carving wood flutes, we could use some new puzzles in the game room. Look!"

Three silver glowfish with pink lights jumped out of the sea. They were chased by a small squid with glimmering skin.

"Seeing this brings back memories of my squid visit," Scree mused. "It's a window into the deep abyss, a world of night and light. Orm, you'd love those amazing living lights."

Orm shuddered. "I'm sure it's exquisitely beautiful, but I have definitely seen enough giant squid."

Arak caught a bright flash in the corner of his eye. A golden star streaked down through the purple darkness. Then another and another, making a rare golden shower. These long-ago ancestors were flying to a new world. He sighed. "On a night like this, anything is possible. I believe I could hear star-song."

Scree fixed her eyes on the sky. "It's a good thing there are so many stars! An empty sky would be dull."

Orm tilted his head back. "I wonder if any of these falling stars is a live dragon."

Arak laughed. "I hope there's a Scree waiting to help, the way she healed me."

Karoon fidgeted. "I wonder how many stars the sky can hold. It's huge. This skiff feels even smaller than it looks."

Arak studied Karoon, who was flicking his tail and staring at the star-lit horizon . . . for the way home. Why had he volunteered? Clearly Dorali loathed him, and Karoon knew it.

Arak remembered well how irritating Karoon could be. This dragon had tormented him for years when they were both younger. He could put a real kink in your tail, but he'd grown into a solid dragon.

Scree motioned him over. "You never liked Karoon. What happened, and why is he here?"

Arak leaned down and signed silently, "Karoon made

life difficult. He never missed a chance to make fun of me. When I was a dragonlet, I was caught in long mind journeys and my body was left behind. Once, Karoon and his friends built a prison of big ice blocks around my empty body. When I returned to my body I was trapped, and it was hard to break free. He may not be my favorite dragon, but this quest needed another dragon and Karoon was the only volunteer. He's nicer now, and I hope he'll grow with the journey."

Scree pointed at Karoon. "Is he the dragon who courted Zarina?"

"Yes. I'm glad Zarina chose me."

Scree turned one of her eyes toward Dorali. "This will be an interesting journey."

Arak smiled and nodded agreement. He turned away and asked Taron, "Why don't you start a game of hand-fist-claw?"

Karoon came over immediately.

Drakor sat down amiably. "What isss this game?"

"Hand-fist-claw. A flat hand is a cloud, a fist is a rock, and claw throws lightning-fire." Taron demonstrated each game sign. "A flat cloud-hand covers rock-fist to win. Rock-fist hurts fire-claw to win. Fire-claw burns the cloud-hand to win."

Driana joined them in a circle and the game took off, with flying hands and laughter.

Dorali sat apart, her back to Karoon, chatting with Scree and Orm.

A few days later, Arak surveyed the gray-green circle of sea beneath a bright blue circle of sky. "I love being in the center of these circles, always wondering how the sky will change and what the sea will bring."

Drakor glanced up from his conversation with Dorali, Orm and Scree, where he was learning new words. "The sea isss interesting but octopus signs are amazing."

Arak checked the skiff-wing and tightened a line. "Drakor, each language is a window into another world. Would you like to learn more? Giant squid speak with light patterns. Scree and I could teach you. Understanding what they say would be useful if you meet them. We fly along the sea, but the world below belongs to others."

Driana raised her wings for attention. "What should we eat today?"

Every eye turned toward her.

Arak held up his hands. "Not smoked fish again, please?" A well-fed crew was a happy crew, and interesting meals were priceless.

"How about plankton soup and grilled shrimp?" Driana suggested.

They all answered as one. "Yes!"

Driana took two tightly-rolled nets from a barrel. "I'll set the fine-mesh net to strain plankton from the sea, and add weights to the other. We could catch some of those dark red deep-sea shrimp."

Karoon stretched and sauntered over to Drakor. "What's in your bag?"

Drakor opened his sack. "I have my rainbow mug, a water flask, a diamond, and metals. Cobalt makes blue lightning."

Karoon looked into the sack and flicked his tail. "That's a big diamond! What's so special about blue lightning?"

"Blue sky means freedom. That isss the most precious gift." Drakor pulled the cork from a small jar and showed him the dark blue powder. "Cobalt makes a lightning bolt that isss bright blue like a summer sky. Dragon-lords and dragon-ladies use blue lightning to choose a mate in the sky dances."

"We use green lightning," Arak said. "A dragon-lord tosses it to a dragon-lady in the cloud dances, and she decides whether to choose or reject him as a mate." He opened his wings for balance as the skiff hit an unexpected wave. "How's your plan?"

Drakor flexed his claws distractedly. "The clan will not want to hear that we need to move. I must fight the leader and win to make the clan listen. But Mardor isss powerful and much bigger. I do not see how I can win."

Taron flicked his claws out and made a lightning pearl. "Your clan should choose the leader by a game of skill, not by size. You'd win at lightning swords."

Arak grinned. "Drakor, winning a fight you can't win is our specialty. Just ask Scree. You'll find a way, and we'll help"

Dorali tilted her head. "If you lose, ice dragons will die. What can you use to fight?"

"Just our bodies. No lightning strikes. We use our claws, tail, and weight. Mardor has more weight and longer arms."

Dorali touched Drakor's arm.

His eyes grew wide. "That isss tiny lightning."

She flexed her claws. "I'll teach you how to micro-zap. It's the magic of cloud sculptors and Healers. These tiny pulses of electricity can heal broken bones or grow a snowflake. This would also distract your opponent. You can't see it, can barely feel it, but the pulse could disorient Mardor like unexpected storm energy."

"Help me haul in these nets," Driana called.

Drakor took the rope from Driana and pulled hand-over-hand, hauling the wide-mesh shrimp net to the skiff. He easily lifted the heavy net up over the stern and shook the catch into a wood box. Red, fist-sized shrimp tumbled down.

Scree, Orm, and Drakor snacked on a few fresh shrimp. The rest were dumped into a huge copper pot filled with boiling seawater and herbs.

Taron pulled in the smaller plankton net and emptied it into another pot. A thick soup was boiled with seawater, sliced carrots, tubers, onions, and pepper; steam made a fragrant cloud over the skiff.

Taron sniffed the scented air and sighed. "Ahhh, plankton soup."

Drakor peered into the pot. "What isss plankton?"

Arak shook the plankton net over a flat plate and some of the remaining specks fell out. "Plankton is the tiny life from the top of the sea. There's a bit of almost everything, and most is too small to see." He handed Drakor a curved glass lens, set in a copper ring with a handle. "Use this glass to make everything look bigger."

Drakor peered through the lens. "They are so small but so complicated. Beautiful."

Scree took her turn. "I see tiny shrimp and jellyfish, gold eggs, and spikey glass balls with holes. Those look like fancy snowflakes."

Orm looked through the magnifying lens next. He turned his skin black and covered it with white plankton pictures. "Sea snow! It's invisible, tasty art."

"How do you make micro-zaps?" Drakor asked, coming back to their earlier conversation.

Arak said, "It's like zapping to light a fire, but using less power and much more control. I've experimented a little but Healers are experts."

"I'd like to learn," Karoon said.

Everyone turned to stare at him.

Dorali narrowed her eyes and snapped her tail. "Why?"

Karoon opened his wings wide, the sign for change. "Our world is changing. Arak says we should stretch our wings. Why should only dragon-ladies learn this magic? And why are there no dragon-lord Healers?"

Arak opened his wings, copying Karoon. "Why indeed? Learning prevents boredom. We should all learn."

Driana glanced from Karoon's satisfied grin to the fire in Dorali's eyes and shrugged. "Why indeed? It's an outdated tradition. Dorali and I can take turns teaching micro-zap control and basic herbs. We could have a skiff-load of Apprentice Healers by the time we return."

Jagged, neon blue lines appeared on Scree's body and raced down each of her arms. "Blue lightning and invisible zaps. I wish I had claws, but I can still micro-zap."

Orm twined arms with Scree. "Words can be as sharp as claws."

Scree nodded. "Words are powerful. I need to learn all of these micro-zaps . . . one saved Scrim's life."

Orm nodded. "Scrim is doing so much better now, but his tiny new arms look odd."

A manta ray the size of a half-grown dragon leapt out of the water and smashed down into the sea, sending up a ring of water. Three more flew up into the air and crashed down.

Orm pointed to the sea. "I think I'll learn to leap like a ray."

The sun was low in the sky, coloring the waves with reds and oranges. "Meal time!" Driana announced. Bowls and plates were quickly filled, and a satisfied silence descended.

* * *

There were no clouds in the blazing blue sky. Crisp, clean shadows of wings and ropes moved across the polished wood deck. The sea was flat calm, the wind was asleep, and the skiff-wing hung loose. They were well beyond any sight of land, traveling in the center of a perfect blue circle.

All four dragon-lords sat on the deck in a circle with Dorali, close together, to block any hint of wind. They each had a ceramic bowl filled with water between their feet.

"Each zap frequency will make a different ripple pattern in the water. Watch carefully." Dorali put the claw of her pointer finger into the center of her water bowl and zapped. A simple series of rings spread out like a bullseye. "Here's another frequency." This pattern was a delicate web with overlapping ripple circles. The third was as complicated as sea foam.

"The water must be still before you try a new zap, or the pattern will be false," Dorali warned. "We'll start low and work up to higher frequencies, since that's the easiest way to learn. Try to match this pattern."

Arak tilted his ears toward Dorali, focused into his bowl, and zapped. His pattern did not match. When the water was still he tried again. And again. "I appreciate

Healer skills even more now."

Taron narrowed his eyes in concentration and zapped again. "So do I."

Drakor's tail flicked up and down as he practiced different types of micro-zaps into the center his water-filled bowl. He studied the ripple patterns with a dreamy look in his eyes. "Free-kwen-see isss interesting."

"Each zap frequency has a different use. The very lightest zap at the lowest frequency will help you grow a snowflake. A higher frequency knits bones and another works on dragon-scales."

Drakor zapped again. "I did not know there were so many patterns. I must learn the bone pattern."

"Why?"

"To help my sire . . . if I can."

Dorali's eyes widened. "I thought he was killed."

Drakor shook his head. "He was destroyed. An ice dragon who cannot fly feels dead inside."

"I understand," she said softly. "Tell me more, later. Now try this zap. It has more energy and a higher frequency, for muscles."

Dorali made a new, fancier pattern in her bowl.

Karoon zapped and checked his ripple pattern against Dorali's. It was a poor match. He stared at his copper claws as if they must be the problem. Then he zapped into his bowl once again. "Arrrgh! How do you zap at the right frequency? I thought it would be easy. Dragon-ladies do it."

Dorali ground her teeth. "Just because dragon-ladies can do something doesn't mean it's easy. You learn through trial and error. Karoon, you can feel/see magnetic lines. There's an inner-mind frequency memory. Try different zaps until you get an overlapping ripple pattern just like mine. Then remember that inner-mind feeling. Make this zap frequency-pattern again and again until it's as easy as a bad habit." She gave Karoon a dark look as if he was a bad habit.

Arak, Drakor, Taron and Karoon continued to zap into the water and check Dorali's pattern. With each energy zap the water grew warmer. Finally, the bowls began to steam.

Drakor jumped to his feet. "The water isss boiling and that isss ruining my pattern!"

Taron laughed with relief. "That's a sign to take a break."

Arak looked up. "That's a great idea. The wind's finally picking up, and we should fly while we can."

Taron took the helm and adjusted the skiff-wing. Dark clouds crept over the horizon. "It's more than wind."

Arak studied the clouds. Then he closed his eyes and looked again. "The magnetic lines are sparkling like stars. It's a true storm. Tie everything down or stash it below!"

Drakor stuffed cookware and empty water bowls in the hold. Black clouds raced across the sky, stealing the light. Wind howled and grabbed at the skiff-wing.

"Sea storms are so wonderfully unpredictable," Taron shouted, as he tightened his grip on the tiller.

Arak shouted back, "This one's growing fast. It's feeding on the sea."

Clouds glowed from within and distant thunder rumbled. Suddenly, a long, jagged spear of lightning struck the sea right beside the skiff. Boooom! The instant thunder tore through Arak like a sharp blade.

Lightning burned through the dark sky, and each

blinding flash lit a wakening sea. The skiff jumped clumsily across choppy gray waves. Then freezing rain struck in sheets, lashing like a waterfall of stones.

Driana dropped the last supplies into the hold and quickly closed the trap door against the rain. Water would add to the weight in the hold, and too much weight would sink them.

Wind screamed at the skiff and piled the water ever higher. Soon the waves were nearly as tall as the mast. Taron guided the skiff while Arak searched the sea, using both regular and magnetic sight. Was that a rogue wave in the distance? He'd seen one once, while questing in trance. An immense wall of water rose up like a tsunami, far from shore, and there was no warning at all.

Arak breathed a sigh of relief. These waves were still dangerous, but there were no rogues.

An hour later he relieved Taron, taking his turn wrestling the wind and waves. Arak's muscles burned with the strain of guiding the skiff diagonally into the surging sea. If the skiff was caught side-ways it would flip, and hitting the waves straight-on could also sink them.

The rain ended suddenly with a hail of ice-stones, but the dark clouds remained. Ice balls bounced and sparkled across the deck. The wind died down to an ominous silence in a gray world. The sea began to relax back to normal waves.

Then the wind roared back to life.

Arak stared. Three dimples formed in the clouds and poked down toward the sea. "Go below or tie yourself to the skiff!"

Three dark gray funnels reached down from the

clouds like long fingers. Each waterspout kicked up a cloud of water as it cut across the sea. They approached the skiff from three sides like a monstrous hand. It reached down to grab them, roaring like a volcano.

Arak glanced from side to side. He adjusted the tiller and slipped through the menacing hand. Seawater sprayed across the skiff from all sides.

Drakor grabbed a sturdy rope. "You can not release the skiff-wing now. Let me do this." He wrapped the rope around Arak twice and tied him securely to the mast. Then he lashed himself to the railing, leaving slack so he could still help.

Another funnel spun down from the darkness above. Drakor stared and snapped his tail. "That isss how I will fight," he shouted above the roar.

Arak shook water out of his eyes and shouted back, "A waterspout?" He guided the skiff away from the new threat.

"I will be a cyclone and whirl so fast that Mardor can not touch me."

"That would be a unique way to fight. Here, take the tiller and hold it steady. The wind's too strong; I need to shorten the skiff-wing." Arak reefed the skiff-wing and took back the tiller.

Dorali tugged on her rope, testing, and frowned. She began to re-knot the rope that tied her to the railing.

Arak flew their skiff east, away from the dangerous clouds. He bellowed into the roaring wind, "Is everyone secured?"

A new finger poked down right above them. The funnel stopped well above the mast but the wind screamed all the way down. The skiff-wing filled with a gale and the line was ripped from Arak's hand.

Dorali was still tying her knot when the wind hit with full force. She was torn from her rope and thrown overboard, where she hung lifeless on the surface. Then she began to sink beneath the waves.

CHAPTER 11: CYCLONE FISTS

Karoon grabbed the knife that was strapped to his leg and cut his rope. He furled his wings against the wind and dove into the sea close to Dorali. The water splashed high as Drakor joined him a moment later, landing on the other side of her. Together they held Dorali's limp body above water while the stormy sea pulled them away from the skiff.

The dark funnel sucked back up into the cloud. A school of small silver fish flopped frantically on the deck among sparkling ice-stones, dropped by the waterspout as a parting gift.

Arak tossed out ring floats, attached to long emergency ropes that were tied to the railing. He and Taron pulled the three dragons back to the skiff, hauling the ropes in hand-over-hand.

Drakor climbed the ladder carrying Dorali over one shoulder. He cleared a swath of deck with one sweep of his tail and laid her down gently.

Karoon scrambled up the side of the skiff and darted to her side. "Is she all right?"

Dorali lay still as death on the deck. Four dragon-lords clustered around her, flicking their tails nervously.

Driana shoved them all aside and knelt beside her, feeling for a pulse. She looked up at the anxious crew-mates. "She lives."

The cyclone victim coughed, opened her eyes, and saw the water dripping off her scales. "I'm all wet." Her whole body shook and her scales rasped like sandpaper against the wood.

Driana laughed with relief. She covered Dorali with blankets and took a jar from her Healer bag. "Nothing's broken, but you'll have bruises. That waterspout knocked you into the sea. Karoon and Drakor dove overboard to save you, but we all would have."

Dorali's eyes rounded in surprise. "Oh. Thank you."

Drakor leaned down and inspected Dorali's wings very carefully. He felt the bones and checked the membranes. "Your wings are not hurt," he said, as if this was the most important thing in the world.

Driana began rubbing salve across her wounds. "The willow and lavender oils will help."

Arak nodded to Karoon. "You were fast. Good instincts."

He slapped Drakor on his back, hard, in their customary manner. "Well done. You're right about the waterspout idea. These cyclones are dangerous, powerful, and unpredictable. No one would expect a fight like that."

Drakor grinned. "When we walk, air feels like nothing. When we fly, air feels thick under our wings.

When air spins fast it feels solid, like a tree . . . or a dragon's fist. It isss an important part of my plan. I will practice spinning until I can do this for one dragon hour." He picked up fish from the deck and tossed them into a barrel. Then he cleared the deck of ice-stones, using controlled sweeps of his long, white tail.

Driana filled the tea pot with water, tea, and spices before breathing dragon-flames.

Arak sat on the deck, inhaling the spice-scented steam. He stretched gently, working kinks out of his tense, aching muscles. His mind still felt those terrible fingers reaching down from the sky. He entered the first stage of the trance-mind. Driana handed him a mug of tea and he sipped it slowly. A much-needed calm washed through him from trance and tea.

Drakor walked over to Orm and Scree. "I saved these for you." He dropped an ice ball into each octopus mug to cool their tea.

"Thanks," Scree signed. "What were you saying to Arak about your plan?"

"I will fight like a cyclone. I must learn how to whirl without falling down," he signed back.

"I can help." Scree spun in her tub so fast that she blurred. "We twirl beneath the waves, and there's a secret. Look at one place while you turn, then let your head whip around. That way you won't get dizzy."

Drakor turned in a circle, watching one spot. He turned faster and tripped over his feet.

Orm sighed. "Feet wouldn't be a problem in the water, but I suppose you must fight on land."

Karoon leaned against the railing, watching. Then he sauntered over. "I can help. I've had more than my share of fights. I'll teach you how to move your feet and how to judge your enemy. Watch the eyes to see what he'll do next."

"So I watch one spot, probably the eyes, and learn how to move my feet." Drakor spun slowly in a circle, watching Karoon's eyes, moving his feet carefully. He spun again, faster, and fell. He lay sprawled across the deck, staring up at the sky.

"It takes practice," Karoon said. "But at least you'll have something to do on this journey. That's better than being bored."

Orm spun like a top while tossing candies from arm to arm. "Eat chocolate before the fight and you'll keep spinning. It's the best energy snack in the world!" He tossed one in a perfect arc to each journey-mate, catching the last in his mouth. "And, it's the tastiest."

"Practice the first stage of the trance-mind until you can stay in it for more than an hour. Learn to fight while you're relaxed and you'll fight better," Arak said.

Dorali limped over to the side of the skiff with Taron's help. She sat down on the deck and leaned against the railing. Driana covered her with blankets, tucking them gently around, and checked her eyes again. "Your pupils are evenly dilated, so you should be fine."

Dorali coughed up more water. "Where is my bag?"

Karoon immediately fetched her Healer bag out of the hold.

Dorali opened the medicine compartment and took out a small, pungent pouch. It was tied with a red warning cord in an elaborate knot. "Drakor, this herb could help you fight longer. Flame flower is powerful. If you drink a brew from this herb, you won't feel any pain. But it's dangerous. You won't know when you're really hurt and should surrender."

Drakor sniffed the pouch. "It even smells strong. I will use it. I cannot give in. If I surrender, the ice dragons will die."

"Remember the other weapon, micro-zaps," Dorali said. "This fits the rules."

Drakor shook his head. "Zaps might help, but that isss not the ice dragon way."

"Stubborn," she muttered. Dorali glanced over the railing. "Look! It's a jellyfish flower." Eight long, clear, sky-blue petals pulsed on the surface. Curly, rose-colored petals were visible through the glass-like center.

Orm looked over the side. "The sea always wins. We even have the prettiest flowers."

Arak took a long look and laughed. "It *is* hard to compete with that."

"It is art," Orm said, as if that settled it.

Drakor nodded approval. "They are fighting flowers. I have felt their stingers."

The next day, when the sun was just past noon, bright colors appeared on the curled, smoky clouds. A wide rainbow skipped across the sky, coloring every patchy cloud and missing every piece of deep blue sky.

"A fire rainbow," Drakor whispered. "This isss very rare."

Arak stared. "Rainbows carry messages from our ancestors in the stars."

Dorali was sitting down, leaning against the railing. She still looked like she'd been slapped by a tsunami, but the cocoon of Healer blankets was gone. She gazed at the brilliant sky display. "Beautiful. It's the first fire rainbow

I've ever seen."

Scree nodded. "Sky art is another reason to travel."

Taron brought a tray full of steaming mugs. "Red root tea with honey."

Drakor reached for his tea and drank it down. "It isss sweeter than berries."

Dorali took small sips. "That's volcano hot. Drakor, when we were practicing micro-zaps, you said your sire is alive but injured. You asked about healing bones. Why?"

Drakor winced. "It happened in winter, when I was not much more than a hatchling. My sire was on the Volcano and the earth shook. He was caught in an avalanche and broke both legs. I tried to help, but he did not heal right."

Dorali shuddered. "Why were you there?"

Arak, Taron, Driana, and even Karoon were listening to the story.

"My dam died soon after I hatched, and my dam-sister grew tired of me. I learned to find my own food and was free to explore. I often followed my sire, so quietly that he did not know I was there. This time, the mountain shook. An avalanche buried my sire. I dug him out of the snow and wrapped his broken legs tight, but they did not heal right. He cannot fly. If we cannot fly, we have no freedom. No one values us. Soon we do not value us. When an ice dragon isss hurt badly he can die from sadness."

Drakor looked out to the horizon, rustling his wings. "I helped him get to the hot springs near the Volcano. Then I made a shelter with rock walls and covered us both with old leaves to keep warm. I gathered lichens for food and caught rock crabs in the surf. We stayed there for dragon-weeks, sleeping near the Volcano. I could sense the magnetic shifts even in my sleep, and the rumbling shakes became a sleep-song. I felt the Volcano's beating heart and breath of steam."

"You have always studied the volcano," Dorali said.

Drakor nodded. "I *feel* the Volcano. The bones of my sire did not heal right. I made leg braces and crutches but still it was hard to walk. He could not launch or land, so he could not fly. When we returned to the clan I brought him food. I asked him to tell me stories, lots of stories. Zardan isss a great story-teller and knows all the legends. I did not want him to give up on life. I did not want to lose him."

Drakor took a deep breath. "I wish I could fix his bones. I want my sire to fly again. That isss why I am learning these zaps."

No one spoke. Lapping sounds of the sea and creaking of the skiff filled the silence.

Then Arak asked, "Who's helping him now?"

"Jardor will wonder what has happened to me. He will help Zardan."

Dorali looked at Driana and she nodded assent. "We might be able to help your sire, but this doesn't always work. Scree could put him to sleep while we break the bones and re-set them the right way. He would need to stay with us while we help him heal."

Drakor's eyes glowed. "He could have a normal life."

Dorali held up a warning hand. "It's painful, and it might not work."

"He would try anything to fly again."

Karoon nodded. "Any dragon would. I understand why you followed your sire. My dam didn't have much patience for a dragonlet."

Arak gave Karoon a penetrating look. Scree said that when you looked with new eyes, this changed what you saw. While he had resented his dam for worrying too much about him, Karoon had been ignored. Had he bullied Arak and called him a worthless Dreamer because he was jealous?

Everything changed when dragons became sick with a crippling illness, turning orange and slipping toward death. Arak searched across the sea and found the rare, precious copper needed for dragon health. "Dreamer" was now a respectable word and Karoon no longer bullied him. Life was change. He studied his old nemesis with new hope.

Arak checked the sky again, using all his senses, and snapped his tail with worry. Everything sparkled. A huge storm was coming. Would they reach land in time?

CHAPTER 12: SUNSET DRAGONS

Arak checked the sky again as they neared their southern stop. "The storm is coming but everything's already tied down. With luck, it won't strike before we reach land. Drakor, Karoon, Dorali, and I will go ashore first. Then we'll take turns. We'll gather honey, cocoa beans, herbs, mushrooms, and those tasty tubers."

Karoon stood by the railing, leaning against it, eyes on the unseen shore. "Land. I can smell it. Room to run, time to fly. I can hardly wait!"

"I will finally see a honey tree," Drakor said with satisfaction. "Now, let us fight."

They cleared a space on the deck and circled each other, eyes on eyes, watching for an opening. Karoon struck Drakor with a quick blow, tilting his claws in so no blood was drawn. Drakor stopped and shook his head in disbelief. "How did you do that? Your arms are shorter."

"How did Scree defeat a giant squid? Size doesn't matter. Success is in your mind. You must believe that you can defeat Mardor."

Karoon and Drakor sparred for another dragon-hour, flipping through the air, darting in and out. Finally, Karoon's wings began to droop like wilted leaves. He held up both hands. "I need a break."

"Then I will practice my spinning." Drakor moved his feet in a pattern as he turned around. He spun faster and faster until he was a snowy blur. The sea flowed beneath him while he moved like the wind. He gradually opened his wings, spiraled up into the sky, and landed with a grin.

"You're getting faster every day," Karoon said.

Drakor's eyes glowed with the praise.

Dorali was watching them from the corner of her eye. Karoon winked and she turned away.

* * *

They reached the coast at dawn under a blood red sky. Arak scanned the rocky shore. "Red sky at morning, dragons take warning. Taron, we need a safe harbor."

"We're flying as fast as we can. If there's a protected cove, we'll find it. If not, we need to head back to sea before storm waves crash us onto the rocks." The sky turned an eerie orange-brown as they hunted for safety. "New World weather is never boring."

"I'll fasten that," Drakor said, taking the damp, slippery rope from Taron. He wound the end around a metal cleat, making a secure figure eight. "What will we look for when we land?"

Arak kept his eyes on the shore. "We'll harvest cocoa, nuts, fish, mushrooms, and tubers first, then honey. I need kapok tree fluff for skiff bolsters, and bamboo." He shivered as the temperature changed in a heartbeat. It was instant winter. Waves of dark brown clouds rolled across a burnt orange sky.

Orm slid down into his tub for safety but tilted his head back for a better view. "Those clouds look like chocolate icing."

Arak laughed. "Dangerous, powerful chocolate sky icing. Even dragons avoid such skies."

Lightning splintered across the sky, making a blinding white lace against the darkness. Thunder followed and chunks of ice pelted down.

Taron shouted above the rising wind. "A cove! It's just beyond that tree. Let's anchor quickly."

Huge trees grew almost to the water's edge, making a sturdy wind break around the semi-circle of sea. They adjusted the skiff-wing, moved to the center of the cove, and set two storm anchors. Arak nodded with satisfaction. "We'll have a few days to harvest, load up, and then travel north. Taron, will you and Driana get five bags of rocks out of the hold?"

"Why do you carry rocks?" Drakor asked.

Taron made a model of the skiff hull with his hands. "The rocks are ballast. A heavy weight at the bottom of the skiff keeps it from tipping over, even in a storm. We'll dump these ordinary rocks overboard and replace them with New World food."

"Especially cocoa," Orm added. He and Scree climbed out of their deck homes and scampered to the railing like huge spiders.

"We'll make sure the anchors are well set before we explore the reefs," Scree promised. She slid eagerly into the welcoming sea.

Arak glanced over the side as two splashes melted into the waves. "It's a relief to have octopus friends to check on those anchors."

* * *

Four dragons flew ashore. Just as they landed, freezing rain lashed across the darkened sky. Three took shelter under an oak. They made their wings into tents that covered the head and wrapped around the body, to shed water. Drakor stood alone in the rain, letting the cold water slide over him. A dragon-hour later, the fast-moving storm blew past and sunshine filled the air. Golden dragons spread their wings to dry in the warmth, while Drakor moved into the cool shade beneath a tree.

Arak patted a gnarled trunk that was wide enough to hide a dragon. "These trees must live a long time, so I call them live oaks."

A branch as long as dragon flight wound through the sky and dipped down to the ground. Karoon ran up the branch, grasped another above him, and swung from branch to branch. He grabbed another and spun around with his wings furled, then leapt gracefully to the ground. "What a great playground! We should have one."

Dorali laughed at his antics. "It's too big to take home."

Drakor scooped up a clawfull of acorns from the ground. "Here," he said, pouring them into her hands. "You can grow a playground for future dragons."

Arak handed Drakor a sack. "That's a great idea. Let's fill up a sack. Acorns are bitter, but they don't taste bad if you soak them in water for a few days. And they make good fishing bait."

"Bait?" Drakor asked.

"Not all fish can be caught by claws on the surface. We push a soaked nut onto a metal hook that's tied to a line." Arak demonstrated with his hands, pushing a cracked acorn onto the claw of a bent finger. "Fish and crabs bite the bait, get caught on the hook, and we pull up the line."

Dorali held a sack open while Drakor, Karoon, and Arak scooped clawfulls of acorns into it.

Arak smiled with satisfaction as he tied off the bulging sack. "That's enough. Now we can gather what we really need."

Herbs and mushrooms were harvested next. Mushrooms were dried in special pans while herbs were hung on hooks below deck. Enticing aromas rose from the hold. Four dragons flew ashore to pick cocoa beans.

Arak landed heavily on the skiff, staggering beneath his load, and dumped his sacks into the hold. The earthy-chocolate aroma of cocoa added to the interesting mix of smells. Drakor landed lightly as ever and added his sacks to the hold.

Arak gave a satisfied smile. "We have plenty of acorns, herbs, mushrooms, and cocoa. Now for the fun part. Drakor, you and I will harvest honey. Karoon, can you and Driana gather more of those huge, tasty tubers? Taron and Dorali will watch the skiff until we're back. Then we'll get bamboo."

"Why bamboo? It's not nearly as strong as oak!" Taron objected.

"But it's much lighter and will float, for a while."

That evening, they feasted on dragon-grilled redfish, honey-roasted almonds, fried mushrooms, and hot cocoa. Scree added stone crab claws and softshell blue crabs.

Orm brought a mesh bag that bulged with seaweed. "I found the tastiest colors: green, red, purple, and gold."

Scree helped him empty the bag. "That's an amazing reef; our whole pod could feast like this every day. We should start a new village here."

Orm rolled his empty bag into a tight bundle, and then restlessly squished it smaller. "This reef is nice, but I prefer our home."

* * *

Arak and Drakor flew inland together, seeking a rare clearing within the dense forest, drawn by its unique scent. Tiny blue, yellow, and purple flowers were strewn among the sun-warmed meadow grass. Drakor landed in the center of a dragon-sized ring of white mushrooms, with caps half the size of his hand.

Arak landed beside him. "This circle grows right here every year, like a magic ring, but the mushrooms are poisonous."

Bright orange dragonflies hovered and darted, catching flies and shiny green beetles. Drakor stopped to watch, tracking one with his eyes. "That dragonfly never misses anything! I think it knows where its prey will be, gets there first, and makes the kill. It anticipates every move. The dragonfly would be a better fighter than Mardor."

"That's a lesson to remember: anticipate every move. If you know how Mardor fights, you can use it against him."

Drakor sniffed the air. "I smell something sweeter than flowers."

"Dragonflies are amazing hunters, but bees are amazing honey-makers. Hear that sound? I called them buzz bees until I tasted the sticky sweetness. 'Honey' is an old dragon word for 'golden treasure'. Now I call them honey bees."

The ancient oak was buzzing louder than a twilight field of crickets. Arak thumped the tree up and down. "This section of the tree has honey inside. It thumps different than a solid tree. I need to know how much honey is stored inside so we don't take too much, because bees must need it to survive."

Arak nodded with satisfaction. "There's plenty. You've had this in tea and candy. Reach into the tree and try it fresh."

Drakor licked his claws clean while bees buzzed angrily. "Ice dragons would love this. You grow seafood. Have you tried raising a honey crop?"

"Once, and I found that bees can't survive the long journey home."

Arak and Drakor gathered honey until dusk, slicing off wax combs with their sharp claws. They ignored the protest of the hive, since dragon scales made excellent bee armor. They filled each jar with honeycombs and pushed in a cork stopper. These ceramic jars had a glassy glaze on the inside to be leak-proof, and they were wound with vines to be shatter-proof.

The sun dipped below the trees as the last jar was filled. Arak sat down among the wild grasses, leaning against a tree. He took a deep breath, savoring the scents of wildflowers, grass, and honey.

"Should we not leave?" Drakor asked.

Arak shook his head. "Wait for the magic."

Twilight shadows moved out from beneath the trees and spread across the grasses. Then fireflies lit the dark meadow, making sparks in the night like visiting stars. Drakor caught one in a cage of claws and watched the yellow light flashing on and off. "We do not have flying stars in my home."

"Maybe your home is too far north," Arak said. "If your clan moves to the New World, you could fly south for an evening with fireflies."

Drakor patted a bag of honey jars. "We would also harvest honey."

Arak stuffed more leaves around the jars to protect them. "Honey would make you popular. Can bees live in the north? Maybe you could move them to a hollow tree when the flowers start to bloom."

"Maybe ice dragons would move here for this," Drakor said, with a hopeful smile.

*   *   *

Scree gazed at a full moon as it rose slowly out of the sea, higher and higher, until the ruddy circle barely touched the blue-black horizon. The moon changed color as it rose beyond the sea, ever higher, until it glowed like a white pearl among the stars. This was the moon of their legends.

Arak lifted anchor and called point with Dorali. They checked for hidden dangers, watching for moonlit ripples and magnetic energy shadows. Taron guided the skiff around a sand bar, a submerged tree, and out to sea. They skiff-flew north through the night, chasing the guide star.

Just before dawn the skiff shuddered to a stop, knocking dragons off their feet. It felt as if they had run aground on a sunken island. Then long, reddish snakes slithered over the sides and four yellow moons shone through the water. Squid!

The giants fastened their powerful suckers on the skiff and shook it. Every dragon grabbed for something solid to hold onto. Cold seawater sloshed across the deck, washing items overboard.

Scree grabbed the pink pearl from her Healer bag and held it high. Arak and Taron reached for their spears, which were stored in rope holders around the mast, poison-point-down. The dragons threatened the giant squid with their spears.

Scree spoke the squid greeting with her arms, making red and yellow spots: "May you surf the tangled currents of the sea forever."

The larger squid returned this greeting with light spots, adding a light pattern for "Scree."

"Veera, it's so good to see you! Please release the skiff now, so my friends don't kill you."

Veera looked Scree in the eye and, with a terrifying/playful smile, gave the skiff one more violent shake. Then the squid and her mate, Tarm, let their arms slide off. The skiff rocked slower and slower, until it matched the natural motion of the sea.

"Tarm said he met you up north, hunting the sky-swimmer." Veera eyed the white dragon. "I see you found it."

Scree rolled her eyes. "Him. He's an ice dragon." There were not enough words, so she added body-pictures to her arm-spot patterns. "Have you seen the three squid who attacked our pod?"

Veera and Tarm both flushed a deeper red. This was their challenging-angry-scared color. Scree watched closely, seeking clues. Were they threatening, angry, scared, or all of this? She said to Tarm, "We defeated those foolish squid, but we did not kill them."

"You made them glow like food-fish," Tarm said, and his tentacles quivered.

Was he mad or laughing? Scree gave a sigh of frustration. Words meant nothing if you didn't know the emotions behind them. "That is bad?"

"It is better to die in battle than to be humiliated," Veera said. "You should know that."

Scree stretched taller and stared up into their eyes. "They broke the treaty. That glow is a warning. If they return, we will not miss seeing them. If anyone attacks octopi or sky-swimmers, we *will* capture and mark them."

"You made your point," Tarm said. He quivered again, and this time she caught the edge of a smile. "Those three are difficult, even for squid. If they avoid our gathering, *I* will not miss seeing them."

Was this a squid joke? Scree took a closer look at Tarm and his smile grew. The giants seemed simple, because they lived free in the sea and often alone. But that was an illusion. They were complicated, with many, often conflicting, emotions. "How are the currents and the abyss?"

Tarm's light-words sparkled. "The currents are stronger, and changing. There is lots of falling ice. Many pieces are bigger than a gathering of squid. These make terrific waves when they hit the sea."

Scree curled her arms with concern. "Is there more falling ice than usual?"

"Lots more."

Scree talked with Tarm and Veera about their journeys by making spots on two arms. At the same time, she interpreted squid-speak for the crew by signing with other arms. Arak was the only dragon who could read squid-lights, but the squid spoke too fast for him to follow.

Stars faded away as the sky grew lighter. Veera said to Scree, "It is time to return to the abyss, but we will meet again. May you surf the tangled currents of the sea forever."

Scree repeated this phrase, which was both a greeting and farewell.

Drakor watched with wide eyes as both giant squid dove beyond their sight. He pointed to the messy deck, which was strewn with their supplies. "Do they always greet you this way?"

Scree nodded. "Friendship with squid is based on respect, and that means a challenge, a test of strength and courage." She made a body-picture of a squid next to a white dragon, both the same size. "Ice dragons fight to be the leader. Are squid truly different?"

Drakor laughed at the comparison. "Squid are similar, but *much* bigger. I want to learn squid-speak. They could tell us where the best islands are."

Arak touched his forehead to Scree's. "This brings back memories. You met a gathering of squid in the deep abyss . . . and survived! I'm really glad you're here to speak to these giants."

Scree gazed steadily back. "Thanks to you, my friend."

She turned to Drakor. "I'll teach you the language of squid. This is their greeting." She made a series of spot patterns, slowly, so he could follow. "Imagine this spot sequence again and again, until it flows together. Learning a new language is like looking through new

174

eyes."

Arak gave Drakor a roll of skins. "These have the marks for 'greetings'. Keep them. Learn the spot sequence and use them to signal back to a squid."

Scree said, "Learning the words is important, but body language means even more."

Drakor looked northeast, toward his home. "My sire says that the hardest part is learning to hear what is not said."

Arak nodded. "That's true, and especially important for a leader."

The crew began to clean up the skiff.

Arak checked the pile of bamboo sticks. "I'm glad these were tied down." He cut each stick the same length, just beyond a natural ring divider. Then he warmed beeswax from the honeycombs.

"What are you doing?" Drakor asked.

"I need to seal each end to keep water out." Arak picked up a roll of tough, fish-skin rope. "A bamboo raft will be light and portable. This could be useful."

Drakor studied the pile of odd, bumpy sticks. "You have a plan."

Arak glanced at Scree and they shared a smile. "Always."

Taron tightened the skiff-wing and they flew north, blown by a steady wind beneath a cloudless sky.

* * *

Arak eased the skiff into a protected cove. He sniffed the wind, noting the different pollens and earthy scents mixed with salty sea spray. This was the middle stop, with their copper mine and trees for building skiffs. Taron set two anchors to cope with the changing tides.

A narrow river fed into the cove, and an endless forest reached almost to the shore. Arak stretched his wings. "We'll mine copper first. Then we'll cut trees and float them to the skiff."

Taron said, "Let's make a quick survey, farther up the river."

They flew over the forest and returned.

Taron landed and snapped his tail. "I saw trees that are perfect for carving flutes! They have a dense wood. Erinite says a boxwood flute plays with tones like a dragon singing, and maple wood makes a brighter sound. I carved more instruments and she made tunes to match. She has three dragons play different melodies at the same time, with flutes made from different wood. It sounds like the stars are singing!"

Arak smiled. "I can't wait to hear this. You and Erinite started a music revolution. Everyone perks up when it's her turn to share."

Taron nodded. "They leap up for Zarina's chocolate."

Arak's eyes glowed with memories beyond chocolate. He and his mate had been apart for too long, but soon Zarina would join him on the journeys. "True. I'm sure the clan would like even more cocoa beans, but we had to save room in the hold. Copper's what we need most, so we'll visit the mine first."

Taron and Driana stayed aboard the skiff while the rest flew ashore.

"The copper mine's just a short flight from here," Arak said.

Karoon had a toothy grin as they flew above the trees. "The famous copper mine."

Arak gave him a sharp look, but Karoon seemed

serious. Had he truly changed from his old, sarcastic, bullying ways? "There's the mine."

The dragons back winged, raising a cloud of red dust when they landed beside a low hill. The hill drew the inner eye, bending magnetic lines into a storm of energy.

Dorali held still and closed her eyes, sensing. "It really is solid sunshine, just like you said. I see it inside my mind. I could find my way here with my eyes closed on the darkest night."

Karoon touched the scraggly grass that covered the hill. "I can feel/see this place like nothing before."

Drakor stepped inside, crouching to enter the dark cave. "Ahhh. It isss cool in here."

Arak followed Drakor into the cave. He pointed to five steel picks that were wrapped in oilcloth on a shelf, waiting. "You can have your pick of the picks." A long, black snake slithered between his legs, fleeing a home that was suddenly too popular.

Arak lit bowls of beeswax candles that were just inside the entrance. Flames flickered in the slight breeze, revealing a comfortably high ceiling and an enchanting cave of crystals. The walls were made of colorful copper ores, like a solid aurora.

Nuggets of pure copper had a thin green skin. A curved wall was covered with glassy burgundy cubes. There were streaks of azurite, a crystalline blue rock that was more than half copper. Bright golden flecks in another rock caught the eye, gleaming against a background of crusty, emerald-green ores. Covellite crystals had an iridescent purple sheen, like the last light on a sunset sea.

Dorali entered and turned around slowly. "It's a

treasure cave. I didn't know another cave could be so beautiful, yet completely different from ours."

Drakor ran his claws slowly down the wall. His eyes glowed in the dim light. "I have never seen such crystals! How can they all have copper?"

Karoon grabbed a pick and swung hard, breaking off a knob of greenish rock. He stared at the gleaming copper cut. "It's ruby gold." He carefully placed this in a bag.

The dragons spread out, each attacking a different section of the cave. The walls glittered in new colors as they uncovered fresh ore. Sparks flew when metal struck against metal, with ringing echoes. Crystals and nuggets fell to the floor in piles that became hills. Drakor's pile quickly became a small mountain. They took short breaks from pounding rocks to fill the bags.

"How are you doing that?" Karoon asked Dorali. Her pile of ore-filled bags was now taller than his.

She grinned. "I have a new way to mine. I found a micro-zap that loosens rock seams, so I don't need as many hits to knock the rocks off. Try it." She opened her flask, poured water into a bowl, and put a claw in the center. Ripples spread from her zap and bounced back in a flower-like pattern. She looked Karoon in the eye. "Match my pattern."

"That should be easy. It's dragon-lady work."

She rolled her eyes. "This dragon-lady has filled more copper bags than you have."

Arak glanced at Dorali's exceptional pile of filled bags, and put down his pick.

Karoon sat down by the water bowl with a serious expression on his face. He copied Dorali's ripple pattern after only three tries.

Her eyes grew wide with astonishment. "How did you do that?"

Karoon winked. "It's easy dragon-lady work."

"You've been practicing zaps."

"Naturally. Dragon-lady work can be useful."

"I need to learn this," Arak said. As soon as the water was still he tried to copy the ripple pattern. Then Drakor learned the new micro-zap.

Pounding resumed with the fierceness of an undeclared competition. Every dragon was soon covered with rock dust, which gave them a strong, earthy smell and dulled their scales.

Karoon glanced at the clear sky outside the cave. "Where are the rain clouds when you need them? I'd love a nice, cold shower. I feel gritty and look like dirt."

Dorali laughed. "Sparkling dirt."

Entrance shadows shifted as the sun climbed high in the sky. "Meal break," Arak called. They moved outside and sat together in the shade of an old tree, eating fish rolls and drinking spiced tea. "Dorali, that's a very useful discovery. Three dragons can do the work of four."

"Orm would call it very efficient." She took a handful of chocolate from her Healer bag. "He sent this."

Arak smiled as he took a piece. "Orm's energy medicine. We're so efficient that we've already filled most of our sacks. Drakor, could you carry two bags to the skiff, empty them in the hold, and bring back extra bags?"

Drakor shrugged. "I have two arms." He hefted the bulging bags, curled his arms around the heavy load, and leapt into the sky.

Karoon stretched his back until it cracked noisily.

"That feels good." He looked to the east, at the flying dragon. "He never gets tired. I think Drakor really can win his fight."

"Tell him. He respects you," Arak said.

Karoon snapped his tail in surprise. "Me?"

Arak nodded. "You. You're helping him with the hardest thing in his life."

Karoon gave a genuine smile that seemed to fill his body. "Of course. He's my friend."

Dorali watched Karoon with a thoughtful expression.

Break over, they returned to the mine.

Dorali shined her light into a deep crack with glassy sparkles. She checked the depth of the miniature cave and busted it open. "Arak! I found a new gemstone seam. It looks like many ice cubes all stuck together. They're pale blue and lilac."

Arak walked over and lifted a few loose cubes in his claws, feeling the light weight. "This is fluorite. It's pretty, but not what we need. There's no copper."

Dorali slipped a few crystals into her pouch. "It's a good souvenir."

During the cool evening, they all flew bags of ore to the skiff and ate a hearty meal. The next day they mined again. Two dragons always guarded the skiff, but everyone took a turn beating on the cave walls.

Salves for sore muscles soon became more popular than chocolate. Willow bark was added to their tea to reduce pain. Dorali and Driana mixed lavender, peppermint, and flame-flower oils. Scree's numbing salve was made from the toxic eggs of quithra, a lovely sea slug.

"Which treatment works best?" Arak asked Driana, as

she rubbed oils into his back.

She shrugged. "Each has its merits. Let's experiment." She used the dragon oils on left arms, octopus salve on right arms, and a mix of the two on their backs. The Healers cheerfully compared notes to see which remedy worked best.

Dorali also experimented with micro-zaps. She ran her gently zapping fingers over Drakor's arms, sending prickly warmth deep into his muscles.

"This isss magic lightning. I do not remember ever having sore muscles."

Dorali began working on his back. "You've never mined copper before. It's fun to discover new zaps. I use micro-energy to change the pattern of a growing snowflake. Now I'm finding new energy patterns for rocks and dragons."

"Life isss energy. You have mastered inner energy, so you have mastered life." Drakor bowed very precisely, legs together, bending from the waist. "Thank you."

Arak was next in line. "Ahhhh. Your latest micro-zap works wonders. You've found another way to increase efficiency."

Dorali laughed. "And to decrease pain, I hope."

Karoon was her last patient. He took a careful step forward, wincing with pain.

Dorali arched her dragon-brows. "You want the help of a dragon-lady?"

He grinned. "Even dragon-lady work can be useful."

She hesitated.

"Please?" Karoon added quickly, with a desperate look in his eyes.

"You do need my help." Dorali used her salves and

zaps on his lower back.

Karoon sighed. "Thank you."

Two days later, everyone gathered on the deck, leaving tracks in the dried sea spray. The hold was now half-filled with copper nuggets and ores. Taron fastened a sturdy net over the sparkling, shimmering, mesmerizing hoard. "This will keep it from shifting in a storm. Ballast has to stay in the right place to keep the skiff stable."

Orm and Scree left their tubs and took a long look into the hold before the hatch was closed. "It's such a sparkly skiff-cave . . . as lovely as an octopus' garden."

Drakor joined them, peering down. "It isss beautiful ballast."

Arak closed the hatch. "Great work! We met our copper quota ahead of schedule. Karoon, Drakor and I will start on the trees. Taron, can you, Dorali, and Driana stay aboard? The skiff needs repairs before we head north."

Taron looked lovingly at the skiff. "I think I have the better job."

Karoon leaned against the railing, eyes fixed on the shore. He snapped his tail cheerfully when Arak chose him and Drakor.

Scree grabbed a collection bag. "It's too cold for coral, but other reefs are interesting." She and Orm slid under the railing, flattening their bodies to fit through the gap. Scree re-shaped into a pointed arrow and dove seamlessly into the sea, without a splash. Orm fell in the normal way, still looking like an octopus.

*   *   *

Scree pulsed through clear, leaf-brown water, feeling the sharp tang of dead leaves and the slippery texture of plant oils. "I could taste my way back here from anywhere. This water changes the color of everything; it's like seeing the world through a topaz gemstone."

There was no living coral, but the rock reefs attracted an abundance of life. Seaweeds, barnacles, and more covered the rocks, while fish swam among them. Scree felt/saw a large shrimp behind her. She shaped herself into a tent-like body net and caught the unwary prey. "I needed a snack."

The sand around a small rock cave had an elegant design made from shells, colored stones, and seaweed. Orm turned green with excitement. "That's an octopus garden!" He peered into the cave, but nobody was home.

Scree pointed to a seahorse with his tail curled around a strand of seaweed. "The fish are home."

They hunted through the reef and found five more octopus caves, but no octopi. "Where are they?"

Scree pulsed with colors. "I want to meet them. I wonder what they're like."

Orm turned slowly in a circle, searching. "Maybe they're out hunting, or hiding from sharks."

"Or riding sharks?"

Orm grinned. "Undoubtedly. We should check back later." They pulsed to the edge of the rocks, until there was only sand . . . a shifting, underwater desert. He pointed and signed, "Look at that!" Dark orange lobsters were walking single file. Every lobster touched the one ahead with their long antennae, making a line that stretched into the distant darkness.

Scree turned the color and texture of sand. She slipped silently toward the living line, arm over arm, matching the movements of a bottom wave. "Lobsters wedge their bodies into holes and hide, so it's hard to catch them. I've never seen them travel together in the open. Where are they going? This journey must be important to take such a risk." She grabbed a lobster, mindful of the sharp spines. "The dragons will love a lobster dinner!"

They each caught eight more, stuffing them into mesh sacks until the bags were bulging with this rare catch. Scree tied the tops securely. "This was too easy. We're hard to see, but they must notice a fellow lobster being grabbed up. They ignored us and simply closed the gaps in their line. Maybe this is a magic sea and we're invisible."

Orm made pictures of lacy white sea-snow on his skin. "We saw invisible plankton with Arak's glass lens. That's like magic."

Scree gave a deep sigh. "I wish there was a magic lens to let us see the future. Drakor is so certain his volcano will explode and destroy his island. If our volcanoes are truly connected, the explosion could destroy all of our homes."

Orm flushed blue with internal stress. He ignored the comment and added more purply-green plants to his collection sack. "This seaweed concentrates copper just like the dragon-weed. It might grow well at our first pod home."

"Orm, it's great that you found another copper source. But that won't matter if our reefs are destroyed and the pods are gone!" She dug gently into the sand around each stalk of seaweed, prying it loose, carefully protecting the roots. "Octopi can move here and have a perfect copper crop to trade with our dragon friends."

Orm sighed. "You're determined to move."

"We need to move to survive, and the reefs here are fascinating. We might have interesting octopus neighbors. Remember Vorm? He said that the entire sea was his home, and he could not understand why anyone would want to be limited to one place. Home is where you are."

"Home is also where our friends are. I would miss seeing the dragons, especially Kragor," Orm said slowly. His color became a dull gray.

Scree twined arms in a comforting way. "I'd miss Arak, Taron, Dorali, Zarina, Driana, Arafine . . ." She flushed gray. "You have a point. But, we could skiff-fly back to visit them."

* * *

Arak, Karoon, and Drakor flew ashore, carrying red-and-blue saws carved from rock. They cut down five oak trees before noon and began sawing off branches. The powerful scent of raw wood saturated the air.

Drakor used his saw effortlessly, as if it was just a fancy claw. "This isss a sharp blade, and pretty. What isss it made from?"

"Corundum. It's almost as hard as diamond. The rock couldn't decide if it wanted to be a red ruby or a blue sapphire, so it's both."

By the end of the day, the dragons were covered in sawdust and their arms were trembling. They dragged the stripped trees to the river. Arak eyed the nearby shore. "It's getting late. Let's rest awhile on that pebble beach. We'll float these trees to the skiff tomorrow."

Sunset colors played across the sea and fled into the night. Water rippled onto the shore, glowing blue in the darkness, colored by tiny, glowing plankton. Three dragons tilted their ears forward, listening to the hypnotic, shushing rhythm of waves.

Arak scooped up a handful of pebbles and tossed them into the sea. A blue glow flared bright in the night wherever stones hit the water. "I'm making fireworks in the waves."

Drakor walked into the sea until only his head showed. He bobbed up and down as he floated with the waves. "This isss like dream flying."

Karoon sprawled flat on his back, shifting back and forth to make a fitted bed in the beach. "Oooh, this feels good . . . a pebble massage. I've never cut trees. Let's stay here tonight."

Arak joined him on the beach. He gazed up at the stars and relaxed to the music of the sea. "Agreed."

They rose at dawn for a quick meal of dried fish and honey-roasted almonds. Then they floated the trees to the skiff and tied ropes around each tree. All the dragons worked together, hauling up tree after tree. Some were cut into shorter sections and stored in the hold. Four long trunks were lashed to the sides for future masts.

The sun was setting as they finished. They celebrated with a communal meal of hot cocoa, fluffy baked tubers, herbed seaweed, and lobsters from Orm and Scree.

Drakor gave a deep, contented sigh. "Lobsters for dinner. Yellow dragons know how to eat."

Arak pointed to the octopi. "It helps to have friends like Orm and Scree."

Taron, Dorali, and Driana stood up together. Moonlight shone on their polished wood flutes. "Erinite made three new tunes for this journey. They run together like the sea."

Taron blew a long, haunting note that hung in the

moist air. Dorali added hers. Then three melodies wove in and out, combining to make chords before slipping into separate streams.

Drakor's eyes glazed over. He stood on the deck, transfixed, until the last note faded away.

Arak snapped his tail in applause. "Taron, you're right. It *does* sound like the stars are singing."

Drakor gazed at the flutes. "Taron carves music. That isss the best possible use for wood."

Arak nodded. "He's our best carver, and now he has a new talent."

Two days later, Arak, Drakor, and Karoon followed the river upstream, treading silently on the thick layer of leaves. Each step released the earthy, moldy scents of the forest. Ancient, gnarled oaks soared above them, with trunks as wide as a dragon. Mottled gray and brown lizards scuttled up into the branches and held still, becoming twigs among the new leaves. Woody shelf mushrooms covered fallen trees. Mushrooms of every color flourished in the moist ground, like a field of odd flowers.

Karoon picked a mushroom with a yellow cap. "This looks tasty." A faint green color tinged the golden scales on his hand. He turned the mushroom over and flicked his tail in surprise. "Where's the green from?"

Arak took a look. "The mushroom dust is green. I think this type is poisonous."

"Naturally, green is not safe." Karoon tossed it aside, muttering, "That's a dragon-lady color."

Arak thumped a tree with dark, winding branches. "Walnuts! We missed the fall harvest, but nuts can last through the Winter Solstice and beyond. Let's hunt for leftovers." He handed out sacks. "Who can gather the most tree nuts? I saw hickory, pecan, walnut, and chestnut trees on the fly-over. Check up in the trees and scour the forest floor. The winner has no campsite duties tonight."

Drakor grinned. "A contest!" He took an extra sack.

Karoon and Drakor flitted through the forest, popping up into trees and running along the wide branches, gathering old nuts. They strolled across the forest floor, using their feet to feel the harvest. Both dragons flicked walnuts and chestnuts up into the air and caught them in open bags.

Arak spotted a patch of wrinkled mushrooms and gathered these, instead of nuts.

As the sun set, Karoon patted his bulging bags with a triumphant smile.

Drakor stared. "How did you win? I am bigger."

"I move more quickly between branches, and smaller feet can feel the nuts under leaves. Sometimes, being smaller is an advantage. Remember that when you fight."

Arak counted the filled sacks. "Excellent! Tonight we feast. Drakor, I'll teach you the secret to making a good nut soup. Tomorrow we'll take our harvest to the skiff."

They made camp by the river, in a clearing beside a giant fallen tree. Arak filled a copper pot with water and hung it over the fire. Soon, steam rose like fragrant ghost flames. He made the soup with three types of nuts, sliced mushrooms, pepper and herbs. Gathering mushrooms took time and cost Arak the contest win, but he was after a bigger prize. Good food made happy journey-mates and a better journey.

Drakor ladled out yet another bowl of soup and slurped hungrily. "This isss great! Ice dragons do not have real nut trees. We have pine nuts. The trees are no taller than a dragon, with long needles and lots of pine cones. We smash the cones and pick pine nuts out of the brown seeds. They have a fatty, piney taste that isss perfect with lichen salads."

"Umm. Lichens." Arak wrinkled his nose. "Ice dragons left our land long ago, when the fish left. They needed more food. Would ice dragons come here for the food? Some conflicts can be solved without claws." He opened his sack, and a pungent aroma escaped. "I found a sassafras tree. It has three different types of leaves: one lobe, two lobes, and three lobes. The leaves are strange, but the roots are even stranger. Smell them."

Drakor took a deep sniff. "That isss a strong, spicy smell."

Arak nodded. He took out his small knife and cut the roots into pieces. "I'll soak these in water with herbs and a little honey. Wait 'til you try it! Root beer is even better than red root tea."

The trio sat down on a thick bed of leaves, leaned against the fallen tree, and gazed into the night sky. Crystal stars sparkled around an aurora. This whisper-thin curtain of white light was folded back and forth, over and over again.

"It's a never-ending blanket. This may be the most unusual blanket I'll ever sleep beneath," Arak mused.

Drakor yawned but his ears twitched. "It isss hard to sleep now. I feel the Volcano rumble even in my sleep."

Arak gazed to the east, flicking his tail with concern. "Driana, Scree, and Dorali all agree that you need this time to finish healing, or you'll have no chance to win a serious fight."

The next morning, Arak, Drakor, and Karoon flew to the dragon-skiff. They stowed their sacks of tree nuts in the hold. Taron joined them to fly up river, where redfish were spawning. They returned hours later with an impressive catch.

Driana sharpened her blade. "These fish are huge! We could use help."

Dorali took out her knife.

Karoon gazed longingly at the shore, then back at Dorali. He met her eyes. "I'll stay onboard."

Dorali tilted her head. "I'll be cleaning and smoking fish. Some would call this dragon-lady work."

He grinned. "It's useful work. I want to learn your secrets for making great smoked fish." He tossed a knife up high and caught it. "And I'm handy with a blade."

Dorali laughed. "Okay. You can fillet the fish."

* * *

Arak and Drakor flew back to the campsite. They walked along the river, peering into shadows on both sides. A faint path veered into the forest and they followed. Arak stopped at a large, unnaturally round structure overgrown with thick, thorny vines. "What's this?" He tugged on the vines, peeling back one after another.

Drakor joined him, easily ripping off vines and tossing them aside. "Dragon sign!"

Tucked among the towering oaks was an old shelter that was nearly big enough to hold an ice dragon. It was made from long, bent branches that were woven together. The remains of a fish-leather cover hung in tatters.

Arak ran an admiring claw along the curved frame. "They soaked oak branches to bend them like this. It's a very efficient design."

They hunted through the woods and found more decrepit shelters. "Look!" Drakor pulled a long bone from beneath a bush. "This isss from a big lizard, bigger than the ones in our Volcano tubes. But I have not seen any lizards in this land."

Arak turned in a circle. "I wonder where they went." A shallow pit was lined with large, fire-blackened river-stones. He poked among the old, charred wood. "These are fish bones. They used fire and cooked their food."

Drakor lifted a heavy, worn bag. The rotting leather fell apart in his hands, scattering smooth stones. He eyed the mysterious markings and shrugged his wings.

Arak studied the carved designs on the stones. "Each one is different, and I have no idea what this means." A sparkle in the dirt caught his attention. The diamond-shaped scale was bronze with an iridescent scarlet sheen. "This is definitely from a dragon. I've never heard of red dragons."

A ray of sunlight sneaked through the dense forest canopy. Arak held the thick scale in the light. He tilted it back and forth, watching the colors shimmer and change. "It's like a rare sunset opal. Arwina will love this." He placed the scale in his pouch. "Scales don't just fall off. Was there a fight?"

Drakor probed through the moldy leaves and found another dragon scale. Light went into the bronze scale and flashed back as orange, ruby, or scarlet. "Beautiful. It isss a sunset pearl. There isss a layer of clear bronze on top of many colors. My sire tells stories of sunset dragons, but I thought they were just stories. His stories always seem real."

Arak studied the ground as he walked in a spiral pattern, moving in wider circles. "There are so many abandoned homes, all falling apart. They must have left many seasons ago. What did he say about them?"

Drakor walked beside him, poking through the ruins with a stick. He picked up one more iridescent scale and smiled. "This isss proof for my sire. Sunset dragons have bright scarlet wings that shine when they fly. When they fold their wings, the red isss hidden. All you see isss the bronze struts. Their scales look bronze in the shadows, like trees. They glow with different sunset colors in the light. They followed the setting sun and live far away in the sunset land."

"This must be the sunset land. What are they like?"

"No one knows. An ancient legend says that these dragons always seemed to know what others were thinking."

Arak flicked his tail nervously. "Like being in trance-mind all the time? That could be hard to live with." He touched the trance-stone inside his travel pack, something he never left behind. "I wonder if we could learn to trance-mind without using a stone."

Drakor gave him a curious glance. "Maybe they just paid close attention. I often know what someone will do just by watching. But what if they *could* read any mind?"

Arak winced. "That would change everything. What happened to the sunset dragons? Why did they leave? Where are they now?" The afternoon sun sank even lower, sending a golden glow across the massive tree trunks. "Let's head back to the campsite."

The night was cold, so Arak made a rough, private shelter. He crawled inside, took out his trance-stone, and focused. His trance-mind rose up through tangled oak branches and into the starry sky. He circled above the forest canopy, searching for smoke or a worn, moonlit path. Where there's smoke, there are dragons . . . maybe. He wove back and forth, crossing tens of tens of dragon-miles, while his limp body remained far behind.

Arak quested further south, trying to sharpen his blurry sight, and found a river. Waterfalls sprayed through pale orange holes in the rock . . . limestone eyes. There must be caves nearby, also carved through rock, that would make a perfect new home. They could live near their crucial copper mine, and the ice dragons. Then he quested toward the north, to check on their next stop.

His thoughts snapped. For the first time ever, he felt a tingling shock at the edge of his traveling consciousness. He jerked away, feeling as if someone had just trounced on his toes. Was this a new ability, to feel in trance? Was it the mysterious sunset dragons?

His mind returned to his body and Arak woke, bone-tired. He felt the thick dragon-scale in his pouch and held it up in the moonlight. Who were these dragons?

CHAPTER 13: CHANGING TIDES

Arak awoke just before dawn and made a quick meal of leftovers. "Let's fly south, inland. That area could be perfect for caves."

Drakor's eyes lit up. "You are truly thinking of moving here?"

Arak slapped him on the back. "Let's see what we find." The sky was just turning blue when he glimpsed the complicated stream from his secret mind-travel. He pointed. "There!"

Arak landed on the bank of a narrow river. His claws clicked against the mustard-yellow limestone. This was even more beautiful than the blurry vision in his trance-quest. Bright green moss, thick mats of ruby-red algae, and yellow sand painted the river with vivid colors.

Water popped in and out of rock holes, spilled down as crystal-clear rapids, and collected in deep blue pools. It disappeared into random tunnels and spurted out as waterfalls. Smells of wet, worn rock and old moss filled his senses.

Drakor landed beside him and stood stock still. "This isss a rainbow river."

Arak grinned ear-to-ear. "Yes. And if there's a cave to match . . ."

Everything they needed was in the New World, except the octopi. And Scree wanted to move here. Ice dragons would make good neighbors if Drakor was their leader. If Drakor lost to Mardor, the ice dragons wouldn't move. Arak's main concern was the sunset dragons that had disturbed his trance. What were they like?

"Drakor, I'll head due west and you search farther south. We'll meet back here at sunset."

This was the only day to search. Blurry mind-traveling was quick and useful, but the trance had its limits. This search would use all his senses.

Arak flew close to the ground as he crossed each stream. He watched for sinkholes made from fallen caves. He flared his nostrils to catch the special scent of cave air.

Arak searched for magnetic wrinkles, for the odd patterns they made above hollow ground. He sharpened his inner eye to feel/see the energy of water running beneath the ground. He concentrated so hard he thought his brain would cramp up.

Golden rays of light slanted across the ground as the sun sank toward the horizon. Arak flicked his tail nervously. What if there was no cave?

Suddenly, a dark cloud flew out from the hillside. Arak sped toward the noisy swarm of black insects. He followed their path back and found a narrow crevice that was hidden by bushes.

Arak peered inside, savoring the taste of cool, damp

air that seeped out. The fading light showed a chamber that disappeared into darkness. He lit a branch, twisted his body sideways, and stepped inside.

This was a cave of dreams.

Arak gazed up at a high ceiling that glimmered with the pale green light of glow worms. There was plenty of room to stretch their wings. This cave would make a great winter shelter!

Damp limestone walls glowed in the torchlight. All three dragon colors flowed together: golden-brown, reds, and white. What would it be like to live near his cousins, to learn new skills and old forgotten legends?

Arak flicked his tail with concern. Were sunset dragons dangerous? Maybe. But crossing the sea to gather copper was also dangerous. If the clan moved here, they'd be near the crucial copper and their favorite new foods. Risk and reward. *Everything worth doing starts with a dream, so I'll dream big.*

Arak walked into the depths of the cave, carrying his torch, peering into dark chambers. He nodded with satisfaction. Dragonlets would fit nicely into this room, far from the entrance. It would be hard for those curious rascals to sneak out.

A circle of light decorated the cave floor with changing sunset colors. Arak glanced up. This natural chimney would give light and good air flow. Perfect! He walked among sleek columns that splashed down from the ceiling like frozen waterfalls. He could see Arwina playing dragon-tag, laughing and running through this stone forest.

Would the clan move here, or at least some of the dragons? And Scree and Orm . . . His mind whirled. He had found a place to live, but friends made a home.

* * *

Scree and Orm pulsed above a rock reef, searching for the missing octopi. An out-of-place movement caught Orm's eye and they jetted down. A rock became a blue octopus, wary and challenging.

"We're just visiting," Scree said, moving her arms slowly, trying not to alarm him. "I'm a Healer." She bent her arms into a triangle, making the Healer sign.

The octopus relaxed his arms but kept the blue color. "We held the final ceremony for our Healer two days ago." One eye swiveled around, as if searching for more visitors. "Where are you from?"

"Far away. I'm Scree, this is Orm. Your garden patterns are amazing."

"I'm Dram." He eyed Scree's Healer bag and added, "We could use your skills."

"Lead the way."

The trio pulsed deep into the reef, to a jumble of rocks surrounded by nervous, color-changing octopi. Four were working together, arms suctioned to a rock, trying to pull it away. The narrow gaps between these rocks would let in light, but not much else. Scree curled her arms with concern. "What happened?"

Dram said, "The sea floor shook. Rocks killed our Healer and covered my mate. Kray is alive, but she's too injured to shift thin and escape. We can't move these rocks."

Orm tasted the rock with an arm. "It's limestone. That's a soft rock, so we can cut through it." He pulled a knife from its sheath at the top of one arm. The blade was razor-sharp, smooth along one edge and jagged on the other.

Scree pulled two small garnet saws from her bag and gave them to Orm. "Share these. I'll see what I can do while you cut through this rock." She shifted flat, becoming so thin that her nerves were squished and she could barely feel. Scree slipped through a crack between the rocks and took her normal shape.

An octopus lay on the sand, eyes glazed, twitching feebly. Two arms were crushed, and pale blue blood leaked from many cuts. Scree spoke with calm, almost musical arms. "I'm a Healer. You'll be out of here soon, but that bleeding must be stopped now." She poked two arms out through the crack and requested items from her Healer bag. Orm passed them down to her.

Scree rubbed oily salve onto Kray's cuts and the bleeding stopped. She added two drops to a vial of water. "Kray, please drink this. It will help the pain. Your arms will re-grow." The patient instinctively swallowed as Scree poured the potion down her throat. Moments later, she slept beyond pain.

Scree tied off the damaged arms at the body. She used a sharp blade to remove the crushed part and repeated, "They will re-grow." This was for her own reassurance, since the patient was fast asleep.

Rasping sounds vibrated through the sea and then a solid thunk. Light poured into the hollow. Dram dropped through the new opening, gazed at his injured mate, and curled his arms in distress.

Scree answered his unspoken questions. "Kray will recover. Two arms were beyond repair, but they should re-grow within a year. She has some deep cuts. Don't move her for a few days, or the bleeding could start again."

Dram twined arms in friendship with Scree. "Thank you." They slid out through the new hole.

Dram's skin sparkled as he twined arms with Orm. "We must celebrate!"

An octopus pulsed slowly to Scree. Her skin was grayed with age, but her eyes were bright. "Enjoy the feast. I'll watch over with Kray." She slipped through the opening and settled onto the sand beside the patient.

The rest of the pod gathered at the feasting circle, which was made from smooth red stones. Octopi painted the circle with food. They made wavy rings with different colors and textures, and soon it looked like a jellyfish flower. The center was a huge pile of mussels with purple-black shells. Next was a wavy ring of clams, then a dark band of mussels, then creamy-gray oysters, and more mussels. The outer star was made from red, golden-brown, and purple seaweeds.

Scree made a skin picture of a grass-like plant with purple flowers and a fat white bulb. "Garlic is a land-plant that will make this taste even better." She added some crushed garlic at each tip of the outer star.

Octopus arms twisted with delight as they tasted this new flavor through the sea.

Scrap, a juvenile, piled clams and mussels onto his shell plate. He added garlic, took a bite, and turned green with pleasure. "Land-food tastes great with sea-food!"

Scree was staring at the shells. "I've never seen so much shell-food from a natural reef!"

"A warm current came from the northeast and the starfish died. The mussels and clams were happy."

Scree turned in a slow circle. "I knew something was

missing from this reef. Starfish add color."

Orm finished eating a huge clam before answering. "Starfish also eat shell-food, so that leaves more for us."

Scree gazed northeast. "That warm current could have come from Drakor's volcano island."

Orm handed her a plate. "Everything is connected. Scree, try the clams."

She added them to her plate. "They're tasty. No starfish means more clams. Change one thing and change the world."

Scree flicked the tip of an arm like the tail of a worried dragon, thinking. What would happen next? A change that seemed good could still cause something bad. She stretched the worry out of her arms. *What will be, will be. And then we'll make it work.*

After the feast, the octopi shared stories with body-pictures. The pod was fascinated by dragons, and Scree's pictures from the abyss were popular. But Orm's stories were the best. The colorful arms of octopus applause seemed like a field of fantasy flowers.

Time passed unnoticed, until Scree felt a lengthening underwater shadow. She checked on her patient and reassured Kray that her arms would re-grow. The elderly octopus who had helped was gone. A youngster was feeding Kray from a shell bowl.

Scree eyed an old, weathered Healer bag that was propped against a rock. She took another look at the small octopus. "Are you the Healer's apprentice?"

"I'm Brie." Her arms were bruised and her face wore the mask of sorrow. "The Healer chose me three moons ago. I still have much to learn. When the world shook, I was hurt and my mentor was killed."

Scree twined arms gently with the youngster. "I'm sorry. It's so hard to lose a mentor."

"I watched when you helped Kray, to learn."

Scree pointed to the bowl he held, which was filled with choice pieces from the feast. "You have the heart of a Healer. Your mentor chose well." She stayed for another hour, explaining the most important items in the former Healer's bag. Then she gave Brie a stoppered bottle that was carved from black coral. "This pain-killer is strong, so use it carefully. Give Kray one drop, two times each day, for an eight-day."

Scree approached Dram, holding her arms formally straight. "I would like to honor your dead Healer."

The pod took their visitors to a ring of purple-green seaweed around a cairn of stones. Scree added a large pearl to the stones that covered the body. She bowed her head in sorrow, feeling the emptiness of loss. It would have been wonderful to learn from another octopus Healer.

An orange-and-pink sea slug twisted through the water, dancing in the late afternoon light that filtered through the sea. Scree checked the shadows. It was time to leave.

"Our reef has enough food for another pod. We could use a Healer," Dram said to Scree. "And a talented story-teller," he added, turning one eye to Orm.

Scree smiled at the invitation. "You'd be great neighbors. We might return." They twined arms with the double clasp of friendship.

Scree pulsed back to the skiff with Orm. "That's a friendly pod."

Orm twined arms and perfectly matched her pulses.

"How could they not like you?"

Scree laughed. "I think what they really want is your story-telling." She playfully changed her rhythm and he matched it. "I learned something new. The world shakes here, too, but I don't taste any volcanoes."

Orm nodded. "I learned that mussels are everywhere. Dragons could gather plenty from the shore."

"You found a farm that grows on its own." Scree twined another arm with Orm and twirled up to the surface.

* * *

Arak focused his inner eye on the night sky, searching for the unpredictable storms. Taron was at the helm, skirting the coastline, ready to seek a safe harbor. They were swiftly approaching their third and last New World stop.

Dorali, Karoon, and Driana sat together on the cold deck. They grabbed handfuls of kapok tree fluff from a barrel and stuffed this into fish-skin tubes.

Karoon picked up a long, fat tube and held it out to Dorali. "What *is* this? It looks like a snake swallowed a watermelon."

Dorali laughed and tied off the end. "They're bolsters, and they do look odd. We'll hang them over the side to protect the skiff. Our next stop may have strong tides."

Drakor gazed to the east, rustling his wings uneasily. "I feel we have little time left."

Arak pointed north. "With this wind, we'll reach our stop in no time. Then we'll head straight to your island." But his eyes were also drawn to the east, and the tip of his tail flicked up and down with worry. When would this disaster happen? Was Drakor ready to fight? He seemed stronger every day. If they reached his homeland before Drakor was ready, he would surely lose. But, if they came too late, it wouldn't matter.

Stars faded and the sea grew louder. They reached the northern bay at dawn, as violet and coral layers colored the sky. Sharp black boulders dotted the sea like flies on honey. These islands were solid rock, taller than the mast, with steep sides and scruffy pine trees on the top.

Debris was piled high up on the rocky shore, warning of dramatic tides that rose and fell the length of a giant squid. The breeze carried stinky aromas from rotting seaweed and the piney scent of trees.

Arak and Taron set three anchors to keep the skiff away from each of the black islands. They used extra-long ropes to allow for the changing tides.

Arak checked the bolsters and flexed his wings nervously. The rock islands were more dangerous than ice-mountains. "These bolsters should protect the skiff if a strong tide pulls it against the rocks."

"We'll check the anchors below, and wedge them between undersea boulders," Scree promised. Then she and Orm slipped overboard.

Drakor leaned against the railing, studying the rocky shore. Ice sparkled on the ground beneath stunted trees. "This looks promising. It isss still cold."

Arak pointed to a distant, cone-shaped mountain. "I think that's an old volcano."

"That isss a good place to start."

"What do you hope to find?"

Drakor gazed at the mountain. "The perfect place would have a quiet Volcano with hot springs, great fishing, pine nuts and lichens. Something to replace our sacred pools would be nice."

Then Drakor's tail drooped to the ground. "Any home isss better than one that will be gone."

Arak looked at each of his crew-mates. "Any of you can come ashore, but we need dragons to prepare for our visit to the ice dragons."

Dorali volunteered to stay.

Karoon gazed at Dorali. "I'll stay, too."

* * *

Arak and Drakor soared inland, flying high to survey the land. They punched through a cloud and landed on the volcano. The windy peak had snow, dry grasses, and short, twisted trees. A beam of light found Drakor; he sparkled like a carpet of diamonds next to the patch of old, crumpled ice.

Arak dug his claws into the frosty ground. "This dirt is thick. I think the volcano has been quiet since the First Dragon spoke."

Drakor flared his nostrils. "There are no Volcano smells and no wandering magnetic wrinkles. It isss sleeping deep."

Arak walked to the edge and faced due east. "What a view! I can see the shore."

Drakor stared down into the valley. "What isss jumping in that river?"

"Fish are heading upstream to spawn. That's a bonus. Let's fly south and check out that forest."

They landed in shadows between pine trees. Arak heard the quiet hum of crickets and faint rustlings in the bushes. Small lizards that he could barely hear, and almost see, jumped from branch to branch. They changed their colors as they moved, with instant camouflage that

204

was nearly as perfect as an octopus.

Arak pointed to tracks in the mud with deep claw marks; water pooled in the big paw prints. "Here's another trace of the large lizards, and it's fresh, but we still haven't seen them. If they can camouflage like the small lizards, we might never see them. Big, invisible hunters. Do they hunt alone or in packs? If they're like the dweer, this could be a problem. We'll sleep onboard tonight."

That evening they flew high over a field of white clouds, heading for the comfort and safety of the skiff. A bright moon rose slowly above the clouds and into the black sky. Red and green lights danced among the stars.

"I will miss my home. But this sunset land has great auroras," Drakor said, with a sad smile.

Arak sighed. "I'm so sorry, Drakor. But there's plenty of room here for sunset dragons *and* ice dragons."

Drakor curved his neck around to look into Arak's eyes. "There isss also room for yellow dragons."

Arak nodded, and they flew the rest of the way in a comfortable silence.

* * *

Arak, Drakor, Dorali, and Driana went ashore at dawn to gather rare herbs. Suddenly, the sky turned gray. Clouds towered high and the sky crackled with energy, but there was little wind.

Arak gazed into the sky. "It's a perfect day for storm dances."

Dorali glanced up and quickly looked away.

"What are these storm dances?" Drakor asked.

"We dance in the sky and paint the clouds with colored lightning. We play dragon games," Driana said.

Drakor snapped his tail. "A new game! What do you do?"

Driana stretched her wings, warming up as she explained. "We catch a small lightning bolt and add metal powder to change the color. Each lightning color has a different game rule. Red: Spin around before you catch the lightning. Orange: Catch the lightning, twirl it on your claws, and release it to the clouds. Yellow: Toss it back twice. Blue: Twirl it on your claws before you toss it to another dragon. Purple: Do a flip in the air before you catch it. That's the hardest one. It's a challenge to remember each rule and do it fast. You need lightning reflexes."

Drakor had both ears tilted toward Driana and his eyes burned with intensity. "Red, orange, yellow, blue, purple. That isss a rule for every rainbow color except green. What about green lightning?"

"Green lightning is only for courting, not games." Arak took a leather box from his pack, with a flip lid and glass vials. "Drakor, you can use my kit. The lightning color is on the stopper of each vial. Pour some metal into a bolt to color it."

Driana's eyes glowed. "Feel that energy! I'm ready to fly."

"Will you play too, Dorali?" Drakor asked.

Arak caught Driana's eye with a silent plea. Dorali was horribly wounded when she was too young to fly, and the holes in her wings healed slowly. She lived at the Healer clinic, apart from the dragon clan. He'd seen Dorali juggling lightning on her own, but she had never played with other dragons in the clouds.

Driana gave Arak a slight nod. "Dorali, it's just a

game with friends. Please join us."

Dorali trembled. Then she released a long sigh and straightened her wings. "Thanks. I'd like that."

Drakor, Dorali, and Driana flew higher and higher until they disappeared inside the clouds. Colored lightning flashed and spun through the gray clouds like fiery sparkles inside an opal.

Arak watched the rainbow clouds from below with a satisfied smile. Zarina would be pleased for her protégé.

* * *

The northern lobster held its ground as Scree approached, clicking strong pincers wider than her arm. She backed away. "These lobsters are as big as we are."

Orm shrugged his octopus shoulders. "They grow big up north. Our lobsters have sharp spines, but these have impressive claws."

Scree drew icicles on her skin with her color cells. "Everything grows bigger here. Maybe it's the cold water."

Orm made a body-picture of icicles that melted away. "I prefer warmth and a coral reef, but this new seaweed is interesting. Let's hunt for some nice, reasonable clams."

They skimmed just above the sand, feeling for the slightest movement below. Then they jabbed into the sand with sticks to find the living rocks below. Working together, they soon filled a sack with clams.

Orm hefted the sack. "We have enough for dinner for everyone."

A strong tide ran out to sea at dawn and swept back to land each night. Scree and Orm relaxed into the pull of this predictable water ride, heading for shore and the skiff.

Scree turned happy-green. "I could get used to this."

Orm matched her exact shade of emerald. "But we would need to plan everything around these tides."

The tide carried them north of the skiff cove, to a place with heavy surf. As they drew near, Scree shot to the surface and caught the top of a wave rushing to shore. She straightened her body like a board, merged all of her arms together, and surfed. She rode the wave faster than a shark!

The water curled over Scree like a hungry mouth and became a tunnel through the sea. She rocketed through the tunnel, hidden by webs of white foam, tingling with the raw energy. The sea flattened out near shore. She took her normal shape, slipped under the waves, and pulsed back to Orm.

He was staring wide-eyed. "What gave you *that* idea?"

"I've wanted to ride a wave ever since I spoke with a squid in the abyss, the one who rode a thunder-wave."

"A what?"

"When an ice-mountain breaks off and hits the sea, it makes a thunder-wave for giant squid to ride."

"Naturally, ice falls to amuse the squid."

"And waves curl over to amuse octopi. You should ride one. It's like being a squid surfing the deep currents, and a dragon riding storm winds, all together."

"If we move to the new reefs, and if our dragon friends move too, I'll celebrate with a wave-ride."

Scree laughed. "I want to see that." Her skin turned a marbled mix of gold, white, and red. "Imagine gold dragons and ice dragons and sunset dragons all living here, together."

Orm scratched his 'chin' with the tip of an arm. "That could be interesting. They're all dragons, but each group seems so different."

* * *

The dark sea sparkled beneath a starry sky and splashed against the hull as they headed for Drakor's home. Karoon and Driana took turns flying the skiff, steering by the stars. A bright aurora rippled in the sky, lighting the busy deck below.

Arak and Dorali finished tying the bamboo stalks together. They rolled this raft into a tight bundle and tied it together; two sturdy wood handles poked out. Arak paused from his work to gaze up at the sky. "This aurora looks like tourmaline crystals, dark pink above and green below."

Scree tilted her head back. "Crystal stars on a gemstone curtain. What a perfect night." She drenched the top of her body in ruby, while emerald green spread down her arms. Sparkly white stars emerged from her skin in a northern pattern.

Orm made the same color pattern in his skin and added southern stars. He twined two matching green arms with Scree and said, with a twinkle in his eyes, "Together we are the world."

Orm kept fish-skin pieces in place, using two more arms, while Scree sewed them together. She held a sharp bone needle in the thinned, curled tip of her arm.

Arak took another look. Scree was actually wielding three needles with three arms. Her arms seemed to move of their own accord, working together with effortless efficiency.

Dorali glanced over and shook her head. "How do you

sew with more than one arm at the same time? You're not even paying full attention."

Scree grinned as she spoke with two more arms. "It helps to have a mind in each arm."

Steaming cups of spiced tea and dragon-roasted almonds scented the air, while fish-skins added their own smell. Taron walked carefully across the deck, carrying a huge tray with snacks and mugs of red root tea. "Scree, that's your third fish-skin rectangle. What are they for?"

Scree stuck her needles into the skins and stretched each arm. She accepted her small mug and turned one eye to Arak. "These are for the ice dragons. Zarina is making sure that the new octopus skiffs are ready for the pods, and I'm helping Drakor." She curled her arms nervously, with one eye facing her home and one eye facing Drakor's island. "I hope everything is finished in time."

Arak slid his bamboo raft across the damp deck, tied it to the railing, and sat down with a satisfied sigh. He swallowed his tea and chewed a handful of warm, smoky almonds. "It's nippy tonight. I really need this energy boost."

Driana grabbed some almonds and joined them. "What's next?"

Arak said, "We need to finish the slings."

"The what?" Taron asked.

Arak held up the huge rectangle that Scree had made. "The slings need sturdy wood handles. When Drakor wins, he'll need slings to carry young dragonlets to the New World."

Drakor flicked his tail nervously. "When? Not if?"

Arak nodded soberly. "You *must* win."

Karoon finished his turn at skiff-flying and slapped

Drakor on the back. "No pressure."

"Why don't we have the ice dragons stay with us?" Dorali asked.

Arak held up his fist and raised a clawed finger as he listed each reason. "First, our skiff could only carry a few ice dragons. We live too far away for the others to reach us. The wind blows the wrong way for them to fly to us, and there's no place to rest."

Arak raised another finger. "Second, even if the ice dragons could reach us, there's not enough food to support so many extra dragons for a long stay. To make things worse, the tsunami that follows could destroy our oyster crop and many of the nut trees. The undersea volcano could destroy the octopus crops. If this happens, we would barely have enough stored food to feed our own clan."

He raised a third finger and gazed to the west. "Third, the ice dragon island is fairly close to Drakor's New World home, and the upper wind-stream flows that way. They should make it there safely in one long flight."

Dorali looked from Arak's fingers to his serious face. "I see that you've given this some thought."

Arak sighed. "Yes."

Drakor signed quietly to himself, "I hope I am ready."

Karoon gave Drakor a concerned glance, then stood up and faced him. "I always feel better when I'm doing something. Let's practice."

When they stopped, Dorali gave them each a cup of tea. "You need to drink more when you practice."

The following day, Arak studied the eastern sky with his eyes closed. "Magnetic wrinkles are gathering like a swarm of locusts. That's a warning sign from your legends. You're absolutely certain the volcano will destroy your home the next time it explodes?"

Drakor shuddered. "I see our Volcano explode, with glowing red eyes and lightning. A cloud of burning dust reaches the wind-stream. Then our home isss gone."

"It must be hard to sleep with that vision. Have you seen *when* this will happen?"

"I do not know. I feel that it will be soon."

Arak flicked the tip of his tail, deep in thought. Finally he asked, "Were there stars in your vision?"

Drakor closed his eyes. Arak waited quietly while he meditated.

"The sky has clouds so I cannot see all the stars." He opened his eyes. "I am not certain, but our night sky should match the Volcano message in three dragon-weeks."

Quiet waves could be heard in the profound silence that followed. Then Arak said, "That's not much time. It will be dangerous to face Mardor and hard to convince the clan that they should leave."

"Yes."

"So I will come, too, and help."

Drakor snapped his tail. "You will help me? Even with the danger? If I lose, Mardor *will* be a danger to you."

Arak shrugged his wings. "Friends help friends. I finally found the legendary ice dragons. Maybe they're not what I expected, but I don't want to lose them now."

Dorali moved closer. "I'll come, too. You may need a Healer."

Drakor's teeth sparkled within his wide grin. "Yellow dragons. What will the ice dragons think?"

Karoon cast a worried look at Dorali and Drakor. "I'll come."

Arak shook his head. "Karoon, I need you here. Two companions is the right number to go ashore; more could be seen as a challenge. And, I have a plan."

Scree's eyes twinkled. "Of course you do."

CHAPTER 14: INTO FIRE AND ICE

Ice-mountains dotted the cold, blue-gray sea. Arak and Taron anchored the dragon-skiff between two white giants, a short flight from the island. They lowered the top section of the tall mast to shorten it below the ice. The floating mountains were smaller now, and their sharp edges had been smoothed by melting. But the stench of rotten eggs was as strong as ever.

Drakor took a deep breath and wrinkled his nose. "I had almost forgotten the Volcano's breath. Even this will be hard to leave. It smells like home."

The Volcano was alive and well, sending regular tremors through land, sea, and air like a beating heart. Magnetic lines shimmered with the force. Drakor drummed his claws together, matching the beat. "The Volcano heart isss beating even faster now."

Arak grabbed the rolls of fish-skins. "Then we must be faster, too. Let's get to work."

The dragons worked at a furious pace, fastening ice-white skins to the top of bamboo poles. Soon a camouflage tent covered the skiff from stem to stern, matching the ice-mountains and hiding the dragons.

"Hiding is safer than fighting. We must protect the skiff and leave within five days," Arak warned.

Dorali tied an extra knot through the last fish-skin. "This place seems almost the same but everything feels different . . . I feel different."

"You're seeing with new eyes," Scree said.

"Waterspouts, sunset dragons, and volcano drumbeats. I'm definitely seeing with new eyes, and new eye-skin," Orm quipped.

Arak arched his long neck and stared into the colored sky. Green light hung in the crystal air, reaching for the snow-covered mountain. "Northern skies are lit every night like colored lightning in the clouds . . . spirals, curtains, and streaks in every color. It's the same in the New World. If ice dragons knew this, they might find it easier to leave their home."

Arak turned to Taron, "You're in charge. You, Karoon, and Driana must protect our skiff. If an ice dragon attacks use sedative spears first, lightning swords if you must. Drakor, Dorali, and I will go ashore and meet the ice dragons."

Karoon gave Dorali a small package. "For luck. It's from the copper cave."

She unwrapped the present and gazed at the bright green cubes. "Fluorite crystals. They're lovely." Dorali raised her head and looked into Karoon's eyes. "Why?"

He shrugged, but his brow had worry wrinkles. "They match the green at the edge of your scales. Please be careful. Drakor is a good friend, but Mardor sounds dangerous."

Dorali studied his face. Then she touched his arm. "Thank you."

* * *

Three dragons flew low over the water under cover of night. The emerald aurora faded away and a deep rosy dawn colored the ice. They glided silently toward shore, each wearing a pack and carrying a heavy bag. A raft was roped to Drakor and it bounced behind him across the waves.

They landed on cold, scrabbly ground. Drakor hid the raft beneath rocks and leaves. They stored the mesh sacks of live clams in the sea. Then they took to the air, speeding along the shore as a red morning sky gradually became the deep blue of spring.

Arak had mind-traveled to the island on their first journey north, before they returned home with an injured ice dragon. He couldn't leave without a glimpse into this legendary land. He had marveled at the frozen waterfalls. How cold must it be to stop falling water?

It was a world of bare trees and snow, black and white, where color came from the sky. Blue shadows lay between boulders. The pink, green, and gold light of auroras played across the snow.

Now spring was here, and Arak marveled at the changes. The waterfalls had thawed into exuberant white sprays that leapt down the steep rock. There were swollen buds on stunted trees. Plants seemed to be growing before his eyes, making the most of this short, warm period. Small lizards darted about, gathering food, already preparing for winter.

As they flew past the volcano, Drakor pointed to a gray haze of steam that clouded the air. The smell of rotten eggs was intense. "Dorali, you said you wanted to see an ice dragon nest."

They landed near the hot spring.

Arak wrinkled his nose at the stench and hopped awkwardly across hot, flat rocks. "Drakor, you're an ice dragon! How do you stand this heat?"

Drakor grinned. "We have thick feet to match our thick heads."

Three dragon-ladies stood together, wing-to-wing, making a protective wall around the nest behind them.

"Three guards for one nest?"

"An egg can't fight, so it needs guards. And it would be lonely here for one nesting dragon." Drakor answered quietly. He bowed to the dragon-ladies. "Greetings. These are my friends, Arak and Dorali."

Dorali bowed and held out her empty hands. "I'm a dragon-lady. May I see your nest?"

The middle dragon-lady looked her over, eyes wide with surprise. "I thought yellow dragons were a myth." She folded one wing against her body so Dorali could see, but her wary eyes followed every move.

Dorali took a long look and her eyes glowed. The nest was made from a ring of fist-sized volcanic rocks with odd holes, like hard black sponges. Golden topaz, glowing rubies, and blue diamonds were fitted into cracks between the black rocks. These sturdy gems caught the afternoon sunlight, flickering like flames. The nest held thousands of fiery, reddish-gold threads. A huge, gleaming egg was nestled within the thick cushion of glass hair.

Dorali's arms trembled, reaching out to touch the egg. She visibly forced her arms to her side and used only her eyes.

Golden dragons had smooth, sandy-colored eggs with spots. This egg had thick, diamond-shaped scales in a whorl pattern, like a pine cone. The dark bronze shell shimmered with other colors. Iridescent, red-gold streaks wrapped around the egg like an aurora, matching the strands inside of the nest. The shell texture and opalescent colors were remarkable.

Dorali bowed low. "Your egg is a precious jewel."

Arak pointed to the glass fibers. "What's that?"

"Dragon's blood from the Volcano," Drakor said.

Dorali nodded. "The nest looks like a volcano on fire. Everything is about the volcano."

"You are born of storm, but ice dragons are born of the Volcano. This isss our history," Drakor said proudly.

They bowed to the dragon-ladies and left, walking together, kicking the loose gray rocks and crunching across dry, shaggy clumps of grass.

Dorali reached for a sparkle among the dull gravel and picked up a clear, nut-sized rock. She snapped her tail. "It's a diamond!"

Drakor smiled at her enthusiasm. "It isss small, but perfect . . . a good sou-ven-ir?"

"Yes." She put it in a special pocket in her pack. "This place has gemstones and gemstone eggs. Our eggs don't have scales, maybe because they can't roll in the sand. Yours would be safer on these rocks." She glanced back and frowned. "When will it hatch?"

"Soon. When the egg cracks, we will gather to welcome the new dragonlet."

Dorali flicked her tail nervously. "This youngster will be too small for the journey. It's too cold in the wind-stream."

"There's room on our skiff for the new one and its dragon-dam. We'll bring them and your sire to your new home, later," Arak offered.

Drakor nodded. "If they will go with you, and if I win."

Dorali picked small blue flowers and put them in her pouch. "This might be a useful herb. Drakor, ice dragon eggs look like sunset dragon scales. Your clan remembers these legends and ours does not."

"Maybe we can read minds, too? Or do we just focus carefully on what is not said?" He stopped near a cluster of bushes that were covered with the pale green fuzz of opening buds. A short plant with small, snow-white flowers grew in the shade beneath them. "This isss special, an ice-flower."

He took a flask from his pack, poured water on the flowers, and the white petals became clear. "Dry petals look like snow and wet petals are as clear as ice. The ice-flower plant has tiny blue berries in the summer, the color of the sky. We make a drink from the berries for the Summer Solstice. Too much will kill, but a little makes us stronger. We celebrate with a feast and games."

Dorali snapped her tail. "I must study this plant. Do you have any dried berries?"

Drakor paused, considering. "Maybe. Look, the butterflies are back!" The pungent, piney scent of a blue-green fir was more powerful than the volcano odor. This short tree was nearly hidden by a cloud of orange butterflies. They hung from every possible spot and nestled between needles. Branches bent beneath their combined weight, threatening to break. "These butterflies come every year."

Arak asked, "Where do they come from?"

Drakor pointed to the west. "They fly here from across the sea."

"That's an amazing journey for such fragile wings."

Drakor nodded. "You must see our three sacred pools. They are connected but each pool isss different. I might miss this most of all." He led the way, and they landed near a round pool big enough to hold several dragons. The water was solid white, but the surrounding ground was covered with fine black dust. "This pool isss the color of ice dragons and holds the black breath of the Volcano."

"There's no black volcano dust on the water. It must be so heavy that it falls right through." Arak reached into the pool and licked his claws. "This looks like snow but it tastes like chalk."

They soon reached the second pool, which was dark red. "This pool isss like dragon blood, like life."

Arak tested the water. "It looks like a ruby gemstone and tastes like iron."

They walked along the stream to a turquoise pool. Drakor's eyes glowed with pleasure. "This isss blue like the sky, like freedom. It isss the most special pool. We drink from it often, to strengthen our claws."

Dorali dipped a claw into the water. "I taste precious copper. This pool really *is* special."

"You have floating ice-mountains, unbelievable auroras, and gemstone pools," Arak said. "It would be hard to leave this."

The smile fled from Drakor's eyes. "Now we must go

to the Meeting Circle." He launched into the sky.

Arak and Dorali followed, pumping their wings hard to catch up. They stopped once to pick up their hidden sacks of clams and nuts. Then they glided together through the cold, dry air.

Short, twisted trees surrounded a stony circle that had been cleared of all shrubs. They landed in a flurry of wings, sending up clouds of black dust.

A young ice dragon snapped his tail with a loud crack and darted across the open space. He thumped Drakor on his back, making a drum of him. "Where have you been? You missed the practice games of Slam."

Drakor's eyes glowed with warmth. "It isss a long story."

"This is Jardor." Drakor introduced Arak and Dorali. "They helped me when I was hurt."

Jardor stared and then bowed. "I never expected to see yellow dragons." He looked Drakor up and down. "You are well? You look fit enough. Everyone has been practicing."

Drakor grinned. "Games are very important here. They help determine status."

A very old dragon-lady approached and looked them over with sharp, disapproving eyes. Her crusty white scales were silvered with age. "This isss my dam-sister, Drikora."

A dragon-lord hobbled toward the feast table, using crutches, and Drakor's eyes lit up. "This isss Zardan, my sire," Drakor said, with true warmth in his voice.

Dorali moved closer to Zardan and studied his ancient injuries with the intensity of a Healer. She silently signed to Drakor, "There is hope."

His eyes glowed as he signed back, "I will tell him."

Other dragons drew near with questions in their eyes. Then a huge ice dragon stalked over. The ground vibrated with each step.

Drakor bowed very low. "Greetings, Mardor. This isss Arak, and this isss Dorali."

They both copied Drakor's low bow. "Greetings."

Mardor regarded them with narrowed eyes and growled, "Welcome. How did you get here?"

Arak offered a small, sweet-smelling bag. "We flew. This is a gift from our clan."

Mardor sniffed the bag, opened it, and crunched a handful of nuts. "What isss this?" A rusty smile creased his face.

Arak bowed again. "These are honey-roasted almonds. We also brought food to add to the welcome meal."

Mardor's eyes gleamed and he nodded to another huge dragon. "Sound the feast drum."

BOOM! BOOM! BOOM! The dragon-sized drum thundered three times, rumbling through Arak's body as he swiveled his ears away. More dragons appeared like magic, answering the drum. They bowed to Mardor, stared at the strangers, and hurried away.

The ice dragons returned quickly and put their offerings on the feasting table. This was longer than two dragons and about half as tall as a dragon. The table was carved from a rock outcrop, a solid mass of garnet crystals. All the garnet colors blended together: orange, red, purple, brown, and a pure green that sparkled more than diamonds. Streaky patches of bright pink and blue shone like an aurora.

Most of the rock had been sanded smooth, but clusters of red, many-sided garnet crystals had been left untouched, like flower accents.

Dorali ran her claws over the smooth table and rough crystals. "This is ice dragon art. They always leave part of it natural, for an earthy feel. I like it."

Mardor raised his wings and there was utter silence. "The clan has visitors. I welcome them with this meal."

Strong odors seeped into the air, as if Arak had trampled on seaweed or sat near a pile of long dead fish. He flared his nostrils and inhaled slowly, testing the scents. He found no herbs or spices. Everything was raw and there wasn't much, but the food was interesting. The salads had a dozen types of gray-green lichens mixed with dried red berries and pine nuts.

Lines formed at the head of the feasting table, one on each side. Arak looked from the meager food to the rather thin dragons.

Drakor's friend, Jardor, followed his glance to the obvious conclusion. "Food isss scarce."

Arak emptied his bag of raw clams onto the feasting table while Dorali added piles of nuts. There still wasn't enough food to satisfy the appetites of these huge dragons. "We brought this from the New World. Drakor helped harvest the food."

Every dragon turned eyes and ears toward Arak. He spoke clearly, knowing that this food would speak more loudly than Drakor's descriptions of the New World. He could help his friend bait a hook to catch dragon minds.

Each dragon took only one piece from an ice fish that was cut into small chunks. They took just a little from the food piles, as if each dragon could perfectly divide the amount of food by the number of dragons. Their eyes glowed when they reached the unexpected piles of nuts and clams. Smiles crept onto their faces.

Mardor watched closely, frowning at the enthusiasm of his dragons and snapping his tail irritably.

Groups of ice dragons found seats on the ground close to Drakor and his friends. All ears were swiveled toward them, listening. Arak glanced from Mardor to the listeners. "How much food is left?"

Drakor held his hands close together. "Very little. We have stores of fish, pine nuts, dried berries, and roots, but most isss gone."

Arak took another bite of food from his garnet plate. "These pine nuts are almost as good as the ones you found near the New World volcano. And just a short dragon's flight south, there are nut trees as tall as five ice dragons."

Drakor grinned, showing a mouthful of sharp teeth. "Remember the river? There were more red fish than we could carry. They are tasty, and longer than my arm! We could store enough food for the longest winter."

Jardor had a dreamy look in his eyes. "We could use more fish."

Dorali added, "Don't forget the clams we brought for this feast."

Arak glanced at the empty table. "They're all gone. The New World food was popular." All eyes were focused on their group. Arak smiled back in a friendly, encouraging way as quiet conversations rippled out.

Dorali asked Drakor, "How do you store raw fish?"

"We dig deep holes in the ground, so deep that it isss always frozen, and line them with stones. The fish are cleaned, frozen on ice, wrapped in seaweed, and put into the holes. Widgers always try to find a way in, so the hole isss covered with heavy rocks. Roots and dried berries are stored in other holes. I will try to find our stores of ice-flower berries."

When the feast ended, dragons piled their rock plates beside the table. Arak approached Mardor and bowed low. "Your ice sculptures are legendary. How can you carve with lightning? I'd like to see this with my own eyes. Your ice games sound impressive, too."

Mardor studied him with crafty eyes. "It will take one day to prepare the ice area, and another to make sculptures and play games. We did not plan for festival feasts."

"We'll gather more food," Arak offered, hiding a smile. This was a perfect opportunity for Drakor to shine, by bringing food and competing in the games . . . especially the lightning sword game.

"Then we will prepare." Mardor spoke quietly to a dragon, who glanced at Arak and nodded to his leader.

Arak smiled pleasantly to Mardor and his helper. He signed to Drakor, "We're being watched. Jardor can't come."

"Is this part of the plan?" Dorali signed.

Arak grinned. "It was expected. A dragon who thrives on power sees a threat everywhere. This time, he's right. If just us three leave he'll be glad to see us gone, but he's suspicious. How could we fly so far? What are we hiding? We'll fly away from the skiff, so our watchers will search the wrong area."

Drakor gave Jardor a private hand signal. Jardor shook his head in protest but stayed where the leader could see him.

"If I fail, Mardor could give him a hard time."

"This will work," Arak promised.

The last purples of sunset colored the water as the dragon trio flew away. Moonlight glinted across the waves and glowed through the edges of ice. They landed on a melting ice-mountain and found comfortable seats near the edge. Waves slapped the base, splashing up as a cold, salty spray.

The dragons took long lines from their packs, baited the hooks, and cast them into the sea. Lines jerked with unseen life. Soon they were landing deep-water crabs, one after another.

Dorali picked a cold, soaked acorn out of the jar. She baited another hook, forcing the water-softened nut onto a bent wire. "This visit has been most educational."

"What have you learned?" Drakor asked.

Dorali pulled up a line and dumped another crab into her sack. "These crabs will take almost any bait. All ice dragons are sparkly white, but dragon-lady heads are a bit smaller than dragon-lord heads." She shrugged her wings. "And Mardor really, really wants to get rid of us. Especially you. You're a thorn between his scales."

"What do you think of my sire?"

"I like him. He has a good energy field. Have you told him about our plan to help?"

"He isss eager to try."

Arak said, "We'll tow him to the dragon-skiff tonight. Tell Zardan to meet us at the shore. He must come alone, in secret. Mardor will be watching you, and he can't know about the skiff."

At sunset, Arak crept into his rough shelter. Hidden

from sight, he entered the trance-mind.

**Scree, We will tow Drakor's sire to the skiff tonight.
You and Driana must be ready**

We will be ready

The rising moon was full, sharing her unwelcome light as Arak and Dorali slipped away. They moved quietly, crouching between bushes and hiding in the shadows. When they reached the shore, Zardan was waiting. He stepped out from between two larger shrubs, leaning on his crutches, and looked from one to the other. Hope burned bright in his eyes.

"I left early, before moonrise. Mardor's dragon followed me, so I walked in circles and scraped lichens off rocks. He got bored and left. Drakor says you can fix my legs."

Dorali held up a warning hand. "We think we can fix them, but there is a risk."

"The chance to fly again isss worth any risk."

Their bamboo raft was well hidden. They pulled it just into the sea, touching the shore. Zardan struggled clumsily to the middle and stared at the water, flexing his claws nervously. "How far will we go?"

Arak pointed out to sea. "It's just a short dragon flight. This raft is light but strong; it bends without breaking. We'll take you to two of the best Healers I know. They fixed Drakor's mangled wing, my broken leg, and Dorali's injuries."

They towed Zardan to the skiff. The following morning Arak, Dorali, and Drakor emptied bag after bag of live, deep-water crabs onto the feasting table. "We caught these using New World bait," Arak said, loud enough for everyone to hear.

Ice dragons added lichens and dried, wrinkled roots from their limited stores of food. Then they formed lines on each side of the table. Seafood scents mixed with earthy aromas and the odor of the volcano.

Drakor added a crab to his plate. "The clan likes our New World food."

Arak chewed on a tough, flavorless root. "They should. This root is a good reason to move."

An elderly dragon-lady flew in from the direction of the volcano and landed. She bowed low to the leader. "It isss time to form the circle."

"Today we welcome a new member to my clan," Mardor announced.

Dorali rustled her wings with excitement. "It's the new dragonlet!" She launched into the air. Arak was a wing-beat behind her. The sky filled with white wings, beating like winter flurries toward the volcano.

They landed near the nest. One dragon-lord touched foreheads with the dragon-dam and peered down at the egg, with a proud arch to his neck. Then he rejoined the crowd. Dragons quietly formed rings around the nest and raised their claws to the sky. Dragon-ladies formed the inner rings, closest to the nest. "They have better control of lightning," Drakor murmured to Arak before he joined an outer ring.

The egg rocked frantically back and forth. Pecking noises filled the waiting silence while the dragon-dam crooned encouragement. The tip of a small nose broke through a crack in the shell. That was a signal.

Sparks crackled up from dragon claws as they called splinters of lightning. Metals were added for color, matching the gemstones in the nest and the fires of the volcano. Electric rings of blue, amber, and red greeted the newest dragonlet as she fell out of her shell and onto the fiery red hairs in the nest.

"Dragons are born of the Volcano," Mardor intoned.

The damp dragonlet stared up at the crackling, colorful circles. She greedily swallowed an entire clawfull of fine-chopped fish. Then she staggered to her feet and began the slow walk to the main gathering, tucked safely between her dam and the elderly dragon-lady. The other dragons flew back to their crab feast.

Dorali sighed. "That was a beautiful welcoming ceremony."

Drakor nodded. "The lightning rings are great, but all dragonlets look the same."

She laughed. "Try telling that to a new dragon-dam."

Mardor leapt up onto a stone block, graceful despite his bulk, and raised his wings. There was instant silence, even from the youngest dragonlet. "The sky isss clear. Tomorrow we will hold a Festival. Come to the new field at dawn."

"Do you use a new field every year?" Arak asked.

Drakor nodded. "The land isss warmer and the ice isss running away, so we must follow it inland."

The next day, Arak flew far inland with Dorali, Drakor, and Jardor. The air grew colder and colder, as if he flew backward in time into winter. They reached a snow-covered mountain that glowed pink in the early morning light. All the dragons landed in a rugged field of ice.

Ten dragon pairs flew to separate ice blocks that were cut from the glacier. Each pair of dragons placed many pieces of magnetic lodestone into their ice block.

"These stones call the lightning like magnetic wrinkles. It takes skill to place the stones. The sculptors know how and where to break the ice, using lightning swords of different sizes," Drakor explained quietly.

Arak just shook his head. How could anyone sculpt with lightning?

The ice sculptors raised their arms high, claws out.

Mardor signaled the drummer.

The loud drumbeat seemed to last forever in the frozen air. Then bolt after bolt of lightning struck each ice block, knocking off pieces of ice. The sky sizzled and thunder boomed; a strong odor of burnt air mixed with the indefinable scents of ancient ice.

Within minutes, rough dragon shapes filled the field. Dragon-ladies deflected excess lightning, making it run down the ice to melt perfect wings. Black diamonds appeared from their pouches, with the clear darkness of a midnight sea. They poked a big diamond into each slushy eye socket, which froze to hold the sparkling gray eyes.

Dragons channeled the power of the sky as if they were spirits of the Volcano. Dragon-ladies melted the surface of the dragon's body, using small splinters of lightning. This liquid skin quickly re-froze with the crackled texture of dragon scales.

When the steam cleared, ten ice sculptures rested on the snow. Each sculpted dragon was larger than life. One held a fish in its claws and another had wings spread in flight. A third dragon sculpture stood tall with its head thrown back, challenging the sky.

Arak stared. "This is amazing!"

Dorali's eyes glowed. "It's like magic."

Mardor declared a winner. This pair of sculptors

spiraled up into the sky, celebrating their success.

Another drumbeat sounded and Mardor announced, "It isss time to play the games of Slam."

Dragons rose up in a flurry of white wings and drifted like snow to a nearby lake. The hard surface was dark blue with white crackling, like a frozen sky with ice clouds. The ice was marked with a huge ring of black stones.

Arak felt a magnetic pull from the black stones. He closed his eyes to better feel/see the silvery shapes of these magnetic lodestones. What a clever idea. Players would know the borders of this game without even looking!

A plain blue stone marked each goal at opposite ends. A sparkling blue, disc-shaped lodestone sat in the center of the ring.

Drakor pointed to the center and whispered, "That isss the game-stone. It isss covered with blue sapphires."

Dragons lined up along the frozen lake, watching with a serious intensity.

Mardor said, "Each game of Slam will last for half a notch on the sun dial. Tails only. No claws or wings may be used to move the game-stone. No flying or carrying. A point is scored when a goal-stone is knocked out by the game-stone."

Four older dragon-lords entered the ice field. Two Attacker dragons walked to the center, on each side of the sparkling blue game-stone. A Defender stood in front of the plain blue goal-stone at each end. At the beat of the drum, the game began.

The Attackers hit each other shoulder-to-shoulder, hard, with wings safely back. One dragon managed to curl his tail around the game-stone and sling it across the ice toward the opposite goal-stone. Shards of ice sprayed from copper claws as both dragons tore across the ice, barely gripping the slippery surface. They slammed into each other again with a jarring thud, competing to claim the stone. It slipped past both dragons.

"Slam is a good name for this game," Arak said to Drakor.

He grinned back. "Body slam isss fun, but tail slam isss better. We hit hard with our tails."

The game-stone was caught by the Defender's tail, wrapped in a tail loop, and slung back; it twirled across the ice with a wicked spin. An Attacker caught the stone with his tail and slung it again. The game continued with no score. Dragons crashed together, tails curled around the sparkling stone, and the piece of solid sky flew back and forth. Finally, a loud crack split the air as the game-stone struck a goal-stone, knocking it from the circle.

"Point!"

Dorali clicked her claws nervously as increasingly battered dragons re-formed the game. "Why are tail hits so important?"

"Our tail isss important for fighting."

She sighed. "Always fighting."

The rough game continued until the drum sounded. Mardor announced the winning team.

Next were pairs of dragon-lord and dragon-lady. This was still a contact sport with impressive body slams. The dragon-ladies had a slight edge in slamming the game-stone home.

"Dragon-ladies are better at keeping their eye on the stone," Drakor said.

Dorali nodded. "That skill would help them keep an eye on dragonlets who like to wander away." She whispered softly, "Like I did."

Three games later, Drakor and Jardor worked together, competing against another team. The game-stone slammed back and forth, flying across the ice. Curious eyes followed Drakor. As the game continued, the crowd began to cheer them on.

Their second game was against a pair of bigger, more experienced opponents. The score was tied when the time drum sounded, so another time-part began. Drakor slung in the winning goal with a perfect tail shot. The crowd went wild!

Drakor and Jardor made triumphant spirals up into the air. Mardor scowled.

Their third game was close. Mardor had a toothy, satisfied grin when Drakor lost.

"We lasted for three games!" Jardor yelled.

A group of young dragons surrounded Drakor and Jardor, pummeling their backs. "You beat Cranart and Dramorg!"

The afternoon sun sank lower, gilding the mountain top with an icy gold. A drum beat sounded and Mardor announced, "The games are now over."

Arak asked, "What about a lightning sword game?"

Mardor's gaze slid to Drakor and his eyes hardened. "Not this time."

Arak nodded. *No, because Drakor could win.*

The games were over, but not the high spirits.

"I'm ready for that feast," said one young dragon.

Another smiled as she stretched her wings. "New World food isss good."

Mardor swiveled his ears toward the New World comment. He stalked by and silence fell like a black cloud.

Arak looked down the steep white slope and simply could not resist. He tucked his wings and stretched his neck. Then he slid down the mountain on his belly scales with cold snow flying in his face, watching for the occasional rock. Dorali and Drakor immediately joined him.

Arak glanced back. Jardor eyed Mardor and then joined the fun. Then most of the younger dragons, and a few older ones, were body-surfing down the mountainside.

Arak reached a bare patch near the bottom and spread his wings, skimming just above the sharp rocks. He soared up into the sky. The others copied his flight, adding twirls and flips. The dragons landed together, smiling and stretching their wings with a cheerful camaraderie, as if they had all broken an unspoken rule.

Jardor's grin was brighter than a winter moon. "That was great!"

"Do you use this slide often?" Arak asked.

Drakor shook his head. "This isss the first time. We gather food and practice for serious, important games."

Dorali gazed up the long, snowy slope. "Games can be just for fun."

The ground rumbled beneath their feet, and loose rocks bounced down the mountain. Arak's magnetic sight was nearly blinded by the energy spikes.

Drakor rustled his wings nervously. "Tomorrow I must face Mardor. That will be no game."

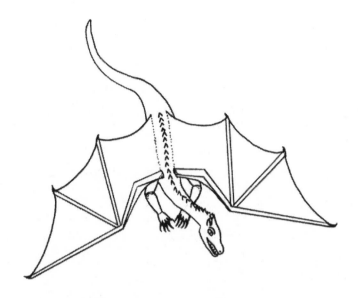

CHAPTER 15: THE CHALLENGER

Drakor left his shelter before dawn, shivering, but not from the cold. He felt the thrumming pull of the Volcano. A magnetic spider web covered the mountain and glowed silver in his mind. Shimmering wrinkles danced above the new cone in a twisted pattern with sharp energy spikes.

He must confront Mardor now.

Drakor gazed into the night sky, seeking the calm beauty of a golden aurora. But the elaborate folds of light were as tangled as his thoughts.

Would Mardor listen? If not, was his wing healed enough to fight? Dragons grumbled quietly, but how did they really feel about the leader? Were they tired of Mardor's rule? Were they hungry enough to follow Drakor if he won the fight? To risk leaving their only home and follow him to a new world they had never seen?

Drakor chewed cold crabmeat with no appetite. As the

sun rose, other dragons left their shelters and began a day of hunting for roots, overlooked cones with pine nuts, and unlucky smidgers. He stretched to loosen his muscles, swallowed a bitter tea, and walked slowly to the meeting circle. He beat the big drum once.

BOOOOMMM!

The entire clan turned toward the unexpected sound. They responded to the summons and gathered in the circle within minutes. Mardor flew to the center.

Drakor bowed to the leader and took a deep breath. "I, Drakor, call for a meeting."

Mardor narrowed his eyes. "That isss your right. Use it wisely."

"Our Volcano has changed." Drakor spoke with a deeper voice, as if he was older. "This has happened before, many homes ago, long before this home. You all know the legend. One day the Volcano heartbeat changed. It beat faster and faster. The smells changed and the ground swelled. Then the Volcano blew up into the sky. All that was left was a hole in the ground. The sea filled the hole and our long-ago home was gone forever. Only ice dragons who were not home survived to tell this story and give us their warning."

Drakor put his feelings into each word. He used every story-teller trick he had learned from his sire. They must listen and believe!

"The heart of our Volcano isss beating faster. You feel this change. You breathe the new smells. Magnetic wrinkles flock to the Volcano, as active as smidgers on a spring day. We must heed the warnings from our ancestors. We must leave this land to survive. There isss a new home waiting for us with plenty of food."

The dragons stared at Drakor. Whispers of fear and interest mixed in the wind.

Mardor flexed his long, lethal claws. "You think our Volcano isss dangerous and we should leave. You remember one legend and forget our ways. We are born of the Volcano and I am your leader."

Drakor kept his claws still, his eyes round. He lowered his neck almost to the ground. Mardor loved this servile pose, a reminder to every dragon that he was in charge. Drakor took deep, slow breaths and focused his mind. He must hang on to his temper. "You would still be the leader in the new place."

"Of course. Where isss this new place?" Mardor growled, raking his sharp claws through the ground with a menacing glare.

"There isss a big land to the west, much bigger than this land, with ice. Huge fish swim in the river."

"How can we get there, if this land isss so far away that I have not seen it?" Mardor asked.

"We can fly high where the wind-stream is fast, and use slings to carry the dragonlets."

Mardor stared down at Drakor. "Isss there a Volcano?"

Drakor sank even lower and Mardor smiled with approval. "There isss a quiet Volcano with no smoke."

Mardor said, "That isss not a good home. We need metals and hot springs."

"There are metals. There isss much food. Ice dragons are strong. We have moved before, in the long ago, when it was necessary. We will live well in this new land." Drakor took a deep breath. "The clan will die if we stay."

"You say we will die, but you cannot know," Mardor

said with a nasty sneer.

Drakor pointed to the Volcano. "The smells are new. The Volcano isss swelling. It rumbles like a stomach that isss always hungry. I have measured the ground and it isss two claw lengths taller. This has not happened before. Ice fish have left. They know it isss time to leave."

Mardor shook his head. "We are smarter than ice fish. We will stay."

Drakor slowly raised his neck. He stood tall and turned in a circle, making eye contact with each clan member. "We may be smarter than fish. But what will we eat when the fish are gone? We are already hungry." He spoke to the new dragon-dam. "Your dragonlet can not escape to safety when the Volcano explodes. It will be too late. Will you let her burn to death?"

Dragons rustled their wings nervously, looking from Drakor to Mardor.

Mardor snapped his tail with a loud crack, like a whip. "I will stay and the clan will stay." He flexed his claws. "You will leave. Now."

Drakor raised his head high. He stretched as tall as possible, trying to stare directly into Mardor's eyes. "The clan *must* leave. I challenge you."

Jardor caught his eye and shook his head, mouthing the words, "Are you insane?" Soon he would know. He flicked the tip of his tail nervously. Losers were painfully marked to remind everyone of their defeat.

All of the dragons backed away from Drakor and Mardor, clearing a space for the fight. Then the dragon-lords marched in a line, silently creating a huge, perfect circle. Their feet struck the ground with martial precision. They stopped and turned inward on some hidden signal, spread their wings wide, and stood wingtip-to-wingtip.

Dragon-ladies made a second circle right behind them. They stood wingtip-to-wingtip in the exact center between two dragon-lords. Each dragon was silent and deathly still, as if carved from ice. Only their dark eyes moved, watching.

Arak, Dorali, and the dragonlets were kept behind this double wall of dragons.

Drakor looked beyond the rings and saw Arak sign to Dorali, "I wonder how often they fight? They all know exactly what to do." Dorali seemed too tense to reply. Then his attention was wrenched back to the challenge ring.

Mardor's second-in-command picked up the huge drum from the meeting area. He thumped it down on the ground, just outside the dragon circles. "This fight begins with the drum beat. The only fight rule isss no lightning blasts. The victor will lead the clan." He looked at Mardor and bowed low, clearly anticipating his win.

Drakor locked his eyes on Mardor. He stretched his wings wide, loosening his muscles for the fight. Had his broken bones truly healed? His ears swiveled backward to face the drum.

BOOOMMMM! The drum beat rumbled through the air like thunder.

Mardor snaked forward. Drakor leapt aside, but five razor-sharp claws slashed like knives across his chest. Dark red lines spread quickly, like mud on snow. *How deep are these cuts?* He felt no fear, just a focused calm from entering the first stage of trance-mind. He smelled the salty blood but felt no pain, thanks to Dorali's bitter flame-flower brew. Now he would either win, or die from unfelt injuries.

They circled each other with teeth bared, eyes battle-bright. Mardor snapped his powerful tail around Drakor's knees like a whip.

Drakor stumbled away, off balance, but quickly regained his loose-knee fighting stance. He feinted left and then leapt high, somersaulting through the sky, and landed behind Mardor. But the leader had already turned and was facing him. They both lashed out with their tails and raked with their claws. Again, only Mardor drew blood.

Drakor staggered away and fell, stopping just inside the border of silent dragons. He struggled upright and glanced at his leg. Dark blood seeped from his new wound, staining his scales, but he did not feel it. How bad was this wound? He was as fast as the leader and knew fight strategy, but Mardor was bigger. Much bigger.

Drakor did not have the reach to strike a single blow.

He yearned to win in the normal way, to be truly acceptable as a leader. He had trained hard for greater stamina and eaten Orm's chocolate for extra energy. But even with all his training, Drakor could not win a traditional fight.

Mardor watched expectantly, smiling with the confidence of many victories. He would cut deep to punish his challenger, drawing blood again and again, until Drakor was too weak to stand. Finally, Mardor would grip his neck in his teeth, the symbol of defeat.

How could he hope to win any fight against this hulking dragon? Drakor shook his head to clear it. He might be smaller than Mardor, and younger, but he had more energy. Now he would use this to his advantage.

Drakor abandoned the traditional way of fighting. He began to spin, with his claws out. His feet moved in a perfect rhythm. He focused on Mardor's eyes until his body had spun around. Then his eyes snapped back to Mardor as he kept spinning. Soon he was whirling like a top around the circle. He did not feel dizzy, and his opponent was always in his sight.

Drakor swerved in, toward Mardor, and slashed with his claws.

The leader stared in disbelief at the red stains. His eyes blazed with anger as he lunged forward. His opponent was already gone.

Drakor's claws bit into Mardor again and again. He spun so fast that he left no open spot for Mardor to strike back. Drakor was made of claws. As he spun he became the wind and his fears fled away. His thoughts were a clear, liquid blue. How long could he spin before his wounded leg was too stiff? Could he really win?

Drakor struck Mardor's left thigh, then his right shoulder, then a leg. He kept spinning and slashing.

Mardor began breathing hard. He slashed uselessly at his moving target. He lashed his tail sideways and stuck out his foot, trying again to trip his challenger.

Drakor avoided Mardor's foot, spinning just beyond it like a waterspout. His leg began to stiffen and he spun slower, mortally afraid of falling. He was no longer sure that he could get back up.

Mardor shuddered with pain and gasped for air like a fish out of water. He staggered and almost fell. He rallied and struck again, always where Drakor had just been.

No dragon had ever fought the way Drakor fought, but he fought with borrowed energy behind a pain-free shield.

He kept spinning and slashing, moving his claws higher and lower, making shallow cuts that would not seriously injure his opponent. Every ice dragon must be able to fly, to escape.

Mardor tried twirling, reaching for a new strategy, and fell hard. He struggled to his feet. His snow-white scales were red with seeping blood and his breath came in loud, rasping gasps. He had never fought this long, always using his greater size and experience for a quick, easy win.

As Drakor's leg became stiff he felt less like the fluid wind. He spun slower and slower, like a top winding down, trying not to stumble. His wounds were deep, his chest was sunset red, and his mind was going white. He moved in a fog. How much longer could he fight? Drakor trembled as the flame-flower drug wore off and his entire body burned with pain.

Mardor struck one last, wobbly blow. Then the leader toppled over like an old, dead tree and hit the ground with a resounding thud.

Drakor fell a moment later.

CHAPTER 16: GATHERING STORMS

Two dragons lay as still as death on the sharp, black ground.

No one moved in the long, profound silence.

Then wings rustled and whispers flew around the rings of dragons. What happened? How could Mardor fall? Who was the leader?

Drakor opened his eyes. He stared at Mardor, as shocked as every other ice dragon, before staggering to his feet. His muscles screamed as he stood tall, ignoring his torn leg. He raised his wings high in victory. Then he folded his wings and turned slowly in a circle, catching the gaze of each stunned, wide-eyed dragon. "I am the new leader."

A dragon-lord with long neck scars rumbled, "This isss not over. You must mark him."

Drakor shook his head. "No. He was a strong leader. I marked him in the fight."

Another dragon challenged Drakor with his eyes and hissed, "He marked me after I lost. Mardor must be marked."

"No. Who challenges my right to lead?" Would a dragon challenge him? He must bind his torn leg soon or forever walk with a limp. Sticky blood dripped down his chest. How much more blood could he lose and still stand?

No one answered. Then, as one, the ice dragons bowed low to their new leader.

Mardor looked up groggily from the ground, clearly wondering what had happened.

Drakor raised his wings triumphantly above his head. "Jardor is my second in command. We will all move to our new home in the New World."

A dragon-dam asked, "How can we fly so far, even in the wind-stream?"

Drakor gazed into the west. "Butterflies come here each year from beyond the sea. If they can fly so far, then dragons can too."

Arak and Dorali dodged between wings, slipped through circles of stunned dragons, and darted into the center ring. Their feet crunched loudly across the gravelly ground.

Arak sprinkled stinging powder on Drakor's leg and bound the wound. "We're all Apprentice Healers now." He rubbed a mustard-yellow salve into the slashes across Drakor's chest. "These cuts are deep enough to scar, but this will fight infection. It's made from goldenseal, lavender, and a bit of yellow tansy."

Dorali checked Mardor and breathed a deep sigh of relief. "I've never seen so many cuts, but the wounds are not deep." She rubbed salve over his huge body and prepared an herbal drink for both fighters. She did not use flames to warm the tea. Ice dragons were fearsome enough without breathing fire, but they would surely learn.

She checked Drakor and asked, "Why didn't you use micro-zaps to distract him? You're both hurt more than was needed."

Drakor winced as he sat down. He drank Dorali's tea, silently sipping the bitter brew. Then he answered quietly, "Mardor would have sensed it, and the clan would not accept such a victory. It isss not our way. I had to win following some traditions. It will be hard enough for them to accept me, for I am too small and too young. The mind isss not as important as size to ice dragons. I want this to change. I want a new way to choose leaders . . . more like yours."

Dorali bowed low like an ice dragon. "Then I, too, accept your victory."

Drakor gave her a genuine smile. "I did what I had to do and nearly lost. I could not have won without the help of golden dragons. Now we must move before it isss too late."

Dorali smiled back. "That's the first time you didn't call us yellow."

Drakor looked deep into her eyes. "You are the most golden of all. You gave me back the sky, the freedom of flight. I will never forget." He touched her face softly. Then he stood up slowly, feeling every slash and burning muscle. He bowed low to Dorali and then to Arak.

The clan watched wide-eyed, whispering to each other. The leader of ice dragons never bowed low to another dragon!

Drakor turned away and walked to the center of the ring, feeling the weight of leadership in the watching eyes of the clan. This was a time of great peril, and all could still die. He spoke in his deepest, most commanding voice, hoping they would listen.

"We will all move. Each of you may bring a pack of food and special treasures to our new home." Dragons grumbled, but they were still conditioned to obey the leader. "We have slings to carry our dragonlets, with three handles on each side. Four dragons will carry one dragonlet, and we will trade off while flying. No one will be left behind."

Drakor turned in the center of the circle, watching the clan as he spoke with growing confidence. "Bring out all the food," he commanded. "We will share a feast to remember! Then we fly." There was less grumbling at the promise of an all-you-can-eat dragon-sized meal.

Arak and Dorali left to complete their last mission for ice dragons.

*   *   *

Stars were shining by the time the dragon-dam and her tiny new dragonlet reached the skiff and climbed aboard. Karoon welcomed them all back, but his eyes were on Dorali. "I was worried."

She smiled. "I'm a Healer, so I know how to fight. What can heal, can hurt."

He laughed good-naturedly. "I'll remember that."

Arak, Dorali, and Karoon flew back to bid farewell to Drakor, Jardor, and their doomed homeland.

Karoon thumped Drakor on the back. "I knew you could win!"

Drakor grinned and thumped back. "Not without your help."

"Keep practicing. You must be ready for the next challenger." Karoon reached into his bag and pulled out a flute. "I asked Taron to carve this for you. Remember us when you play magical music."

Drakor snapped his tail with enthusiasm. "How could I forget?"

Dorali watched with interest. Then she handed Drakor a small bag. "This has salve for wounds and tea for pain. You must win to make changes."

Drakor's eyes lit up. "You do understand. Thank you."

Arak handed the ice dragon a clear crystal ball. "I made you a new trance-stone from ice quartz. Use this to enter trance-mind on the eve of each moon phase. I'll call you at star rise on your shore."

Drakor had a gleam in his eye. "I will keep practicing until I can cross the sea with my mind and call *you*."

Arak grinned. "I'm sure you will." He gave Drakor a hefty bag of chocolate. "This is from all of us, for extra energy during that long flight. There's enough for each of you."

Drakor inhaled the enticing aroma. "Chocolate isss treasure, but your friendship isss a treasure beyond measure."

Arak smiled sadly. "Now we must leave to reach home in time."

"What will you do?"

"Arafine and Kragor will make sure everyone is safe. Zarina is smart and capable. I'm not really needed, but I need to see my dragon-lady and Arwina. Then I'll fly the skiff far from shore, beyond the claws of the tsunami."

Drakor nodded understanding. "I must fly with my clan beyond the fire of our Volcano." He bowed low to Arak, then touched forehead-to-forehead in the respectful manner of golden dragons. He repeated this display with Dorali and Karoon, while the ice dragons watched in silence.

* * *

Dorali sighed. The voyage back was swift, and now she was home. She missed the adventure, the beauty, and the camaraderie. Lightning sparked in the clouds as golden dragons gathered for the storm dances. Dorali stood near a lone tree, almost hidden, watching.

Dragons flew up into the lightning clouds, wingtips barely touching as they spiraled higher. By custom, mated pairs were first to fly. Then other couples formed and joined them. The clouds glowed brightly, lit from within as dragons played catch with colored lightning.

Dorali waited on the ground, alone. Her eyes were fastened on the beautiful, flashing clouds. Perhaps this beauty alone was enough, but a corner of her heart yearned for a mate of her own. For a dragon who could love her just the way she was.

Dorali flicked her tail in surprise as a dusty wind blew against her.

Karoon landed right beside her. He straightened his wings and looked into her eyes. "Dorali, will you join me in the clouds?"

Dorali trembled inside as she searched his eyes. Her heart still ached from his last insulting offer. During the journey they had become good crew-mates. But were they more? He could make her laugh. Then she remembered the rare green crystals that he saved, just for her. He was worried when she went to Drakor's island, and asked her to be careful. Did he truly care? Why did he ask?

"You're not as handsome as Drakor, but you are a well-grown dragon-lord."

Karoon snapped his tail. "Is this an insult?"

"No. It's true. Why do you offer again?"

He bowed his head. "You were right. You have your own beauty. You're sweet, incredibly capable, you'd make a terrific dam, and . . ."

"My scars?" Her eyes held years of unshed tears.

"I've grown used to them. They're like frost."

Dorali nodded. "That's what Drakor says."

Karoon stiffened. "Do you prefer him to me?"

It was a serious question, and her turn to be surprised. "No . . . not really. Drakor and I are good friends. I've noticed you since I was a dragonlet, and you've grown. Inside. You were always a handsome dragon-lord. Now you're also likable."

"What about lovable?"

Dorali tilted her head, considering. Then she gave Karoon a slow smile. "Yes." She leapt off the ground. He followed in an instant, and together they spiraled up into the rainbow clouds.

*   *   *

Arak studied the stars in the night sky. It was time. He focused into his aquamarine globe, sank deep into trance, and sent his mind north. Magnetic wrinkles covered the volcano with secret, silvery light that sparkled against the darkness. Then colored lightning danced above the mountain in purples and gold. Thick red ropes ran down its side like dragon's blood.

BRROOOMMMM!!!

The mountain screamed as it was torn apart! An explosion beyond anything the world had ever heard knocked Arak back toward his body; the sound chased him home.

He sat up gingerly, disoriented, and gazed north. Dark clouds towered into the rumbling sky, already visible even so far away. He looked south-west. Magnetic lines shot up to the stars as Scree's volcano erupted. No one could survive those blasts.

How many beings had escaped into the west? How many still lived?

The star-studded sea breathed in and out with a normal rhythm. When would the terrible waves strike? The dragons had moved three hills in from the shore. Was that far enough to escape the wrath of the sea?

Zarina reached over and touched his arm in a comforting gesture. "Did everyone leave in time?" She had insisted on coming along when he flew the skiff to safety. Their dragonlet, Arwina, was fast asleep below deck, worn out by the excitement. Karoon and Dorali were also onboard.

"I mind-talked with Drakor after their flight. Everyone made the trip safely except for one. He was quite old, but refused to come with us."

"And the octopi?"

Arak flicked his tail as he gazed into the west. "Scree made sure there were enough skiffs. It took some persuading, but the last octopi finally left yesterday. She and Orm are leading this group, and the skiffs are heavily loaded. Scree persuaded many blue-ringed octopi to leave with them. They survived a sea storm and should reach land within two dragon-weeks."

Zarina followed his gaze. "I feel in my bones that they will make it."

Arak leaned against his mate, grateful for her company. But he could not tear his eyes away from the sea. "The explosion was even greater than I expected. Tsunamis will attack the clan from two directions. What will be left of our home?"

"We'll survive. Then I'll finally fly beyond the horizon with you." She stretched her wings wide, the sign for change. "We'll have such interesting neighbors. I wonder what sunset dragons are like?"

Arak turned to Zarina and his eyes glowed. "Do you mean . . ."

She smiled. "I would miss Scree and Orm, and Drakor. We'll move."

GLOSSARY: WORDS AND SCIENCE
Science within the science fantasy

Abalone – This sea animal is used for food. The inside of the shell has colorful mother-of-pearl with overlapping layers of silvery pink, green and blue. (a-bah-low-nee)

Arak – A golden dragon, explorer, and dreamer. (A-rak)

Boisterous – Noisy, rowdy, jolly, not restrained or quiet. (boy-stir-us)

Camouflage – An octopus can change its shape and skin color to match, and hide within, its surroundings. This is an example of natural camouflage. (kam-oo-flaj)

Cloth-of-gold –Thin, strong, golden thread is made from the wiry roots of the pen shell. Cloth-of-gold fabric is woven from this thread, and was once used to make beautiful gloves for ladies.

Dam – A dragon's mother. Zarina is Arak's mate and Arwina's dragon-dam. Arafine is Arak's dragon-dam.

Dorali – She's a golden dragon and Healer. (Door-a-lie)

Drakor – He's a young ice dragon. (Dray-kor)

Dweer – This scaly, rust-colored, wolf-like predator has a blunt snout and sharp teeth. Dweer are wingless and smaller than dragons, but dangerous in a group. (dwee-er)

Giant squid – These animals have eight long arms and two extra-long arms. Giant squid usually live in the deep ocean. They are intelligent, aggressive predators that may grow up to 60 feet long. Giant squid have a long head and huge eyes that can be almost 12 inches across. (skwid)

Ice flower – There is a real plant like this called skeleton flower. The chalky white flower petals turn clear under rain, and it has tiny blue berries.

Iridescent – Shining with different colors, a sparkling rainbow effect. (ih-rih-deh-sent)

Juveniles – These are the young, immature members of a group. Puppies are juvenile dogs, children are juvenile humans, dragonlets are juvenile dragons. (joo-veh-niles)

Lodestone – This stone is a natural magnet. (lode-stone)

Mesmerized – Amazed, fascinated, almost hypnotized by someone or something. Drakor was mesmerized by the flute music. (mez-mer-izd)

Octopus – This intelligent sea being has 8 flexible arms and no bones. The proper plural is "octopuses". "Octopi" is sometimes used, and this sounds more science-fictiony.

Quithra – This imaginary sea creature resembles a sea slug. Slow, colorful creatures are often toxic and taste bitter; this is their defense. Medicines sometimes use the natural chemicals from bitter-tasting animals and plants. (kwi-thra)

Sire – A dragon's father. Kragor is Arak's sire. Arak is Arwina's sire. (Sii-er)

Solstice – The winter solstice is the shortest day of the year; then days become longer. The summer solstice is the longest day of the year. (sol-stiss)

Spawn – To release many small eggs into the water.

Sturgeon – This large, primitive fish can grow to 12 feet long. Sturgeons are covered by diamond-shaped scales. The females make thousands of tasty, oily eggs. (stur-jun)

Tentacle – This is the flexible, boneless arm of an octopus or a squid. An octopus has strong, sensitive suckers to touch or hold. (ten-ta-kel)

Titanium – This shiny, silvery-gray metal was named for the Titans of Greek mythology. The chemical symbol is Ti. Titanium is very light, strong, and resists breaking down in sea water. It's found in volcanic rocks and was first found in black sand. It's greatly concentrated in horsetail and nettle plants. I've never put titanium in fire or lightning to see if it turns black. (tie-tay-nee-um)

Tsunami – This is a huge wave, a rare wall of water that strikes the shore. (sue-nah-mee)

Tunicate – This small, soft, primitive sea animal grows in clusters that are attached to a surface. Many sea creatures glow, so some tunicates might glow. (too-nih-kat)

AUTHOR'S NOTE

In Arak's world, golden dragons are large, lively, and intelligent. They share shadow-stories, carve glaciers, and grow fantasy snowflakes. These dragons love festivals, surfing the storm winds, and playing games with colored lightning. They learn to breathe fire, talk mind-to-mind, and manipulate energy.

Ice dragons are even bigger than golden dragons. They have a more rigid society, like the ancient Vikings who also lived in a harsh climate. All dragons have ancient traditions and legends.

Octopuses are much smaller than dragons, very curious, and clever. Once, on a research cruise, I saw a deep-sea octopus. He was less than two feet long, with head and arms as clear as glass. His head was a bit smaller than mine but his eyes were the same size, a lovely yellow-gold color with black pupils. I looked into the eyes of the octopus and he gazed right back at me. This was truly an alien intelligence, and I wondered what the sea-being was thinking.

Octopuses have unusual senses and abilities, amazing intelligence, and distinct personalities. They show emotion by changing colors. Scientists recently discovered a village of octopuses off Australia . . . after the first Dragon Dreamer book was published.

Many octopus types are natural shape-shifters who can change their color, texture, and shape to perfectly match the background; they disappear in a heartbeat. Some types mimic other species so realistically that people don't realize it's an octopus! The mimic octopus "is one of nature's greatest shape-shifters: it is able to assume the form and coloration of at least 15 other species, including crabs, stingrays, and jellyfish." (Time's *Living Wonders* book, 2008). Scientists thought the octopus was truly the animal it copied.

If an octopus can choose to mimic so realistically, why not choose to make skin pictures using the natural octopus color cells? Especially to talk to a dragon.

This snowflake is made of seals and kelp seaweed, because everyone needs a "seal of approval".

ABOUT THE AUTHOR

J.S. Burke has worked as an author, artist, chemist, and marine biologist, studying creatures of the dark abyss and diving on coral reefs. She lived on a ship far from shore, and learned to walk with the sea. Once, three waterspouts grew down from the storm clouds and headed for her ship. She lives in Georgia with her family and rescue pets.

The Dragon Dreamer is the first book in the Dragon Dreamer series, and *Dragon Lightning* is the second. *Fantasy Snowflakes Coloring Book* has fantasy snowflake mandalas drawn with animals and plants in Celtic designs. Her Crystal series has hands-on math/science/art books: *Crystal Geometry* and *Crystal Colors* have activities with crystals for ages eight to adult.

Website: www.jennysburke.com
Facebook: www.facebook.com/Jenny-S-Burke-721518861218158/?ref=aymt_homepage_panel
Amazon: www.amazon.com/J.-S.-Burke/e/B00NVRVHWE/ref=ntt_dp_epwbk_0
Twitter: www.twitter.com/TheDragonDreamr
Goodreads:
www.goodreads.com/author/show/8283255.J_S_Burke

To all you marvelous readers, THANK YOU. If you enjoyed *Dragon Lightning*, could you please leave a rating and/or review on Amazon, Goodreads, or another site? Just a sentence or two about what you thought is all it needs.

Made in the USA
San Bernardino, CA
16 October 2016